T0245504

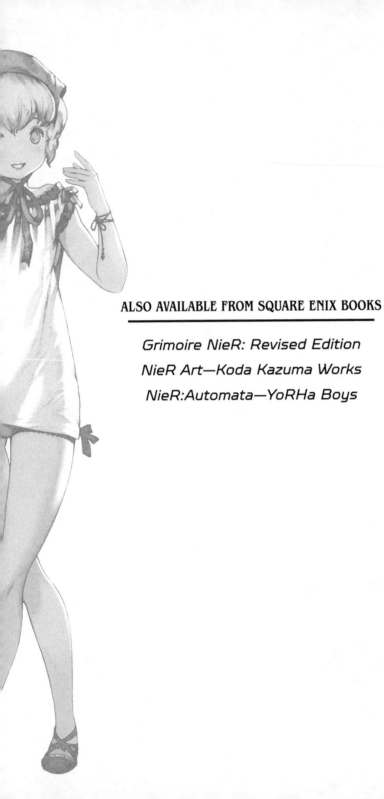

ALSO AVAILABLE FROM SQUARE ENIX BOOKS

Grimoire NieR: Revised Edition

NieR Art—Koda Kazuma Works

NieR:Automata—YoRHa Boys

NieR Replicant
ver.1.22474487139...

PROJECT GESTALT RECOLLECTIONS

FILE 01

Written by Jun Eishima
Original Story by Yoko Taro

English Adaptation by Jasmine Bernhardt and Alan Averill

SQUARE ENIX
BOOKS

NieR Replicant ver.1.22474487139...
Project Gestalt Recollections—File 01
© 2021 Jun Eishima
© 2021 SQUARE ENIX CO., LTD. All rights reserved.

First published in Japan as *NieR Replicant ver.1.22474487139... Gestalt Keikaku Kaisouroku* in 2021 by SQUARE ENIX CO., LTD.
English translation rights arranged with SQUARE ENIX CO., LTD. and SQUARE ENIX, INC.
English translation © 2023 by SQUARE ENIX CO., LTD.

Based on the video game *NieR Replicant ver.1.22474487139...*
© 2010, 2021 SQUARE ENIX CO., LTD. All rights reserved.

Library of Congress Cataloging-in-Publication Data

Names: Eishima, Jun, 1964- author. | Yokoo, Tarō, 1970- author. | Bernhardt, Jasmine, translator. | Averill, Alan, translator.
Title: NieR Replicant ver.1.22474487139... : project gestalt recollections / written by Jun Eishima; original story by Yoko Taro ; English adaptation by Jasmine Bernhardt and Alan Averill.
Other titles: NieR Replicant ver.1.22474487139. English | NieR (Video game)
Description: First edition. | El Segundo, CA : Square Enix Books, 2023- | "First published in Japan as NieR Replicant ver.1.22474487139... Gestalt Keikaku Kaisouroku"
Identifiers: LCCN 2023009048 (print) | LCCN 2023009049 (ebook) | ISBN 9781646091836 (file 01 ; hardcover) | ISBN 9781646096619 (file 01 ; ebook)
Subjects: LCGFT: Dystopian fiction. | Novels.
Classification: LCC PL869.5.I7 N6613 2023 (print) | LCC PL869.5.I7 (ebook) | DDC 895.63/6--dc23/eng/20230412
LC record available at https://lccn.loc.gov/2023009048
LC ebook record available at https://lccn.loc.gov/2023009049

Manufactured in the United States
First Edition: September 2023
1st Printing

Published by Square Enix Manga & Books, a division of SQUARE ENIX, INC.
999 N. Pacific Coast Highway, 3rd Floor
El Segundo, CA 90245, USA

SQUARE ENIX
B O O K S

square-enix-books.com

CONTENTS

A NOTE ABOUT THE CONTENTS

This book is an updated and expanded edition of *NieR RepliCant Recollection: Gestalt Keikaku Kaisouroku* (NieR RepliCant Recollection: Gestalt Project Retrospective), originally published in Japan in 2017.

The story "The Boy 1" also appears under the title "Red and Black" in *Grimoire NieR: Revised Edition—NieR Replicant ver.1.22474487139... The Complete Guide*.

REPORT 01

Going forward, we will be submitting regular reports using a new format. We made this decision after observing a rise in the frequency of irregular incidents recently—had we stayed with the old format, we would have been forced to increase the number of reports significantly. Though there will be a slight increase in superfluous information, we hope you understand it is a result of our wanting to prioritize accuracy.

The situation in our district is growing worse. Our farmland has become less and less fertile, leading to food shortages. Additionally, pollution in the river is making it increasingly difficult to secure the water necessary for both farming and daily activities. Shades and plague also continue to be a threat to the residents, and we believe their fear of these things is an indirect cause of the frequent, irregular incidents.

When a person believes tomorrow will be the same as today, they act out their usual routine in order to preserve their circumstances. However, if a person believes their peace will vanish tomorrow, they change their behavior in an attempt to avoid the worst. The choices resulting from that trial-and-error process may be leading to the incidents.

That said, we admit the possibility that we

are reading too deeply into this, and we will await reports from other districts regarding our observations. In the meantime, we intend to keep a very close eye on all everyday matters, as ignoring or downplaying them would be a dereliction of our duty as village leaders. We are in charge of Nier's village, after all, and we feel it would be foolish to judge the importance of things based on their magnitude. They say the smallest signs often herald the greatest disasters, after all.

In fact, we fear the case we are currently observing may be exactly such a sign. We will write about this in more detail in our next report.

Record written by Popola

The Boy 1

1.

AS NIER REACHED down to pluck an egg from the dew-soaked grass, birdsong echoed in the distance, signaling a pleasant day ahead. *Looks like this is the last one,* he thought. *Can't leave any behind when they lay only one a day.*

"That all of 'em?"

He turned to see the owner of the chickens coming up a nearby rise. Nier held out the basket to the other man, who took it from him and quickly tallied up the count. "Nice work, boy," the man said. "Oh, and the wife's fever broke, so I think she can go back to collecting eggs after today. Can't thank you enough for everything you've done for us."

"Happy to help," responded Nier.

"I got the payment you asked for, but are you sure you don't want money or food or nothing?"

"No, a baby chick is fine. Yonah will love it."

"Well then, pick whichever one you want from the basket."

The man gestured to a gaggle of chicks born the day prior. Nier had no idea how to tell one from the other, so in the end he chose one that seemed especially energetic. As he went to grab it, the chick began running around the basket as if fearing the idea of being separated from its fellow hatchings. But after a couple of stops and starts, he was finally able to cup his hands gently around the animal and head for home.

When Nier had gone to collect the eggs, he had been the only villager stirring, but now things were beginning to buzz with the morning energy of merchants and shoppers. As he walked down the street exchanging greetings with various merchants, the owner of a grocery shop called out to him.

"Nier!" she cried. "Hey, hold up. I hear Popola asked you to pick medicinal herbs today, and I'm hoping I can pile on and get you to grab some mushrooms."

Though sudden, such a request was not abnormal. Wild beasts roamed the area outside the village—as well as other, darker things that lurked in the shadows—and people didn't like to stray far from the walls of the town unless the sun was at its zenith. And with only a few hours a day where that was the case, Nier was often the one they turned to for morning or evening adventures.

"Mushrooms? You got it."

"Oh, you are just a delight! When you get back, I'll give you a pumpkin. I just got a big one in that I know your Yonah will love!"

"Sounds great!" replied Nier as he dashed away. He quickly found himself approaching the little brick house where he lived with his sister, Yonah. It was all they had left of their parents, but along with the kindness of the villagers, it had been enough to keep them healthy and happy for some time now. After a second, he spied Yonah waving at him from a window and picked up his pace.

"You're back!" cried Yonah, who burst out from inside the house before Nier could even open the door. Her breath was ragged from having rushed down the stairs.

"I sure am. Also, didn't I tell you not to run around before and after bed?"

"Oh . . . right."

Yonah was a sickly girl who fell ill when the seasons changed, became feverish if she stayed up later than normal, and started coughing if she moved around too much. She also wasn't much of an eater, and had thrown up her dinners more times than Nier cared to remember.

"I'm sorry. Am I going to start coughing again?"

"You'll be fine so long as you eat your breakfast and behave. Now let's get inside before we both freeze to death in the wind."

As Nier pulled the door shut behind him, he turned to Yonah and smiled. "Oh, hey! I have a present for you."

As his sister squealed with delight, Nier brought his hands up to her ear. The peeps of the chick inside were quiet, but they proved enough to reveal the surprise.

"It's a chick!"

"Yep. Now hold out your hand." He gently placed the chick onto her palm, where it huddled and shivered in shock from the sudden flood of light.

"It's so warm and fluffy," whispered Yonah.

"Yeah, it's still pretty little, so we can keep it in the house until it grows."

"WE CAN?!"

"Sure we can. We used to do that all the time back when Mom was still alive."

Saying this caused Nier to think on the early days of his childhood, when it had been his job to feed the chickens that lived in the garden. Their mother was too busy managing the household to take care of animals, and their father was often away on business in some faraway land—the same place he died not long after Yonah was born.

Nier could barely recall his father's face, and the man's passing had had little effect on the family's daily routine. Their mother raised vegetables in the garden and sewed clothes for the villagers; so far as Nier knew, his mother's hands didn't stop working until the day she died five years ago.

Nier was ten and Yonah not even two when it happened. The evening had begun like any other, with their mother stirring a pot of stew in the kitchen. She turned to Nier and asked him to fetch some bowls from the shelf, then collapsed to the floor with a heavy thud. Unable to comprehend what was happening, he burst from the house and ran to Popola in the library, figuring the woman in charge of all those books would know what to do. But although respect for Popola's wisdom was a sentiment shared by all who lived in the village, she proved unable to help his mother, simply shaking her head when she finished examining the body.

Nier found it hard to accept this most sudden of changes. It had seemed less like life leaving a person and more like an object suddenly breaking. And yet, when he saw the look on Popola's face, he knew without a doubt that his mother was no more.

When Popola's older twin sister, Devola, helped put his mother's body in a casket, Nier felt nothing. When the villagers began preparing for the funeral, Nier felt nothing. It was as if his mind had gone numb. He never even felt an urge to cry until a moment at the service when his eyes began to well up. The pit of his throat began to squeeze shut and his vision went blurry, but he pushed the emotions down because Yonah had started crying herself. Though she wasn't old enough to understand her mother's death, the fact her brother was ready to cry was enough to upset her. But when he smiled down at her, her tears immediately stopped—and once he wiped the wetness and snot from her face, she began to smile again.

Both of our parents are gone now, he thought in that moment. *Which means I'm the only one who can protect Yonah.*

2.

ONCE THEY WERE done with breakfast—simple left-overs from the day before—Nier began preparing to leave again.

"Can I come with you?" Yonah asked. "I want to help."

The medicinal herbs he needed to collect were most common just outside the eastern gate at this time of year, and he'd taken his sister there before. But before he could answer, she was over-come by a series of short, staccato coughs.

Nier had heard worse, and he felt no fever when he put his hand on her forehead, but the answer was already clear.

"Sorry, Yonah, but no. We can't take the risk of you getting worse overnight."

She appeared dejected, but didn't push the issue as Nier looked on with concern. A fever had left her bedridden just a week prior, and while her temperature had gone down and her appetite was back, the lingering cough still concerned him.

"Look, you can go outside for a bit if you want, okay?" he said in an attempt to make amends. The moment the words escaped his lips, her energy came roaring back.

"Can I go on an errand?!"

"You can buy one onion and one carrot. All right?"

"Can I buy the smallest carrot?"

"What? No. Remember how Popola said carrots are good for you?"

"Fine, I'll eat my carrots. That should cure my fever and my cough, too, right?"

By way of an answer, Nier reached out and patted Yonah on the head before placing a single bronze coin in her hand. Considering he would be paid for the herbs that day, a single coin seemed a reasonable price to make his sister happy. But as she grabbed her shopping basket and dashed out of the house, thrilled to be leaving for the first time in a long while, Nier caught up to her and took her hand.

"I thought you were going to the eastern gate," she said.

"I'll go with you to the fountain."

The gentle slope from the house to the fountain made running a tempting option, but past that there were more people about, which made Yonah less likely to bolt. At times like this, he often wondered if he was being overprotective, but made his peace with the matter by reminding himself he didn't want to see his sister in pain.

"Nier, look! Something splashed! Is it a fish?"

As Yonah pointed to the canal with gleaming eyes, Nier readjusted his grip on her hand to ensure she was secure. "The fish in the canals don't jump. Some of the ones in the sea do, but these guys are pretty calm."

"I want to get some water," said Yonah after a second's pause.

"Nope. Sorry. Buckets get really heavy when they're filled with water, and I don't want you falling into the canal."

As said canal was a precious lifeline for the entire village, people could only fish in certain areas and children were not permitted to splash around. This was why the majority of the villagers—including Nier and Yonah—didn't know how to swim. If anyone ever fell in the water, there would be no one coming to save them.

"Aw, boo," said Yonah. "I wish I could help you more."

"Hey, you're going on an errand, remember?" Nier reassured her. "That means you are helping."

As Yonah nodded in delight, the soft plucking of strings came drifting on the wind. Soon they saw Devola playing her beloved instrument and singing softly as she sat next to the fountain. Nier couldn't imagine the village without her voice in the background—it would be like having the library without Popola.

Yonah let go of Nier's hand and ran to Devola, and this time he didn't stop her. She looked up to Devola and Popola like they were her mothers—or perhaps older sisters—and preventing that most innocent of meetings seemed unnecessarily cruel.

"Morning, Yonah!" said Devola as she reached out to pinch the younger girl's cheeks. "Is your fever gone?"

"Yep! And did you know I'm going on an erra—"

Before Yonah could finish, a dry cough exploded from her lungs. Devola looked up at Nier as he approached a few moments later, concern written across her face.

"Her fever went away three days ago, but the cough is still sticking around," he explained.

"Mm, I see. Well, at least it doesn't seem like a bad cough."

Devola was right. It wasn't the phlegmy cough Yonah often got with a throat ailment, nor was it the kind that left her wheezing whenever she inhaled. It was a dry, almost weak thing—but while his sister didn't seem too bothered by it, the fact she'd never had this particular sort of illness made Nier nervous.

"You should drop by and see Popola when you're done with your errands," Devola suggested. "Last night she made a cough suppressant for the lady who runs the weapon shop, and I bet she has some left over."

Yonah wrinkled her nose as she recalled Popola's bitter medicinal brews. Her dismayed expression caused Devola to laugh.

"You know, I bet Popola would be happy to read to you if you drank the whole thing."

"Will she read me the book about the big tree?"

"You bet."

"Okay, then I'll go see her. I don't like it, but I'll take her icky medicine and then she has to read to me!"

"*After* your errands, yes?"

"Oh yeah!" cried Yonah. "I'll be right back!"

Devola grinned as the girl spun on a heel and took off for the shopping district, and Nier gave a polite nod before setting off on his own task. He retraced his steps to the house, climbed a steep hill, and soon found himself standing before the eastern gate, where the usual guard was stretching and trying to blink the sleepiness out of his eyes.

"Good morning," said Nier.

"Morning," replied the guard. "And hey, be careful out there today, all right? Word's going 'round that one of the guys spotted a Shade just outside town."

Shades were dark creatures that attacked people indiscriminately, and they were far more dangerous than any wild beast. The terror they inspired was the reason most people never wanted to leave the safety of the village walls.

"Nice day out, though," the guard added. "So they'll probably leave you be."

Sunlight damaged Shades, which meant they rarely showed themselves on warm, bright days. However, that made dim nooks and thick brush all the more dangerous during cloudy days or when the afternoon moved to evening. Yet because their weakness was to the sun specifically and not merely any light, even the brightest torch had no effect on them. No one knew why this was—and in fact, they all had far more questions than answers about Shades. Were they alive? What did they eat? How did they proliferate? Did they have any degree of intelligence? Even these most basic facts were a mystery to all.

Fortunately, Nier had never heard of Shades appearing near the eastern gate. Goats, on the other hand, did. Those grumpy critters were far more temperamental than the sheep on the plains, and a careless approach was likely to be met with both hooves and horns. So as Nier passed through the gate and began gathering his herbs, he made sure to give the grazing animals a wide berth. Someone once told him that people long, long ago used to keep domesticated goats and sheep, but he wasn't sure if that was true. He couldn't imagine raising such creatures like you would a pig or chicken. In fact, he had no idea how you'd keep them calm at all, unless it was through some kind of magic.

While thinking on the past, he remembered how someone once told him the night was pitch-black in ages past. He could scarcely believe this, either, but if true, it meant there hadn't been any Shades back then—if the sky went dark after the sun vanished behind the horizon, they would have wiped out humanity in no time. A shudder ran down his spine as he imagined a world that ended in darkness every day, and marveled at how people once went about their lives free from the terror of Shades. He decided to stop his musing there, because there was no point in imagining what things were like long ago; it wouldn't make their lives easier, nor would it make Yonah healthier.

Once his bag was full of herbs and his basket overflowing with mushrooms, he looked down at the shadow at his feet. He was done earlier than expected, and there was still plenty of time before the weak gloam of evening arrived. If he went a bit farther, he could reach the tree that bore Yonah's favorite red fruit. But despite having the time, he decided to head back to the village anyway. For a reason he couldn't put his finger on, he just wanted to be with Yonah today.

3.

"YONAH CAME AND left not too long ago," Popola said with a smile as she took the bag of herbs from Nier. "You just missed her. Honestly, I wish I could have read her another book—but when letters come in, I have to read them. Duty calls and all that."

"It's all right, Popola. I'm sorry she was bothering you while you were working."

Popola's job included a wide array of things. While most of their responsibilities revolved around managing the library, she and Devola were also in charge of all matters concerning life and death in the village and surrounding area. They helped deliver every baby that was born and arranged funerals for every person who died. That, combined with Popola's seemingly endless supply of general knowledge, made her a treasured resource. Whenever trouble visited a community, they dropped everything to send letters and messengers in search of her wisdom.

"Her cough is different this time, isn't it?" asked Popola in an almost offhand way.

Mixed emotions immediately rose up in Nier: anxiety that he'd been right about the oddness of her cough, as well as relief that Popola didn't seem too worried about it.

"I didn't give her a suppressant," she continued. "I thought it better to just keep an eye on her for now."

"I'll be sure she gets to bed early," replied Nier, his mind already whirling with plans. *I'll need to feed her soon, then make sure she has enough blankets. After that, I'll have to see she doesn't leave the house tomorrow, and also—*

"Enough," chuckled Popola. "I see your gears turning. You're going to end up sick yourself if you worry this much."

"But—"

"Seriously, stop. You're doing fine."

Hearing those words brought Nier genuine relief, and he was again struck by how the twins took such a personal interest in Yonah and himself. After leaving the library, he delivered the mushrooms and received a pumpkin in return before heading home. It was an especially sweet variety of pumpkin, and he planned to boil it for dinner, which was one of his sister's favorite meals.

As he approached the house and looked up at the second-floor window, he noticed it was empty. Yonah was always glued to the glass when it was time for him to come home, and seeing it bare caused a horrible feeling to form in his stomach. Screaming her name, he ran to the door and practically kicked it open, only to find her sitting on the floor with a confused look on her face and the baby chick in her hand. A wave of relief almost knocked him off his feet as he realized she hadn't been upstairs because she was caring for the hatchling.

"What's wrong?" she asked.

"Nothing," muttered Nier as he started to feel silly for picturing his sister collapsed on the floor in the midst of some coughing fit.

"Our little chick ate so much!" Yonah announced as she happily ran a finger over its head before gently placing it back in the basket. "Oh, and Popola said I don't have to take any medicine! She just wants me to stay warm, go to bed early, and . . ."

As usual, Yonah began rambling on about everything that

happened that day, almost as if she wanted to reclaim the time they'd been forced to spend apart. Relieved, Nier let her talk as he set down his things and began preparing a fire in the kitchen. But a moment later, her monologue was interrupted by a dry cough—and in an unexpected turn, it didn't stop, but instead began to get worse.

"Easy, Yonah. You're talking too much. Try to stay quiet for a little bit, okay?"

Just as he was about to turn back to his business, he heard a quiet splat like she'd just coughed up her lunch. He whirled around, ready to run over and help, then froze. Yonah's hands were pressed to her mouth, and a thick black fluid was leaking through her fingers. A grim odor, clearly not vomit, filled the air, and it took him a moment to recognize the scent of blood.

"It . . . hurts . . ." moaned Yonah. She attempted to stand as tears filled her eyes, but another coughing fit kept her planted on the ground. Globs of dark red blood began to pour from her hands and puddle on the floor, almost as if some creature inside her was attempting to burst out.

As he looked on, a thought forced its way into his mind—a thought of a disease so horrible, it was nicknamed "the Reaper." The Black Scrawl.

4.

"THAT SHOULD KEEP things calm for now."

Popola's eyes shifted to the door, silently urging Nier to leave the room. Devola, who had stayed by Yonah's side until she finally fell asleep, nodded.

Nier didn't remember exactly what had happened after he thought about the Black Scrawl. He knew he ran out of the house with Yonah in his arms, he knew she cried about her back hurting, and he vaguely recalled running into Devola and having her send him back to the house. His first truly clear memory was cleaning up the blood on the floor with Devola, then Popola arriving with medicine. But even though they were the two people he trusted most in the world, their presence did nothing to stop his anxiety.

When our father died, Mom was still around. And when Mom died, Yonah and I had each other. But what happens if Yonah *dies?*

He was unable to think beyond that; it was as if his thoughts were being swallowed by a dark and bottomless abyss.

"Why Yonah?" Nier asked a little later when it was just him and Popola alone on the first floor. "Is it because I didn't take good enough care of her? Was my food bad?"

"Of course not. You take very good care of her, and you feed her quite well."

"Then is this . . . is this Mom's . . . ?"

His voice quivered and the question died in the air, but his mind was more than happy to finish it for him: *Is this Mom's fault?*

The Black Scrawl had killed their mother without warning five years before, but it was a long time before Popola revealed this information. Their mother apparently didn't think her children would understand, so she'd kept her symptoms hidden and continued to push herself without pause until the very end.

"This is no one's fault," Popola had said at the time. "While it's true no one knows the cause of the Black Scrawl, it isn't a genetic condition, nor is it contagious. There's also no relationship between it and constitution or lifestyle, so it's not unusual for perfectly healthy people to contract it."

Nier suddenly stopped musing on the past and stared at Popola. "Did you know?" he asked. "Did you know Yonah had it?"

He suspected one of the sisters knew, especially since Devola was the one who told them to visit Popola when she heard Yonah's cough. But then Popola opted not to give her a suppressant, saying they would keep an eye on her instead. So maybe she knew normal medicine wouldn't help at all.

"I hoped I was wrong," she replied in a whisper. "But Devola and I have seen so many cases of the Black Scrawl now that I . . . I just . . ."

"What's going to happen to her?"

Nier couldn't bring himself to ask the real question on his mind: *How long will she live?* He knew the Black Scrawl was fatal, and that no drug or treatment could cure it. The Black Scrawl scared *everyone*, which was why everyone knew a thing or two about it. After it claimed his mother, he found himself listening carefully whenever adults started talking about it.

"It's different for everyone," began Popola, "but the fevers, cough, and pain will last for a while. Some people complain about aching in their arms or legs, but since Yonah said her back is hurting, that means her pain is coming from her bones."

Popola went on to explain how the pain would eventually spread through the entire body, rendering Yonah bedridden. Even lying motionless would not dull her agony, and each time she coughed up blood, the symptoms would grow worse. The description made Nier's heart clench as he thought about how their mother had managed to bear such agony while still greeting them every day with a smile.

"Once you see black writing appear on the body, it means the end is close," finished Popola sadly. "I'm sorry. I truly am."

"There must be something we can do," said Nier. He knew it was a stupid sentiment, but that was precisely why he felt the need to bring it up.

"We can manage the pain somewhat with medicine, but as for a cure . . ."

"Then let's stop the pain. We'll worry about the rest later." He couldn't stand the idea of his sister suffering, so if there was a way to take that away, he was more than happy to pursue it. But Popola quickly brought him back to earth with a small shake of the head.

"That medicine isn't something we have on hand, nor is it a thing we can make by scavenging materials that grow around the village like we do with our cough and fever cures."

Which means it's going to be expensive, thought Nier. Since he was the one who gathered materials for the village, Popola usually gave him medication whenever he needed it. That clearly would not be the case this time.

"But still . . . it's Yonah."

Popola, looking woeful, cast her eyes downward and said nothing more.

5.

THIS IS YONAH, and I'll do anything for her.

Nier's sentiment as Yonah's older brother was genuine, but reality was not so forgiving.

He was able to purchase the first order of painkillers by draining their savings. After their mother died, Nier found letters from their father along with a small pile of coins. He never touched the money, instead saving it for the day they absolutely needed it—which was likely the reason their mother hadn't spent it either. Meager as they were, having emergency funds around proved reassuring—so much so that when Popola first told him the painkillers were expensive, he knew he would manage somehow.

When he finally got the first order, he was pleasantly surprised at how well they worked. They did nothing for Yonah's low-grade fever or cough, but those had been light to begin with. In fact, the cough caused by the Black Scrawl wasn't as bad as the one she got when the seasons changed, which often kept her up all night for days on end. So as long as the pain of the Black Scrawl was held at bay, the physical burden on her was practically absent.

But this was only a temporary reprieve; once they ran out of medication, the pain would return with teeth and talons bared. Sadly, sooner than he ever imagined possible, they had drained the last coin of their savings.

"Are you going out already?" asked Yonah as she sat up in bed and rubbed her eyes. Nier had done his best to get ready without making any noise, but she had sensed his movement anyway.

"I'm picking royal ferns today, so I need to leave early. Now go back to sleep."

"Are you going out to where the scary sheep are?" she demanded as her face clouded over. She knew royal ferns were abundant in the northern plains, along with Shades and the surprisingly terrifying wild sheep.

"I'm sorry," she continued. "This is all because I'm sick. That's why you have to—"

"Don't worry about me. No sheep could ever beat your big brother. Remember when I brought home that mutton?" He left out the fact he'd been with an adult from the village at the time, and that the sheep had already been weakened from a trap. "Besides, I'm only going to pick ferns today, but I promise to bring some mutton home soon."

This wasn't merely a lie to make her feel better—he truly was stronger and faster than he had been a year ago. In fact, if he had a real weapon, he could likely take down as many sheep as he wanted. Acquiring such a thing, however, was a challenge currently beyond his means.

"I'll be back later," he said with a smile. Yonah raised her hand to wave goodbye and wish him luck, but the gesture was stopped short by another cough.

Nier quickly made his way to the southern gate. Most of the villagers were still asleep at this hour, and the market street was nearly deserted. For a long while, the only sounds were the echo of his own footsteps, but then he made out the faint creak of the waterwheel and some clucking hens. He figured the chicken keeper's wife was probably out collecting eggs, and a moment later, his guess was rewarded by the sight of a familiar face by the gate.

"Good morning!" he called from several paces away, making sure not to accidentally crush any eggs hiding in the tall grass.

"Heya, Nier!" replied the chicken keeper's wife. "Another early morning for you?"

"Sure is. Speaking of, I was wondering if you had any work for me." Nier needed as many jobs as he could handle in order to afford Yonah's medicine, so he'd made a habit of asking any passing villager if they could use a spare hand.

"Sorry, but we've got things sorted for now," said the woman in an apologetic tone. She and her husband never raised more chickens than they could handle between the two of them—not that the grasses and bugs in the area could support a great number of chickens anyway. If they got more, they'd have to go out of their way to buy feed, and they didn't have the money for that kind of expense.

"Actually, you know what? If you ever get a job that takes you to Seafront, pick up some seashells for me, okay?"

Seafront was a long way to go for a single errand, and not a place Nier was very fond of. While he'd only been there once, the experience had given him some very unpleasant memories.

"Why shells?" he asked in an attempt to hide his discomfort.

"I heard that feeding crushed shells to chickens helps 'em lay better eggs."

"Well, I'll be sure to pick some up if I get a job out that way, but it will probably be a little bit."

"Oh, sure, no rush. Just whenever you happen to be in the area."

Their chat complete, he continued down the empty market street to the northern gate, where he discovered one of the two guards on duty. As always, Nier asked if there was work available, but the guard only gave a troubled shake of the head.

"Sorry, no," he said. "But I'll ask anyone who passes through for you, so stop by on your way back."

"Thank you."

"Sure thing. Wouldn't expect too much, though."

The guard's warning was understandable, for while the villagers were all kindhearted, theirs was a particularly destitute hamlet. The scrap wheat and tiny river fish that served as chicken feed and bait in other towns were precious sources of food in the town. In addition to lacking food, most people didn't have the financial leeway to hire workers, which meant jobs were in incredibly short supply. Even the villagers who were comparatively better off had their hands full paying for basic tailoring and mending fees. If you didn't run a shop, work a farm, or guard a gate, your only option was to look elsewhere—which was what sent Nier's father far afield.

This meant the jobs Nier took were essentially charitable errands that could be completed in exchange for food or pocket change. While the villagers knew how hard it was to make money based on such tasks, they recognized a fifteen-year-old wasn't going to be hired on in a larger town. Nier was painfully aware of all of this, and desperate to grow up as fast as possible. Because at the rate things were going, he wouldn't have money to eat tomorrow, much less pay for medicine.

He spent half the day picking royal ferns before returning to the village. As predicted, the guard who asked passersby about work opportunities had come up empty. After thanking him, Nier decided to speak with Devola, who spent a good deal of time singing in the village tavern and chatting with folks who needed to blow off steam. She wasn't the voice of wisdom her sister was, but she was always willing to lend an ear and a shoulder—which made her keenly aware of who was looking for help at any given time. When Nier asked about work, however, Devola could only frown.

"Sorry, Nier, but I've got nothing. Oh, but I *did* just come across an old lady looking to buy a house! She said her son and daughter-in-law are coming home after being away for a while."

Nier blinked. "Devola, wait. Are you suggesting . . . ?"

"It wouldn't be so bad! There are plenty of empty rooms in the library, so the two of you would always have a place to sleep."

Nier had never considered selling the house. While it was old and small and probably wouldn't command much of a price, it was still money that would free him from the worry of not being able to afford Yonah's medicine for a while.

"At least think about it?" Devola suggested.

Considering their savings were depleted, Nier knew the smart thing to do was nod in affirmation, sell the house, then ask Popola to let them stay at the library. But while he understood the logic, he still couldn't bring himself to agree. Yonah spent nearly all her time in their house because of how sickly she was, and it was special to her. It was also the only connection she still had to their late mother, seeing as they had sold her old clothes and personal effects to buy medicine. The house was all they had left to remind them of her, and he just couldn't bring himself to sell it.

"Yeah, I don't know if . . ." Unable to finish his sentence, Nier trailed off and hung his head.

"No, of course not," replied Devola. "That's fine. Don't worry about it."

Nier was happy he didn't need to explain himself at length, and pleased that Devola and Popola understood his family better than anyone. "I'm sorry. I know you brought it up because you were trying to help."

"No, *I'm* sorry! I had a feeling you were going to say no."

With no more work to do and nothing set for tomorrow,

Nier felt his heart growing heavy. Sighing, he pushed open the weighty tavern doors and left. On his way home, he saw a young mother dragging a child behind her and berating him, which only brought his mood lower. He had a suspicion the local mothers forbade their children from playing by Nier's house lest they catch Yonah's Black Scrawl.

The villagers all knew the disease couldn't be passed from one person to another, so they treated Nier as they always had after Yonah was diagnosed—but that didn't mean they weren't scared. While they were *told* the Black Scrawl wasn't contagious, everyone had more questions than answers. What if it could be passed on in rare instances? Why did it affect some people and not others? All the uncertainty surrounding the Black Scrawl served to muddle what few truths they had.

It was why their own mother chose to hide her condition—not only for the sake of her children, but out of fear she would stop receiving even the smallest of jobs. No matter how much the pain plagued her, she decided it was better than not being able to support her family.

Nier wondered how things would have turned out if the villagers had learned the true cause of her death. Would they have been as kind to him and Yonah? Would that kindness remain now that Yonah had the very same illness? And was a simple warning not to play by their house the worst of it, or was there more to come?

As Nier pondered such things, another thought suddenly occurred to him: *When was the last time I watered the garden?*

With all their money going to medicine, they had nothing to spare for food. He knew their yard had been a vegetable patch when their mother was alive, so he'd weeded it, dug up fresh earth, and scattered what few seeds he had—but how long ago had that been now?

Please let there be time, he prayed as he ran. When he reached their house, he vaulted over the crumbling wall that protected the patch, then fell to his knees when he saw how the few leaves that had managed to emerge on the sprouts had all withered and died. As his mind reeled, he remembered how obsessive his mother had been about watering the garden. Though she was happy to leave the chickens to Nier, she never let him near the garden, likely because she knew how hard it was to grow things in poor soil. But his day had begun early today, yesterday he had been running errands from morning to night, and the day before that had been the same. With all the work, the garden had simply slipped his mind.

Maybe it just wasn't possible for two children to live without support in a poor village like this. Maybe his only choice was to sell the house. After all, they had already sold off everything else they could.

No. Not everything.

That's right. He did have something else to sell—one last thing. As he considered this, he found himself unable to stand, almost as if a terrible weight had settled on his back. He needed to get inside, feed Yonah, give her the medicine, and prepare for tomorrow. But though his list of tasks cried out for attention, his body simply would not obey.

6.

"WHERE ARE YOU going today?" asked Yonah. She could tell he was going somewhere far away based on his clothing, and the nervousness in her voice was palpable.

"I've got an errand in Seafront," he said as Yonah clung to his coat suspiciously. "The chicken lady said her birds lay better eggs if she grinds shells into their feed, so she asked me to go get some. Honestly, I'm still not convinced chickens can eat shells."

It wasn't a lie—and secretly, he was glad he'd encountered the chicken lady the day before. Regardless, Yonah refused to let go of his coat.

"Is that all?"

"Huh? No, I've got other jobs! Seafront's too far away to run over there just for shells. You know the lady at the flower shop? She wanted me to buy her some tulip bulbs they only sell out there."

Now *that* was a lie—no one else had asked him for anything. He knew he was talking too much and too quickly, but he couldn't stop. He had a feeling that if he didn't pile lie upon lie, Yonah would see right through him.

"Oh, and then the man at the material shop asked for—"

"It sounds like you've got too many errands to come home tonight, huh?"

Nier felt a wave of relief when he saw her head drop. She hadn't seen through his lies—she was just sad. She'd probably remembered the last time she spent the night alone six months ago and felt uneasy. While he hated to make her stay alone, Seafront was a long way away—not to mention that the southern plains between there and here were home to a fearsome Shade, making midday the only safe time to travel. No matter how urgent his business, getting there and back in a day was simply not possible.

"You stayed by yourself once before, remember?" he reminded her. "You're a lot more grown-up now than you were then. Besides, staying here and making sure everything runs smoothly is an important job."

She finally seemed to accept this and released her hold on his coat. He turned away from her uneasy expression, closed the door behind him, and began to run without looking back. He was afraid if he stopped, he wouldn't be able to push himself any further, so he ran and he ran until his breath finally gave out. When he stopped, the village was already out of sight, so he slowed his pace and began measuring each breath.

He needed to conserve his energy in case he bumped into a Shade at some point in his journey. The only way to survive an encounter with one was to run as fast as you could the moment you saw it in the distance.

Soon he found himself on the outskirts of the southern plains, home of the massive Shade. Since he'd been here before, he knew just how much distance he needed to keep and exactly which places were safe to stop and rest. Despite that, he found himself much more nervous than he was last time.

Said time was a mere six months ago, when he got his first job sending him to Seafront. He was asked to deliver an urgent letter to someone in the city, buy tulip bulbs, and pick up some natural rubber. He'd been a bundle of nerves at the prospect of leaving Yonah by herself, and when he saw the massive Shade in the distance, he started running across the plains as fast as his legs would carry him.

Upon reaching the city, he saw the ocean for the first time in his life. Though it was beautiful, the fishy odor that lay over the city proved too much for him. His hair and skin grew sticky as he walked around, making him feel disgusting. It was only after speaking to the woman at the flower shop that he learned the sea breeze caused this discomfort.

Once he had the bulbs and other materials, Nier ventured into a district full of large houses to deliver the letter. The streets wove around like a maze while buildings blocked every sight line, making it hard to get his bearings. When he finally managed to make the delivery, he realized he had no idea how to get back out again. And either due to the time of day or because residents simply didn't like going outside, there was no one to ask for directions. After a number of exhausting dead ends, he finally sat down by the gate of a large house.

"Whatcha doing there, kid?" came a man's sudden sharp voice from the direction of the house.

Thinking he was being scolded, Nier scuttled away from the gate in a panic. "Not from around here, are you?" continued the voice. "You lost?"

Relief coursed through him as he realized he could finally ask someone for directions, which was why his guard was lowered when the man stepped through the gate, and why he answered honestly when the owner of the voice asked if he was alone. A moment later, a wolfish grin flashed across the man's face. Nier stumbled back, but the man grabbed his arm—he was *so* strong—threw a hand over his mouth, and began dragging him into the house.

"You want some money? Huh, kid?"

The whisper in Nier's ear sent chills rocketing through his body. He used every ounce of strength to shake himself free, and as he ran away, he heard the man behind him laughing and laughing and laughing.

"Come back when you want money, kid!"

His desire to escape the voice was overwhelming, so he ran as fast and as far as he could. And once he reached the shoreline, he still kept running, because the voice seemed to follow him no matter how far away he was.

After he returned home, the echo of the man's laughter gradually faded from his mind. Nier had little cause to go to Seafront—incidental errands for the villagers if anything—and over the next six months the unpleasant incident was forgotten.

But now, as Seafront slowly came into view, Nier's steps grew heavy. *Maybe I'll get lost again*, he thought. *Maybe I won't be able to find the house.* But in a terrible twist of fate, the residence he was looking for sat right next to the town's main entrance.

He stopped to consider the home. It was nice—quite nice, actually—which meant the owner must be a man of some means. The moment that thought crossed his mind, the sickening laugh replayed in his head and his legs shook.

You can't go back, you know. Once you step across the threshold . . .

He realized he was looking for an excuse, any excuse, to turn back. *Just forget about everything*, he told himself. *We've had enough—you have had enough. You can't burden yourself like this anymore. But if I turn back now, what happens to Yonah?*

Yonah had been Nier's emotional support ever since their mother's passing. When he thought about what to feed her tomorrow, it gave him an excuse to ignore the distant, uncertain future. When he was busy caring for her, he could forget their mother wasn't around anymore. Though still a child himself, his younger sister gave him the strength to work hard and carry on.

"This is for Yonah," he murmured as he slowly pushed the gate wide.

7.

YONAH REMAINED IN a state of remission in the weeks after Nier returned from Seafront. While she still had a cough, it was no longer accompanied by blood—and with her pain gone, her appetite came back. She even managed to feed their chicken outside and spend some time in the library. Yonah only expressed loneliness and unease when Nier made his trips to Seafront every few days, but she was all smiles the rest of the time.

It was good. Everything was good. Nier had brought Yonah's joy back, and now he was focused on keeping her safe. That was all he needed, even if it did feel like more and more of him broke off and blew away every time he got the money to buy her medicine.

Nier walked through his village as those thoughts swirled in his mind. This always happened when he came home from Seafront, and he wished more than anything that he could simply empty his mind like a sieve and sleep. But somewhere, somehow, the road back home had become much more painful than the journey there.

Dazed, he thought he heard someone call his name and turned around to find Devola, who he hadn't realized was at the fountain.

"Hey there," she said. "You okay? You sick?"

Nier shook his head. He wasn't sick—only very, very tired. "Just thinking," he said eventually.

Devola gave him her usual grin, but for some reason he found it utterly stifling. "Hey, if you say so. Oh, and I meant to tell you that I love how you're tying your hair up now!"

"Yeah, it was getting in the way," he said, leaving out the part about how he'd started wearing it like this since *that time.*

"So practical," said Devola as she reached out to pat him on the head. It was a simple act, one she'd done hundreds of times since they were little, and his rational mind understood this. But as her hand landed on his hair, memories of the previous night came flooding back, and he smacked it away with all his strength.

He'd hated his hair ever since he started going to Seafront— and not just having it touched, but having it touch *him.* It was such a sickening sensation, and each time it happened, memories came flooding of the man grabbing his hair, as well as what came after. No matter how he tried to forget, the memories always returned, and with them came a pain that was etched into every crevice of his being. He'd considered shaving his head, but knew people would want to know why, and he couldn't come up with a good answer. Not to mention that every time it came up, the memories would rise with it. Eventually, he just decided to tie it up so it wouldn't touch him, which was the best solution he could come up with.

"Sorry," said Nier in a voice so hoarse and dry he hardly recognized it as his own. He knew he should say something, spout some explanation to ease Devola's suspicion, but nothing would come.

"Oh, that's my fault!" she replied, cheerfully oblivious. "You don't want me mussing up your new 'do, huh?"

She lifted her hand back to her instrument and prepared to play, but then stopped. "Oh, right. Popola was asking for you, so swing by before you go home . . . And, Nier?"

"Yeah?"

"Don't push yourself too hard, okay?"

Nier gave a vague smile. He appreciated Devola's concern

about how exhausted he was, but he valued her ignorance even more. If she ever found out, she wouldn't be this considerate. Instead, she would begin to look at him with contempt, like he was an undesirable piece of filth.

When he found Popola, he wondered if she would ask after his health as well or remind him to take it easy. But instead, she simply said, "I have a job for you."

That breezy, almost casual statement felt like salvation; right now, he much preferred being treated with indifference over worry or sympathy.

"But it's extremely dangerous," continued a hesitant Popola. "I'm not even sure if I should be asking you to take it on, but . . ."

"What is it?"

"Killing Shades."

An image of the enormous black mass in the southern plains appeared in his mind. It was folly to think a single person could keep that thing contained, much less slay it—yet he agreed to the offer without hesitation.

"You won't be alone, of course," Popola said. "There should be three others joining you from other areas around here, which makes you the fourth."

She went on to explain that the job was to exterminate one of the Shade dens in the northern plains. Thankfully, the creatures involved were all small, so even amateurs had a good chance of coming back successful.

"The other hunters are adults, and I don't think these Shades are particularly strong, but . . ."

But we're still fighting Shades, thought Nier. He would have to be ready for a minor injury, or perhaps a major one. And of course, there was always the possibility he wouldn't come back at all, which was likely why Popola was so hesitant. Still, Nier knew exactly what he wanted.

"I'll go, Popola. The more Shades there are in the northern plains, the more danger for the village. Besides, I need money for Yonah's medicine."

And the job keeps me away from Seafront.

"In that case, you're hired. Oh, and I promise that the pay will more than match the risk."

When she told him how much he'd be earning, Nier almost couldn't believe his ears. How many times would he have to go to that man's house to earn the same amount? How many times would he have to endure humiliation?

"The risk is fine. I'll do it."

"Just please take care of yourself, all right?"

There was a dark cast to Popola's eyes as she said this. It wasn't sadness or pain, nor was it sympathy or compassion. But the moment Nier saw it, he realized that she *knew*—and likely Devola as well. They knew how he was getting money to pay for Yonah's medicine, and they knew the true cost of such actions. And once they found out, they arranged for a job with a salary that dwarfed his current earnings, despite knowing the dangers that came with it.

The moment he realized this, his face went hot with shame. Yet at the same time, he was thankful the two of them had continued to treat him as they always did. Why did he think they would scorn him? They would never do such a thing.

"Thank you, Popola," he said finally. But despite how much he meant it, the darkness never left her eyes.

Their village was small and rarely visited by outsiders, so when Nier saw two strange men standing by the northern gate, he knew they were his companions on the job. But the newcomers had clearly not been told they would be fighting with a young boy, and their brows furrowed as he walked up to them.

"Go home, son," said one. "This is no game."

"I know that, but—"

"I'm serious. Get lost. I don't wanna lose sleep because some boy gets torn apart in front of me."

Nier didn't want to lose this rare opportunity—he had to do something, *anything*, to be part of the operation. But just when he was about to defend himself, a familiar voice rang out behind him.

"What's all the fuss about, eh?"

Nier didn't even need to turn to know who was speaking—it was a voice he would have recognized anywhere.

"Well, well, well! Look who's here. I forgot you're from this village, kid."

It was the Seafront man, and if Nier had any questions as to what he was doing here, the blade hanging from his hip quickly dispelled them. He'd seen a myriad of different swords in the man's house; he spared no expense in his collection and often bragged about how each one held a trace of murder. Of course a monster like him would have equally monstrous hobbies.

The Seafront man already seemed acquainted with the other two. As they talked among themselves, Nier learned the trio often worked together on jobs like that—jobs where the Seafront man could put his collection to practical use.

"You know this boy?" asked one of the other men.

"Oh, we know each other *real* well," the Seafront man said with a leer. "Don't worry, he won't get in the way—he's got enough strength to push a grown man around, and fast little legs too."

He was clearly speaking of the moment they first met. Nier looked away, disturbed, which only amused the man further. He leaned in close, trying hard to keep his face in view, and said, "He's got a face like a girl, but he's fierce. And he's good at toughing things out."

Nier's arms and legs stiffened and refused to obey him. He couldn't even shake off the hand resting on his shoulder in an overly familiar fashion.

"I got a feeling he might end up being surprisingly useful. 'Course, personally, I wanna see him shake and cry the moment the first Shade shows up."

"Well, if you say so," one of the other men said. "I guess we can bring him along."

The man Nier couldn't hate enough had now enabled him to keep his job. What could be more humiliating?

This is for Yonah. This is all to keep her safe.

He was repeating that mantra to himself and clenching his fists when he felt a sudden grip on the back of his head.

"What's with that look, kid?"

Grip was the wrong word—it wasn't tight enough for that. Yet it froze Nier in place all the same.

"I told you not to go tempting anyone else, remember?"

His voice was low enough that the others couldn't hear, his hot, sticky breath clinging to Nier's ear like poison. He felt new strength come into the fingers toying with his hair, and a moment later, it came loose and fell to his shoulders as the man danced away with a laugh. When Nier stooped down to pick up the fallen hair tie, he realized he couldn't stop his hands from shaking.

8.

THE SHADE DEN had been spotted along the mountain range facing the plains. People had known for a long while about the cave at the end of the narrow, winding path, and it made sense Shades would live there, considering their hatred for sunlight.

By the time they pushed into the mountains, the tension in Nier's arms and shoulders was constant. This was his first time holding a sword since he'd gone hunting with adults from his village—but while he'd wielded a dull blade suitable for taking down small animals that time, he now held an old, one-handed sword Popola found in the library storeroom. He didn't know how to look for traces of homicide on the blade, but the dark glint of the steel told him it had drawn blood more than once. Yet despite the weapon's ominous air, it felt perfectly comfortable in his hands, almost as if it had been waiting for him.

"The wind is oddly damp," said the man leading the way. The moment he did, Nier realized the air was indeed cool and heavy, much like how it felt before a rain. Yet when he looked up, the sky was a brilliant, cloudless blue.

"Let's get this business done and go home," the man continued. "Don't wanna get caught in some downpour."

With some way to go before the cave, the group's pace quickened. Even though there were no clouds in the sky, it wasn't unusual for the weather to change without warning. A few minutes later, the group realized the damp wind wasn't portending rain, but fog, and they soon found themselves unable to see the color of the sky anymore.

"Should we head back and try again later?" asked one.

"Fog won't matter once we reach the cave," said the other. "Let's just hurry up and . . . Oh damn! Shades!"

The group screeched to a halt as several black silhouettes emerged from the white mist. They whirled around to find several more approaching from the rear. They were surrounded, and by far more Shades than any of the men had expected to find. Suddenly it dawned on them: Shades thrived not just in caves, but in any area without sun. The foggy, narrow mountain paths were a perfect breeding ground for the creatures.

"These Shades weren't just living in a cave . . ." breathed the man in front. "This whole area belongs to them!"

"Look sharp! They're coming!"

As the dark silhouettes rushed at them, Nier swung his sword, letting the weight carry his momentum forward. The impact raced through the weapon and up to his hands, reminding him of what it had been like when he killed a sheep. A moment later, warm blood splashed across him—blood with the same acrid scent as the liquid Yonah coughed up. It was Nier's first time seeing a Shade bleed, and it caused him to hesitate.

While Shades looked like shadows, they tore apart like flesh when attacked, and bled the same red blood as any living creature. The only difference was that they didn't leave a corpse behind upon death, instead vanishing into a dark mist with just a small puddle of red left to let the world know they had ever been there at all.

What are *these things?*

This wasn't the time for questions, so Nier quickly shoved the thought aside and focused. Though the Shades were indeed small and weak, they were great in number, and he soon found himself falling into a kind of trance where his only thoughts were swinging his sword and watching the blood fly. Yet no matter how many he killed, they continued to pour out of the mist. Things with heads. Hands. Feet. Upright gaits. In fact, the more he slaughtered, the more they came to resemble humans, and he soon lost track of whether he was cutting down people or Shades. Were these members of his species? Was this sticky red liquid actually human blood?

When conscious thought finally returned, he found himself standing beside the Seafront man. So engrossed was he in testing his prized blade he didn't notice Nier. There was a faint smile on his face, and the blood that covered him head to foot made him look less a man than a monster.

Nier stared at him, wondering if he'd been wearing the same expression himself right until that moment. There was no question he had been killing Shades with a smile on his face—or that a secret piece of his heart had reveled in the slaughter. He even felt a bit of pride that he'd managed to take down so many of the creatures in succession. So who were the real monsters here? The Shades? Or them?

The mist grew even thicker as they continued their grim work.

9.

NIER'S MIND WAS numb. His thoughts a jumble. He'd
lost count of how many Shades he'd killed, but he knew that the
area seemed to be cleaned out. Exhaling loudly, he turned and
began heading back the way he'd come.

While he hadn't been seriously injured, he was covered in
scrapes and bruises, and there was a dull pain radiating across
most of his body. The blood on his arms and legs had dried, pulling his skin tight when he moved. He was also certain he smelled
terrible, but couldn't confirm that as he'd long since grown ac-
customed to the odor. He wanted to wash himself off as soon as
possible, but lacking the energy to run, he settled for walking as
fast as he could.

As the mist finally melted away, he caught up to the men
who'd tried to send him away back at the gates. One was dragging his leg behind him, and the other's left arm was twisted
in an unnatural direction. Seeing them, Nier couldn't help but
think how lucky he was to escape with the few injuries he had.

When the two men saw him approaching, their eyes widened
in shock. "You're alive!" cried one. "I honestly never expected to
see you again."

As Nier nodded in response, the man continued. "You were
real impressive out there, you know that? Weren't in the way at
all, and you practically had energy to spare. Our friend was right
about you for sure."

Suddenly, the expression on the man's face clouded. "Wait, where is our buddy, anyway? Isn't he with you?"

This time, Nier shook his head, which caused the man to let out a grievous sigh. "I was afraid of that. We had no idea there'd be that many of 'em, so it's basically a small miracle any of us are alive—especially you, seeing as you're still so young. I imagine it was pretty rough out there for you, huh?"

"It was fine," said Nier. "I did it for my sister."

It was true. He had done it for her, and he would continue to do anything for her. No matter how dangerous the job or dirty the act, he would keep doing what was necessary to keep her healthy and alive.

"Well, I'm just glad you're okay," said the man with the injured arm. He gave Nier a friendly slap on the back, then offered a shoulder to his friend as the three of them began the long journey home.

Nier remained silent as they walked through the mountain path and cut across the plains. They moved carefully, knowing none of them were in any shape to fight off even a single Shade, and grateful that luck had decided to bless them with a bright, sunny afternoon.

As he walked, Nier suddenly thought about the massive Shade he'd seen in the southern plains. It had hands and feet, and it had walked upright.

"I never knew Shades were so similar to people," he thought out loud.

He used to call the creatures "shadow monsters" when he was younger, since a shadow was exactly what it looked like when he saw his first real Shade. But not for a moment had he ever made a connection between them and actual people.

The two men tilted their heads in response to Nier's statement, so Nier elaborated. "I mean, you cut them and they bleed. Plus, the way it feels when you hit one . . ."

"Heh," said one of the men. "You might as well point out that goats and sheep bleed and all that when you cut 'em. Hacking apart Shades didn't feel particularly different."

The two men laughed at Nier's odd thought, then one continued talking. "Killing an actual person might feel different from doing it to Shades and sheep, but that's not something you can just test out."

"Well . . ."

Nier stopped to look down at the dried blood caked on his hands. The color gave no indication of whether the source was human or Shade. The Seafront man was dead, and Nier would never go to his house again.

"You okay there, son? Something hurt?"

The question snapped Nier back to reality. He looked up from his hands and shook his head. "Just thinking about how I need to get home."

He pictured Yonah at the second-floor window, waiting for him to return and greeting him with a smile like always. There was nothing else he needed to think about besides keeping her safe, which meant his life would be an easy one now.

He felt a great weight lift from his shoulders as he looked up at the sky. It was the same shade of blue it always had been, and as he watched, a single fluffy cloud drifted slowly.

REPORT 02

We have witnessed a tentative conclusion to the case under ongoing observation that we mentioned at the end of our previous report (please see attached documents for details).

We feared the incident would turn into a long-term situation, but this was luckily avoided. However, we are still unsure if the outcome was the correct one. While we are pleased the matter was settled quickly, the manner in which it concluded was less than desirable. In a way, it may have actually been the worst possible result, even though it was the best outcome for Nier himself.

Though we did not foresee this outcome, we remain responsible. We did not enjoy seeing Nier suffer in poverty, so offered him a dangerous job. We did not enjoy seeing him take up the dangerous job, so gave him a lethal weapon. One cannot help but think that the resulting circumstances changed Nier's way of life, if not the boy himself.

Now that he has learned to eliminate obstacles with his own power, he will likely approach future difficulties differently than he did in the past—and new events will most certainly arise as a result. Who can say this will not serve as the seed of a fresh, unplanned disaster?

This incident, which we referred to by

code name "Red and Black," was a minor matter resolved in a short period of time. Under normal circumstances, our report on the incident would have remained local. However, we went out of our way to designate it a shared incident because we could not ignore the possibility of it serving as the catalyst for something larger.

We sincerely hope the concerns we carry about our inference turn out to be groundless.

Record written by Popola

The Boy 2

IF ONLY THIS were still a dream; he would have been happy to accept everything as a terrible nightmare he never had to face again.

"YONAH!"

Nier called his sister's name over and over as he ran. His own shrieking would have woken him if he were in a dream—if it were one of the many dreams he'd had where she suddenly vanished. But in a cruel twist, this was no dream. Instead, what lay before him was the very narrow—and very real—path that led to the Lost Shrine.

Lunar Tear? That's a silly name.

I guess. But people say finding one will make you rich beyond your wildest dreams!

Could a Lunar Tear make me better?

He shouldn't have told her that. Yonah had always been a curious girl, and he should have realized that even the name of the flower would be enough to pique her interest. Plus, no matter how many library books she had, he knew spending so many days cooped up inside their small house was boring her out of her mind. He just wanted to tell her something interesting to relieve the boredom, so he chose a story he'd heard from Popola about a flower called a Lunar Tear—one said to grant any wish to the person who found it. And while Yonah's eyes had lit up at the story, Nier never imagined she would do something like *this* when he saw the joy on her face.

His heart sank into his stomach when he got home and didn't see her waiting at the second-floor window. She didn't tackle him in a hug as she normally did when he returned, nor did she welcome him with an unending barrage of chatter. Her bed was empty. She was gone.

He searched every nook of the library and looked in every corner of town, then rushed *back* to the library to see if Popola had any idea where his sister might be.

"She just asked if I knew where Lunar Tears grow," said Popola. "She's so cute."

She went on to explain how Yonah had visited the library earlier that day and asked all sorts of questions about Lunar Tears. "I told her how they used to grow around the Lost Shrine long ago, but . . . Oh no."

There it is, Nier thought as his conversation with Yonah came rushing back. When she'd asked if a Lunar Tear could make her better, he had not realized how deadly serious the question was.

As he dashed away from the library and toward the edge of town, he still couldn't quite believe it. Yonah was so small, after all—could she *really* have left the village by herself? But then he found a hair ribbon lying on the ground in front of the eastern gate. It seemed like any old ribbon at a glance, but a closer examination revealed that the ends were slightly frayed. Nier had tied her hair up using that very ribbon; there was now no doubt she was heading for the Lost Shrine.

He flew through the gate and dashed up the stone steps. His mind was a whirl of panicked, terrible thoughts. If he couldn't find her soon, any number of horrific things could happen on the narrow, treacherous road that led to the shrine. But though he ran as fast as he ever had in his life, all manner of unexpected obstacles arose to slow him down. At one point, an aggressive goat wandered over to stand in his way. At another, he had to make a detour around a path blocked by a rockslide. Yet these things wouldn't have deterred Yonah. The goat had likely been grazing elsewhere when she came through, and she could have easily fit through the gaps in the rocks.

Nier clambered up a boulder, then proceeded down a narrow path flanked on either side by rocky cliffs. He couldn't see very far in front of him, and frequently found himself doubling back on his own trail, wasting even more time. With impatience burning in his chest, he crossed a rickety rope bridge and finally found himself at the entrance to the Lost Shrine. Yet no matter how many times he screamed Yonah's name, she never responded—which could only mean she had already gone inside.

"How in the world did she make it here on her own?"

Though Nier left the village on occasion, he'd never come close to the Lost Shrine, much less gone inside. He hadn't known the building was surrounded by water, nor that its roof was hemmed in by a series of uneven walls. Frankly, the entire building seemed rather unkempt.

His surprise only grew when he ventured inside and found a massive tree growing in the middle of the shrine—one that would take several full-grown adults to encircle its thick trunk. Its upper branches had burst through the ceiling and stretched up into the sky, allowing sunlight to filter in from the outside. And it was not just the ceiling that let in light—broken sections of the outer wall also helped in that regard. All that sun meant the threat of Shades was considerably lessened, yet there were still enough dark patches here and there to give him pause.

"Yonah?"

Though he didn't speak loudly, his voice echoed far more than he was expecting. He called for her again, more strongly this time, and heard her name repeat over and over. Yet no matter how much he strained, he could sense no living presence in the shrine, much less hear Yonah. His only company was the sound of his own breathing; his sister had gone somewhere his voice could not reach.

He knew she would have strained her little head to think of all the places flowers might grow. Since flowers grew in bright, sunny places, and not the shaded interiors of buildings . . .

"I bet she's on the roof."

Nier considered the unsightly roof and its uneven walls for a moment. Popola said Yonah had come by the library in the early afternoon, and considering it was now evening, there had been more than enough time for a child to reach the roof. He sprinted to the spiral staircase that stretched up from the tree's roots and began to climb. The stairs were worn almost to the point of collapse but remained bright in the sunlight. If Yonah had indeed come this way, she definitely would have used the stairs.

If you leave the village, never go into the shade. Always walk where the sun is shining.

He'd told her this over and over again when he brought her outside the village gates, trying as hard as he could to burn it into her mind. Though Yonah was little, she had a sharp memory—he trusted that she would have remembered his words.

As he continued his mad dash up the stairs, he suddenly heard an echo of Yonah's voice in his mind.

I'm sorry. All I do is cause you trouble.

I love you sooo much!

If I get better, will you stay home more?

Hearing her words caused him to curse his carelessness anew. Why had he told her about the wish-granting flower?! Why hadn't he thought about how lonely it was for her to stay home alone all the time?! All she wanted was to find a Lunar Tear, cure her illness, and live happily ever after—and that desire had caused her to leave the village and come all the way out here. He couldn't imagine her *not* being afraid as she squeezed through tiny gaps in fallen rocks, crossed the rickety rope bridge, and made her way up the creaking spiral staircase. As he pictured her mustering up the courage required for such things, he felt as if his heart were going to burst.

Please be safe, he thought to himself as he ran. *Please be safe.*

Nier checked the halls and side rooms in the upper floors just in case, but didn't find any sign of her. What he did find, however, was a dark shadow the size of a child. It was swaying back and forth next to a stack of crates, and the sight of it caused his feet to freeze in place.

Was there only one Shade, or multiple? Should he press the attack, or fight only if it came at him first? After considering these questions, he began slowly backing away, keeping his eyes on the monster all the while. A moment later, the dark shadow began making its way toward Nier with slow, drunken movements. Perhaps it was drunk, at that, because it made no attempt to avoid a patch of sunlight illuminating the floor in front of it. As Nier stopped to watch, the Shade began to burn and fizzle in the light.

Though the creature ended up posing no danger, he couldn't shake the eerie feeling it caused to rise in his stomach. He never thought he'd see a Shade *choose* to walk into sunlight. Clearly the ones in the shrine weren't as smart as those on the plains—that was, if Shades even had any intelligence to begin with. Relieved that he didn't have to draw his sword, he smacked his cheeks a couple of times, forcing himself to get back on track.

When the spiral staircase came to an end, he was forced to climb several ladders. As he roamed through passageways looking for the next one, he spied a door sitting ajar. A thin ray of light filtered in through the gap, suggesting it led outside—and when a gust of wind rushed over him as he pushed it open, his suspicions were confirmed.

The corridor it opened onto was less a hallway and more a shoddy hodgepodge of wooden boards. He could tell at a glance it had been hastily thrown together as a stopgap measure. The boards were worn in places, their hues faded to a variety of different colors. One step too forceful or one leap too aggressive would likely cause him to go crashing through the floor, so he made his way onward and upward at a slow, agonizing pace.

Wind whipped around Nier's head when he finally emerged on the roof. Like the inside, the top of the shrine was in a terrible state. Crates sat cracked. Walls stood crumbled. Vinelike plants—either roots or branches—tangled around everything, writhing across the floor as if hoping to trip an unsuspecting traveler. As Nier wondered how he could possibly get past them, he encountered another obstacle: stone walls that sectioned the roof off into a series of small areas.

As he wandered, Nier realized this wasn't the structure's original roof. Instead, he was standing on what used to be the top floor, and the things he'd thought of as fortress walls were, in fact, the same ordinary walls that lined the rest of the building. It had clearly been a taller structure at some point, but the top floor—including the roof—had crumbled away and been lost. The unsightly ups and downs he'd spied from a distance had not been built deliberately. They were the result of a portion of the building being destroyed by unplanned circumstances.

Knowing the reason for the unusual architecture, however, did not make the shrine any easier to navigate. With passages and stairs made by human hands long gone, Nier was forced to squeeze through gaps in broken walls and climb mounds of debris. He even made use of a ladder some thoughtful soul had left long after the destruction.

Though he called for Yonah every step of the way, she never responded to his voice. But if she wasn't on the roof, where *was* she? As he shook his head violently in an attempt to clear away an increasingly terrible series of thoughts on the matter, he spotted something that looked like a ladder sticking out from an unnatural spot. Cheered to realize there was still a portion of the roof he'd yet to search, he walked over to the ladder and saw it led to a set of sturdy doors.

Yonah is beyond those doors. The reason she never answered my calls was because they were blocking the sound. She's safe. She's safe!

He quickly slid down the ladder and burst through the doors, finding himself in the middle of a large, grand room. It was so long, it took a few seconds for him to look from one end to the other, and the ceiling was high enough above his head to make him dizzy.

The moment his gaze finally reached the far side of the room, relief pooled in his chest. Yonah was lying on a platform by the wall, one just tall enough to serve as a bed.

She must have fallen asleep after all that walking.

Though all his instincts screamed for him to run to his sister, he paused a moment to look at something odd. Standing in front of Yonah were two massive stone statues, one with a single horn and one with a pair. Though they lacked typical human forms—with limbs seeming to sprout directly out of their heads—they still stood upright, wore armor to protect their bodies, and held weapons at the ready. Nier couldn't tell if they were swords or staves; each was a long shaft that ended in a kind of half circle. The more he examined the statues, the more disturbing they became. Yonah must have been *unbelievably* tired to fall asleep with those things around.

I need to take her home. I need to feed her warm food and put her to bed before she comes down with a fever.

Nier's feet, which had begun to move at this thought, suddenly came to a halt. A number of dark shadows stood swaying at the statues' feet, their size and movements similar to the Shade he'd seen on the way here. This time, he did not wait for the sun. He drew his sword and began to cut them down without mercy. The creatures didn't run at his approach—instead, they hopped about and vanished as he hacked and slashed, not even bothering to fight back.

Though they seemed to be harmless little things only interested in wandering aimlessly, their numbers were impressive. Considering they weren't moving to attack him, he decided to ignore them and focus his efforts on his sister. But though he wanted to run to her and scoop her into his arms, he couldn't. Something was blocking him. Even though she was right there, some invisible force held him back.

"What the hell?!" he cried, annoyed.

In the space around the statues' weapons, a faint pattern could be seen floating in the air, one that glowed with a dim light. As Nier stared, he realized they were creating the barrier between them. While Yonah had been able to crawl through a tiny gap as she did with the rocks, he was too large to make the attempt.

"Dammit!"

He swung his sword at the barrier with all his strength, then stopped when he noticed what appeared to be a masked book floating in the middle of it. Was *this* the thing blocking his way?

"I don't have time for this!" cried Nier as he began pounding the barrier over and over, mowing down more of the pitiful Shades that had placed themselves there with each swing.

"Give . . . my sister . . . back!"

The moment he said this, a brilliant white flash exploded out and consumed his vision, forcing him to raise a hand and shield his eyes. He heard the low, soft thump of something falling to the ground, and then all was silent once more. Cautiously opening his eyes, he saw that the statues had lowered their weapons—most likely because his attack had activated some sort of mechanism.

"Oh, thank god. Yonah!"

He vaguely heard a voice say something about "pounding," but couldn't have cared less in the moment.

"Yonah! Say something!"

Annoyed, he realized there were still obstacles between him and his sister. Another barrier had appeared behind the statues, and new Shades were also beginning to swarm. Pausing a moment to consider his options, he suddenly heard the voice again:

"By the heavens, I have never been treated in such a manner!"

"Then move!" shouted Nier.

The masked book was now floating in the air, but Nier wasn't interested in that. He shoved the book to one side and reached for Yonah—but once again, the barrier blocked his way. There was no other option: Yonah would have to come to him. Sadly, the girl remained fast asleep no matter how much he yelled.

"I am a being of incalculable importance, and yet you approach me as a common cockroach!" the book huffed. "This is why I loathe dealing with people."

The grumbling was starting to get on Nier's nerves. He had bigger issues to deal with—namely, how he was going to save his sister when he couldn't seem to wake her up. But the tome would not be denied his complaining.

"You stand in the presence of ancient wisdom! I am a text of the darkest, most arcane type, and I could be of great assistance to you."

Wisdom? Assistance? Nier hadn't even thought to wonder why the book was talking until that very moment, but it suddenly seemed possible he might be able to help after all.

"You're a *what*?!"

"I am Grimoire Weiss! My very name brings kingdoms to

their knees! Bow your head and accept my power, or go it alone and fail."

"Could this power save Yonah?" asked Nier as the book began floating around his head, flapping his pages with a palpable arrogance.

"Oh yes. Once I destroy these Shades, the magic barrier preventing your passage should simply disappear."

"Then do it already, Weiss!"

"You will refer to me by my full and proper name!"

The next thing Nier knew, he was surrounded by so many Shades they blotted out the floor. Nevertheless, Grimoire Weiss remained perfectly composed.

"You should not have turned your blades on me, foul creatures!" he cried. "With a single word, I, Grimoire Weiss, can shatter the very universe itself! Now! Prepare to . . . Er . . . Oh dear."

Grimoire Weiss fell silent. Though Shades continued to approach, the tome said no more.

"Oh *dear*?" repeated a shocked Nier.

"It seems the frantic bludgeoning you gave me earlier has caused my memory to escape me."

"Are you kidding me?!"

Nier had no time to think. He could only swing his sword in an attempt to cull the Shades' numbers, however slightly. Grimoire Weiss had said something about destroying the Shades to remove the barrier, so if the book couldn't find a way to make that happen, Nier would just have to do it himself.

The Shades kept coming, and soon Nier found himself falling into a kind of battle trance. It had been a long time since he'd fought so many enemies at once, but the familiar routine soon came back to him. He swung his blade with the smallest possible movements, trying not to waste any of his energy. He felt resistance as the sword sliced through creature after creature, then braced himself for the inevitable spray of blood before they vanished into black dust. But soon, he noticed something different: instead of spraying out in all directions, the Shades' blood was being absorbed by Grimoire Weiss.

"Did you just suck the blood out of those things?" asked a bewildered Nier.

"Blood is sound . . ." the book replied ominously. "Sounds are words . . . And words are power!"

"Oookay?"

"Is this . . . my memory?"

Nier saw that Grimoire Weiss was trembling—perhaps because he'd struck him so hard with his sword earlier. "You all right, Weiss?! Hang in there!"

As Nier called out, small, gravelly orbs of light surged from Grimoire Weiss. The orbs lashed out at the Shades, smashing them to bits, and the dark blood that remained seeped into the tome.

"Hmm," Grimoire Weiss murmured, his tone dignified. "It would seem I can regain my powers by defeating these monsters."

"Powers? Like *magic* powers?"

"Indeed! This is the true ability of—"

Nier didn't wait for the sentence to finish; he already understood that the more Shade blood the flying book absorbed, the more power he could use. He was gaining the ability to destroy Shades, and that knowledge alone was enough.

"Hold on, Yonah! I'm coming!"

Nier cut down Shade after Shade around Grimoire Weiss and watched as their blood was absorbed and turned into magic. More blood came in. More magic came out. Countless Shades were blown to smithereens, and as Nier swung his sword without pause, he found himself bemused by how quickly his foes were decimated. No matter how many poured out of the shadows, Grimoire Weiss obliterated them at an even greater speed.

"Is that all of them?"

Before Nier knew it, the last black shadow was gone. They had destroyed the Shades, which meant the barrier would finally fall. Shoulders heaving with ragged breaths, he began making his way to Yonah.

"Stop," said Grimoire Weiss.

Even before the book's warning, Nier was already freezing in place. Before him, the statues' eyes were beginning to glow—blue in the one-horned one, red in the other. It was as if they'd waited to awaken until the horde of Shades was gone. As he looked on, the statues began to lift their heavy legs in an attempt to walk.

"It seems our task is going to be more difficult than I first envisioned," Grimoire Weiss remarked gravely.

The statues raised their weapons and made their way toward Nier. Each time their feet connected with the ground, the shrine shook and the air rumbled. With each leg being easily as tall as Nier, it only made sense they would be incredibly heavy.

"A talking book and moving statues?" muttered Nier. "Really?"

"It is all too real, lad!" the tome replied. "Keep your sword high!"

One of the statues suddenly swung its weapon at Nier, cutting off any reply. The boy deftly leaped out of the way, feeling steel brush past the tip of his nose before embedding deeply into the floor.

"Watch their blades at all costs!" Grimoire Weiss cautioned.

The statue's weapon was no mere knife to be used on a carrot or a pumpkin—it had destroyed a portion of a solid stone floor and was clearly a destructive force to be reckoned with. A shiver shot through Nier as he considered what might have occurred to him had his leap been even a second slower.

"Keep your distance!" cried Weiss as Nier attempted to stay out of the statue's reach. "Let your magic do the work! . . . No, not like that, fool! Circle around them and attack!"

"Maybe you can stop talking and help me out with magic like you did before!"

"Oh, what nonsense! I *have* granted you the power of Grimoire Weiss! It is now imperative upon you to make use of it!"

"You did *what*?!" cried a confused Nier. He'd watched Grimoire Weiss destroy the horde of Shades, so what was he talking about when he said he'd already granted him his power?

"Stay calm, lad. You simply must fight 'like you did before,' as you said a moment ago."

"Still don't know what that means!" yelled Nier. He hadn't *done* anything before aside from wielding his sword as he always did. At a loss for a better option, he focused his attention on the one-horned statue, raised his sword, and hoped something would happen. Suddenly, orbs of light flew from his weapon and struck home, causing the statue to howl. He'd done it—he'd used *magic*. And while he had no idea how or why it worked, it seemed enough to know that he was wielding a new power.

"Dealing with both at once may prove to be a daunting task. Focus on taking them down one at a time!"

Grimoire Weiss didn't have to tell him twice—he knew he couldn't possibly handle two foes wielding such daunting weapons. Nier decided to attack the one-horned statue since it was closer, but this seemingly random decision turned out to be a sound choice. The moment he plunged his blade into its glowing eye socket, the statue let out a great cry. Black blood then erupted from the wound and flew across the room and into Grimoire Weiss.

"This thing's . . . a Shade?!"

Nier had known from the moment it lifted its weapon and started walking that it was no ordinary statue, but he never imagined it could be a Shade—even though he knew the creatures came in all shapes and sizes. Though typical ones were similar in height and stature to a human child, he'd also seen some the size of adults in the northern plains. He'd seen tall Shades and skinny Shades—and even heard rumors of fat, stout Shades—but he'd never heard anyone speak of Shades that looked like *statues*. Still, there could be no doubt as to the source of the dark blood that was now spurting from his foe's wound.

"They seem to be much the same as those other monsters," Grimoire Weiss remarked as he absorbed more of the blood. "Now take heed! The one-horned statue has gone berserk!"

"Got it!"

When adults from his village first took Nier sheep hunting, they taught him that the most dangerous animal was an injured one—and that it was best to kill such a creature as quickly as possible. Thinking of this, he took a moment to watch the one-horned statue move around the room, waiting for an opening to attack.

"There!"

Having finally grasped how to wield the magical power Grimoire Weiss had given him, Nier unleashed the entirety of his might on the blue light in the statue's eye sockets once more. The impact caused it to sail through the air before landing on its back, and Nier knew he could not allow it to stand again.

"Now!" cried Grimoire Weiss. "Put it out of its misery!"

The sword in Nier's hand seemed to swell with magic. He created a picture in his mind of himself slicing the one-horned statue in two, then brought his blade down. His magic became a giant thorn, then a lance, before boring directly into the statue's eye socket. It was an attack that felt more powerful—and more *final*—than the orbs of light.

"Is this more of your power?" he asked Grimoire Weiss.

"Mmm, it would seem so."

The enormous, magical lance pierced the statue's body, causing dark red blood to fly. After a final, deafening shriek, the blue light in its eyes faded away and the one-horned statue crumpled into a heap on the floor.

"Is it dead?"

"Stay on your guard, lad! One yet remains!"

"I know!"

The two-horned creature tilted toward the heavens and roared, causing the red light in its eyes to shine brighter than before.

"That statue does *not* look happy," Nier commented.

"Anger is but a form of negative energy," responded Weiss. "Nothing to fear!"

A Shade *angry* its companion was killed? Impossible. If its attacks were becoming more powerful, it was not because of anger, but because the thing was desperate to turn the tide of this battle back in its favor.

Fireballs larger than an adult's head erupted from the statue's mouth and flew at Nier. He leaped to the side, but the fireballs followed, proving there was nothing random about this attack. When one grazed the side of his face, he smelled the horrible odor of his own hair burning.

"Take advantage of the delay in its attacks!" Weiss chimed in.

All well and good for him to say, but Nier couldn't tell what kind of "delays" Weiss was talking about. The moment the fireballs seemed to relent, the statue charged in with its weapon at the ready. Chunks of stone and rock flew into the air each time the half-moon blade struck the ground. Even worse, the statue was moving faster than before, and almost got behind Nier more than once. Whenever he managed to evade the blade and create some space, the fireballs reappeared. Evading all these things at once took everything he had, leaving no time to analyze his foe's strategy.

No, wait. *There* it was! There *were* delays in its attacks! Whenever the thing spewed fire, it would stop moving for a moment— apparently it lacked the dexterity to run and gun at the same time.

Realizing this, Nier made a show of backing away, hoping to tempt the creature into unleashing its fire. The moment it did, Nier was ready—he knew the weak point of the statue was its eyes, and he thought he had a chance to emerge from this in one piece if he could just get in a couple of good shots.

Nier let fly with his own orbs of light, which caused the statue to pause. He then waited for Grimoire Weiss's signal, which came . . .

"Now!"

Nier gripped his blade as Grimoire Weiss's magic poured into him, taking the form of five pitch-black spears. When he brought down his arm, they flew out and lodged not only in the statue's eyes, but its forehead, arms, and legs as well. A massive limb splintered. Blood exploded into the air. Light vanished from its eyes. Finally, it crumpled to the ground and moved no more.

With the barrier between himself and Yonah finally down, Nier ran toward his sister, screaming her name. As he neared her, her eyes fluttered open, causing relief to flood through his system.

"I . . . I'm sorry . . ." she whispered as he helped her up. "I just wanted to help . . ."

"*I'm* the one who's sorry—you must have been scared out of your mind! Are you okay?"

As he went to help her up, he felt a low rumble from below his feet—one lower and deeper than the one caused by the statues. This was followed by a faint trembling in the air around them.

"Perhaps we'd best depart, hmm?" Grimoire Weiss suggested.

It made sense that all the jumping and slicing and stomping from the statues had weakened the shrine, and as Nier looked up, he saw a stream of dust and grit begin to trickle from the distant roof above.

"C'mon, Yonah, let's go!" he said, hauling his sister onto his back. "Hold on tight and keep your mouth closed, all right? I don't want you biting your tongue."

Committed to following his instructions to the letter, she nodded and gripped his clothes for all she was worth. Nier broke out into a run, trying to be cautious of the holes that were opening in the floor. He shoved the door to the massive room open with his shoulder, burst outside, and kept running. He felt erratic trembling under his feet and heard a deep rumbling that could only be sounds of collapse. Each time it happened, he picked up his pace a little more.

Only when they reached the far end of the long rope bridge did Nier set his sister down. There was a dreadful roar from the earth as he did, and he whipped his head around to see a wall collapse across the entrance they'd just come through. A chill ran through him as he realized that could have been them had he been a few seconds slower.

"I'm so glad we made it," he said. He hadn't realized how on-edge he was until he heard how his voice trembled. The moment he spoke, he felt the tension on his shoulders and back ease. Though sweat was pouring across every inch of his body, he knew they were safe at last.

"I tried," Yonah said quietly. "I really did."

"What?" said Nier as he turned to look at her.

"I couldn't find a Lunar Tear, and I'm so sorry." Yonah hung her head, the sadness in her tone palpable. "I just wanted to make you rich."

Nier had always assumed she wanted money to buy medicine and make herself better, but her wish had never been so selfish. Instead, she only wanted her *brother* to be rich.

Without another word, Nier pulled his sister into a hug. He didn't need anything else so long as she was safe. He didn't care about being rich so long as he could live with his little sister. When he pulled away and looked at her, he was greeted with the sight of black writing moving slowly across her body.

"Yonah? What's going on?!"

As he stared in horror at the sinister letters that slithered across her wrist and over the back of her hand, Popola's recent words to him suddenly came to mind:

Once you see black writing appear on the body, it means the end is close.

REPORT 03

I wish I could say I have nothing to report, but I'm afraid that's not the case. Nier found Grimoire Weiss. I'm not sure if this event is a coincidence or an inevitability, but in any case, the seal on the Lost Shrine has been undone.

If Nier asks about it, I'm going to say Grimoire Weiss is mentioned in the lyrics to the Song of the Ancients instead of attempting some awkward evasion. Popola's also going to show him a bunch of ancient documents on the Grimoire, and we're hoping one or both of those is enough to satisfy his curiosity. But Popola said that if he shows further interest, we'll use the opportunity to guide the situation in our favor.

Unfortunately, it seems likely that Nier and Grimoire Weiss's encounter will bring about other irregularities, and we'll probably have to interfere in order to course correct. Luckily, Grimoire Weiss seems to have lost his memory, and it's unlikely he'll sniff out our intentions or expose Nier to any more danger.

On the other hand, Yonah's condition continues to deteriorate, which means they'll be spending more on medicine and falling deeper into poverty. As such, we're planning to offer him more work. While the jobs are dangerous, they pay really well—and since we can't be their parents, we feel we should at least do this much. It's hardly a perfect solution, but we also need to remember our responsibility to be impartial with all villagers under our supervision.

I spend time with Yonah on a personal level beyond what my job requires, but I'm not doing it merely out of goodwill. Honestly, anyone would want to humor a sweet kid who comes up to talk to them. If that's how *I* feel about a girl I'm not even related to, I can only imagine the level of adoration Nier is dealing with.

If we need any further proof that a brother's love surmounts his animal instinct, just look at how he eats her cooking with a smile. I once joined him at a lunch made by Yonah and would definitely turn down a second invitation because it was DISGUSTING. She used a recipe Popola taught her, but I have no idea what she did to make it taste like *that*. Afterward, I warned Popola to stop with the cooking lessons because it might actually cause health repercussions down the line. Of course, that now seems like an overreaction on my part. Poor kid won't even be able to get out of bed soon.

As the one in charge of this particular task, I pray their life together lasts as long as it can, plus a day. Also, I realize this report was a little on the long side, but you can now consider it concluded.

Record written by Devola

NieR Replicant
ver.1.22474487139...

The Boy 3

1.

NIER'S MEMORIES OF arriving home after escaping the Lost Shrine were fuzzy, but he did recall how uncharacteristically heavy Yonah felt on his back. Her exhaustion, coupled with her unwell state, had caused her to fall asleep there, and when he tucked her into her actual bed, her eyes fluttered open for a moment before closing again. By the time her head hit the pillow, she was asleep once more.

"Yonah . . ."

"Best let her sleep, lad," said Grimoire Weiss in a low tone. Nier nodded at his suggestion and got up to leave the house. When he pulled the door closed behind him, he leaned back against it, feeling that he would simply topple over otherwise.

"This is so unfair!" moaned Nier, who couldn't seem to stop talking once he started. "Yonah hasn't done anything! Why do terrible things keep happening to us?!" He vaguely heard Grimoire Weiss offer to help if there was a way to do so, but he ignored it. The words simply wouldn't enter his head. "Yonah's just a little kid. She doesn't deserve this."

The ground at his feet blurred. He didn't want to think anymore. He didn't want to do *anything*. Even moving felt like a great burden, so he stood in place with his head hanging low until he lost all track of time.

"I say! Is someone singing?"

Grimoire Weiss's question gave Nier the strength to lift his head. As he did so, the wind carried a familiar tune to his ears—one sung by Devola—and his feet immediately began to move. He wasn't hoping she could do something about his situation; he simply found comfort in her lovely voice and the sound of the plucked strings.

"Hey, you're back!" Devola exclaimed when he approached the fountain. "I was worried about you. I heard you went through the eastern gate, and . . ."

Her gaze drifted to Nier's side as her words faltered. He hurriedly opened his mouth to explain why he was now accompanied by a floating book, but Grimoire Weiss beat him to the punch.

"I am Grimoire Weiss, and you will treat me with the proper respect!"

"Wait, you're Grimoire Weiss? Oh, that is so cool!"

It was Nier's turn to be shocked. "You *know* him?"

"Of course! He's the white book I was just singing about."

"He's in your song?"

"Yeah, the Song of the Ancients. It's an old tune that's been passed down through generations of villagers. But it's in a forgotten language, so I doubt you could make much sense of it."

Nier had no idea the song Devola was always singing in front of the fountain had such a name. "Do you know what it means?" he asked.

"Well, it's not like I've studied it or anything, but I can tell you bits and pieces. See, there's this terrible black book that shows up and starts spreading disease all over the place. But then this white book shows up and saves the world, and everyone's happy. You know how it goes."

A black book that spreads disease; a white book that saves the world. Black and white. Could it be?

"What is it?" Devola asked as she peered up at Nier.

"Ah, it's—" *Nothing* was what he wanted to say, but he cut

himself off. It was okay to ask the question, even though he didn't have much basis for it. He was just asking, after all—he didn't have to expect anything in terms of an answer.

"So how exactly does this white book save the world?"

"It's just a song, yeah? I don't really know the details."

Nier felt the wind vanish from his sails. He'd told himself not to expect much from her answer, yet it seemed a small part of him had ignored that advice. Was the disease spread by the black book meant to be the Black Scrawl? And if so, did "saving the world" mean curing the disease? Could he possibly save Yonah with Grimoire Weiss?

Ah, but nothing was ever that easy. The lack of reaction from the white book in question only served to disappoint Nier further.

"Aw, don't be sad," said Devola. "Look, why don't you ask Popola? She's got a big brain. Maybe she knows something."

"Yeah, you're right. Thanks."

Because Popola managed the massive library, if there was something Devola didn't know, it was likely her sister did. Perhaps she even knew why Grimoire Weiss had lost his memory—that was the only explanation Nier could think of as to why he showed no reaction when he heard of the Song of the Ancients.

"Is something the matter, lad?" came doubtful prodding from Grimoire Weiss. Nier brushed it off with a vague answer before hurrying to the library, where he found Popola in her office. She was surrounded by books as always, hands folded on her desk, eyes downcast.

"I heard about Yonah," she began. "I . . . I don't know what to say. I'm sorry."

Any number of villagers had seen Nier rush home with a limp Yonah slung over his back. One of them must have let Popola know. They surely also mentioned the black writing covering her arms and legs, and Nier decided not to think too deeply as to whether this was an act of kindness or a warning borne out of fear or aversion. He had more important issues to deal with at the moment.

"What do you know about the song Devola was singing?"

As he asked the question, Popola's gaze drifted to the item floating next to Nier. "Wait. Is that . . . Grimoire Weiss?"

"You know Weiss?"

After staring at the tome for a long moment, Popola finally murmured, "Yes, well, the Song of the Ancients. Let's see. I came across it in an ancient record once, but that was a while ago . . ."

Popola stood and pressed a finger to her temple, an act that told Nier it was an old tale indeed. She then reached for the bookshelf behind her, her fingertips gently swaying left and right before finally coming to a halt.

"This book is a compendium of old scrolls," she said as she pulled down a thick tome with a tattered cover. It seemed ready to fall apart at any moment, and Nier had no idea what could possibly be inside.

As he watched, Popola gently flipped through the pages until she found what she was looking for. Then she set the book on the desk, displaying the image of a creature with a staff in its hand, along with something that could have been a shield or a plate with three eyes. It was impossible to parse what the picture was supposed to be; the only clear portions were a group of people and two books.

"When the great black book, Grimoire Noir, brings calamity upon the world, the white book, Grimoire Weiss, will appear with his Sealed Verses. He will then use them to vanquish Grimoire Noir and purge the calamity he wrought," Popola said, pointing to the image. Though Nier still didn't understand what he was looking at, it was clearly something of great significance.

"Sealing verses?"

"Sealed Verses. No real records remain about them, so I can't say anything for sure, but they seem to resemble some form of magic."

Magic was, so to speak, the magic word, and the moment Nier heard it, everything clicked. He had been right all along!

"That's *it*!" he cried.

"Er, what is?" Popola asked.

"So the song says Grimoire Weiss purges the world of this calamity, right? And he does so using 'Sealed Verses' . . . ?"

"Ho!" declared an excited Grimoire Weiss. "And you believe the matter I infused in the shrine is one of these Sealed Verses?"

"Exactly, Weiss!"

When Popola said Grimoire Weiss would use Sealed Verses to vanquish Grimoire Noir, the first thing that came to Nier's mind was what Weiss had muttered when he first absorbed the blood of a Shade: *Blood is sound, sounds are words, and words are power.* And if words were indeed power, maybe they were enough to defeat this Grimoire Noir.

"Exactly, Weiss! With your power, we could cure Yonah!"

"Guys, don't get too excited," Popola warned. "This is just some old legend."

"Hey, Weiss was just some old legend yesterday, but here he is. And if he's real, the rest of it must be too. He can cure the Black Scrawl—I know he can!"

The book turned his stern face to examine Popola. "That said, do we know anything regarding the whereabouts of this Grimoire Noir?"

"Sorry, but there's nothing about it in any of the records. All I can say for sure is that there are a number of Sealed Verses out there."

Nier had assumed they'd found the one and only Sealed Verse

when they killed the Shades at the Lost Shrine, especially considering how much more powerful his magic was after the battle. But now he realized things wouldn't be quite so easy. In a way, however, the fact that their path was going to be difficult somehow made his belief in the idea swell all the more.

"We still have quite a few unknowns, but it appears that Shades and these Verses are intrinsically linked," said Popola.

"Then we'll go kill every Shade we can find," proclaimed Nier. If there were other Sealed Verses, they needed to acquire them. He didn't care if there were a hundred or a million Shades standing in the way—if all he had to do was kill them, then kill them he would.

"What an absurdly reckless plan!" remarked an astonished Grimoire Weiss.

"So I should sit around and do nothing while Yonah suffers? I don't think so."

"Well, it's clear I won't be able to talk you out of this," said Popola as she returned her book to the shelf. "In which case, I've heard the Shades are gathering near a village called The Aerie."

"Where?"

"Remember how they were repairing the bridge in the northern plains? It's a bit past that point."

Nier recalled how the bridge repairs had taken longer than expected, which was why he'd taken a Shade-slaying job. If the creatures were gathering out that way, it was likely a Sealed Verse could be found there as well.

"Once you arrive, be sure to visit the village chief," Popola continued. "He lives in the house on the highest point in town."

"Got it."

"And be careful!"

"I'll be all right, Popola."

A ray of sunlight had appeared from between the clouds of

Nier's despair. He didn't care what danger he had to face, so long as it meant curing Yonah—he'd push himself to the limit and straight through for her. With this thought in mind, Nier dashed down the stairs with steps much lighter than when he arrived.

2.

YONAH HAD FALLEN asleep without eating, so Nier woke early the next morning to make her breakfast. He took a thin broth to her bed and attempted to feed her, but she slipped back into slumber after only a couple of spoonfuls.

He was sick with worry at the prospect of leaving her alone in her current condition, but the knowledge it would only grow worse meant he had to act. For unlike previously when he could only give her painkillers, he now had tangible hope for a cure.

After leaving a few things by Yonah's pillow that she could eat without much trouble, Nier quietly went down the stairs and out the door. Though the chicken-keeping couple were usually the only ones awake at this hour, he heard Devola's singing on the breeze the moment he stepped outside.

"Morning!" she said from her usual seat next to the fountain. "How's Yonah doing?"

"She's a bit better than yesterday. Doesn't seem to have much of an appetite, though."

"That's no good," she said as her brows knit together and her fingers continued to dance across the strings. "Oh hey, Popola told me you're going to go find the Sealed Verses. Is that true?"

"Yes."

Devola's playing came to a sudden halt. "But that's crazy-town! Do you have any idea how hard that's gonna be?!"

"Doesn't matter. I'd do anything for Yonah."

Devola briefly cast her eyes downward, a reaction shockingly similar to Popola's reaction the day before. Of course, it only made sense that a pair of twins would have identical responses.

"Popola said she'd check on Yonah today, so don't worry about her," Devola said finally. The moment it was out, Nier realized she had gotten up early and waited for him simply to let him know his sister would be looked after.

"Thanks, Devola."

"Sure thing. Take care out there."

With that, she resumed her playing. Nier nodded his thanks a final time before rushing off across the dew-soaked grass and toward the northern plains. Once he exited the village, the brilliant sun and bright blue of the sky stung his eyes, while shadows cast by the stony mountains lay dark on the ground. Without a Shade in sight, sheep munched grass here and there, comfortable in the ownership of their domain.

All these things led to a journey far easier than Nier expected. When he encountered a single Shade at the foot of the newly repaired bridge, he simply dispatched it with Grimoire Weiss's magic and continued on his way without halting his stride.

"You can save Yonah, Weiss," he said at one point as they traveled. "Heck, maybe you can save the whole world!"

This simple fact was enough to make Nier feel as if he was walking on air. So much so that he scarcely noticed when Grimoire Weiss murmured his doubts on the matter. Nier had seen his companion turn Shade blood into magic, after all—and the fact that a talking book even existed in the first place was nothing short of a miracle. He'd been so focused on saving his sister at the Lost Shrine that he simply accepted the existence of Grimoire Weiss, sparing no thought for how odd the situation was. The idea of his saving the world was just another portion of this belief.

"I guess I won't use you for kindling after all," Nier mused.

"You should really treat omnipotent magical beings with more respect."

"Mm-hmm."

After some time moving across the plains, Nier eventually came to the barrier that was the mountain range. According to the map, The Aerie lay just beyond. As he drew closer, he saw a small tunnel in the mountains that could serve as a way in. Two thin strips of metal snaked deeper inside, with only a meager strip of light visible at the far end.

"It's through here, I guess," he said.

"What ever is the matter?" asked Grimoire Weiss.

"Just dark, is all. There might be Shades."

While the walls were lined with torches, the majority of the passage was shielded from the sun. It was the perfect place for Shades to live, and Nier knew he would be in danger if he stepped inside unprepared. But Weiss clearly didn't share his concern; he responded to the boy's words with a hearty peal of laughter.

"If Shades harry you, you need only destroy them with my magic! They will not be able to get close enough to do harm if you proceed in such a fashion."

"Hey, that's RIGHT!" cried Nier. The reply was much louder than he intended, and his cry echoed around the tunnel.

"Lower your voice, fool," muttered Grimoire Weiss.

"You're so smart, Weiss!"

"I told you that you are to use my full and proper—"

Before the annoyed book could finish, Nier fired a magical bullet into the darkness, watching as the orb and its reddish glow were swallowed by the gloom. He fired again just to be sure, but nothing stirred in response. The tunnel appeared to be free of enemies, at least for the moment.

When he stepped inside, he found the path not only dark, but treacherous. The two strips of metal that led down the tunnel were connected by planks of wood as wide as Nier's shoulders. Stone slabs of a similar cut were placed beneath both metal and wood. He had no idea what purpose such a thing was supposed to serve. He knew only that it made walking in the gloom difficult and annoying.

Just as he was getting used to traversing the terrain, he arrived at a spot where the wall was torn open. Outside, a small, flat patch of ground was encircled on all sides by stone walls that reached up to the heavens. Though the area sat in shade now, there was likely a time of day when it was filled by the sun, and small flowers dotted the grass here and there. Sitting against the stone wall was a little hut. Since it was the only dwelling in the area, Nier knew he hadn't reached The Aerie.

The hut was in sad shape, with a roof that was little more than a sheet of cloth pulled taut across poles stuck in the ground. There were no doors or windows of any kind. In fact, he could see straight inside the thing.

"Does someone live here?" Nier called. "Hello?" He waited for a response, but nothing came but the howl of the wind.

"It appears to be deserted," observed Weiss.

"Yeah. Let's go."

Nier felt a striking curiosity about what sort of person would be comfortable living in such an unsafe location, but the more pressing matter was finding the village chief. Placing his own questions aside, he once again set off for his destination.

Though the light at the end seemed bright when seen from within the darkness of the tunnel, it wasn't particularly so once they exited. The strong wind they encountered, however, caused Nier to shield his eyes. A few paces beyond the exit found them standing at the edge of a terrifyingly sheer cliff. A rope bridge extended before them, stretching across the deep ravine. There were no flat spots of land anywhere, and the only sounds were the howl of wind and the rattling of various weather vanes.

"This is a weird place for a village," Nier remarked.

The village's name also served as a description of the place. The cliffs that towered over the deep ravine were dotted with dark-colored, cylindrical tanks that clung to the rock face—most likely the houses Popola had mentioned. Their rounded roofs reminded Nier of eggs more than houses. This thought made him think of clusters of insect eggs laid on tree bark, which sent goose bumps shooting up his arms.

Squinting, he noticed a series of pathways and ladders across the cliffs that created passages between the tanks. They looked similar to the outdoor path he'd seen on the Lost Shrine, and they were likely made of wooden planks. The only other things that stood out were the numerous weather vanes and strips of cloth hanging from the bridges. These things seemed designed to show how strong and from which direction the wind was blowing, which were crucial elements of life in such a place.

"Popola said the chief's house is in the highest spot, right?" asked Nier. After searching for a moment, he saw a tank far above the others, one painted a slightly different color than the rest. "That must be it."

"Indeed. But how one might reach such a place remains a mystery."

The tank in question sat squarely in the middle of the cliff to the right of Nier and Grimoire Weiss. However, there was no direct path to it that they could see. Instead, it seemed they would be forced to take the long way by crossing the rope bridge, climbing up the opposite cliff, then doubling back via another bridge.

"Might as well get going," said Nier as he stepped out onto the bridge. The sheer strength of the wind through the ravine caused it to shudder, and he couldn't help but think of how far the fall would be from that point. If the worst happened, he would be beyond saving.

By the time he reached the middle of the bridge, a cold sweat was trickling down his back. This part of the bridge was wider than the rest, and it formed a kind of small, circular plaza. Unlike the narrower parts, this area did not tremble with every step.

"This bridge is *really* long," Nier observed. "I bet the villagers stop here to rest."

Weiss snorted. "They were right to put such a thing here to counteract its length, yet it is unlikely it was constructed solely for relaxation."

"You don't think?"

"Long bridges are unstable, and their strength is difficult to maintain," began Weiss in the dull tones of a lecturer. "Therefore, bridges are often supported from the middle, with supports placed directly in the ground below."

"Okay, so this plaza thing actually helps the bridge stay up?"

"More likely it is a spot to allow those coming from the opposite side to pass. A bridge of this construction could easily flip if two parties passed each other along the way. Also, as you said, it would provide a spot for children and the elderly to rest."

"So it *is* for resting."

"Not primarily! Bah, did you hear nothing I said?"

The conversation took Nier's mind off the dangerous crossing, and before he knew it, they'd reached the other side. "I can't imagine delivering letters to these people," he said. The thought hadn't crossed his mind when he saw the mailbox by the village entrance, but he now sympathized with mail carriers after crossing the long span.

Now free of the bridge, they found themselves navigating a series of wooden paths so narrow they made him yearn for the cozy confines of the Lost Shrine. They lacked railings of any kind, and powerful gusts of wind buffeted them endlessly from all directions. Nier proceeded forward with caution. One slip from this height would be the end of everything.

"They're a lot smaller than I thought they'd be," said Nier as he stared at one of the tanks. The front doors were tiny, shrunken things, as were the windows—and both had been shuttered tight despite it being daytime. Nier wondered briefly if there were sick people inside, but then realized all the other houses were shuttered in a similar fashion.

"Maybe they don't mind the dark," he mused.

"More likely it is a way to protect their homes from powerful ravine winds," said his companion. "I wager their homes are shaped this way for similar reasons."

"You sure know a lot, Weiss."

"You still underestimate me, lad! But even in all my wisdom, I cannot comprehend why these people would deliberately choose to live in such a terrible place."

They descended a ladder, proceeded down a path, took another ladder back to the previous level, and then proceeded to a second rope bridge. Now they could *finally* reach the cliff that held the village chief's house.

"I can't believe we have to go through all of this to get there," grumbled Nier. "They should just add a path from the entrance."

"I thought the same. There must be a reason why . . . My word! Shades!"

Black shadows suddenly shimmered into existence atop the bridge. Despite it being daytime, the lay of this part of the land was bathed in shadow from the mountains. On top of that, the residents had strewn crates across the bridge seemingly at random, adding even more spots for the creatures to hide.

But Nier had Grimoire Weiss's magic, and the fact that the

Shades were clustered together on the narrow bridge made them easy targets. Confident, Nier drew his sword and took a step forward. He just as quickly stumbled back in a panic.

"What are those?!" he cried as a series of orbs flew at him. Their reddish light reminded him of Grimoire Weiss's magic.

"That's magic, you fool!" barked the book. "Seek cover!"

Nier leaped behind a nearby crate, watching the orbs fly in neat little rows before dissipating after they collided with his cover.

"They are not so powerful, but their sheer number makes this tricky," Grimoire Weiss remarked.

"I bet they'd hurt if they hit me."

"Wait for an opening, then take them down in a single strike!"

When he said a *single* strike, Nier knew that referred to his massive black lance. Unlike the magical bullets, however, he couldn't cast the lance right away, nor could he use it multiple times in a row. Nier concentrated, taking careful aim, then unleashed his magic.

He hadn't faced an enemy that used magic since the statues at the Lost Shrine, but these proved much easier to defeat. They weren't even close to the strength of those statues. They were more akin to the Shades in the northern plains. Still, Shades were Shades, even if they were weak.

"I can't believe there are *Shades* in this village!" he said to Weiss as they resumed their journey.

"Though those tanks seem small to us outsiders, I imagine the villagers felt that they were the best way to stay safe against the creatures."

The pair had yet to see a single resident, which lent credence to the idea that they were hiding from the Shades. Another result of this strategy was that Nier and Grimoire Weiss were unable to achieve their objective when they reached the village chief's home. He met them with a resoundingly negative greeting from behind his sealed door.

"Begone, strangers!" he barked.

"Wait!" Nier yelled back. "Please, we're—"

"Leave!"

"But we just—"

"Enough! Leave this village at once and never return!"

"What a pathetic bunch of rabble!" muttered Weiss. Speaking to another villager in the chief's stead did not seem to be an option. They couldn't even ask a random passerby, since no one was bothering to pass by.

Still, Nier decided to try knocking on a few doors to see if their luck might change. He went from house to house asking in the kindest voice he could muster if the inhabitants knew anything about the Sealed Verses, but if they didn't respond with silence, they let fly a series of negative invectives.

"We don't trust your kind!"

"Leave our village at once!"

"Go away!"

Some of them, however, seemed to lump Nier in with some other person: "You're just like her. Like Kainé!"

"Someone needs to put an end to that Kainé!"

He had no idea if this Kainé person was another villager or an outsider, and the people he spoke to weren't interested in enlightening him. To top it off, Shades appeared once again as Nier and Weiss were attempting to complete their task. Though the creatures were weaker than the ones who used magic, they still left Nier feeling exhausted, perhaps because he'd just dealt with a pack of cranky villagers. He'd have felt less tired if he'd encountered a large Shade, because at least that would have presented the exciting opportunity for a Sealed Verse.

On their way back from the chief's house to the mailbox at

the entrance—and all the paths that journey entailed—they were attacked by multiple enemies that were all easily dispatched.

"It would appear there are no powerful Shades here," Grimoire Weiss remarked.

Which meant none of them had any Sealed Verses, since such a thing was likely to exist only in a Shade of some size and ability.

"Yeah," Nier replied, his voice pitifully weak. "Let's go back to Popola and figure out a new plan."

He gave his final statement in a louder voice as he began his journey back up the tunnel—but not before firing a bit of magic into the darkness, of course. If Shades were appearing in the village, it only made sense that some would be in the tunnel connecting it to the outside. Luckily, just as the first time, the tunnel was empty as a tomb.

"What a cheerless village that was," grumbled Weiss.

"I didn't even want a warm welcome," said Nier. "I just wanted to talk to them."

I suppose people who keep their windows shuttered during the day have their hearts shuttered too. After a time, Nier spoke up. "Hey, Weiss? Do you think the person who lives in that hut is back yet?"

They had come again to the break in the tunnel, the one that led to the dwelling without windows or doors. Perhaps someone who didn't live in a cheerless tank would be willing to talk to them.

Though he'd only peered at the hut from a distance at first, Nier decided to walk over to it this time. He briefly wondered how the owner dealt with rainy days, but he soon spied a thick canopy of fabric wrapped around a log that lay across the house. The mystery owner would apparently stretch the fabric toward the ground to block out any inclement weather.

Nier halted and stared at a series of beautiful white flowers inside the hut. They were so enchanting that he practically forgot he was poking around inside a stranger's home. True, the world was filled with white flowers, but these were something else entirely. Their color was not the white of a cloud or a pearl, but a paleness that held a warmth and luminosity reminiscent of moonlight.

"They're lovely."

"Those are Lunar Tears," Grimoire Weiss replied. "Legendary flowers of almost perfect beauty."

"You're kidding," he said as he reached out to touch one of the flowers. "Those are—"

He was about to explain to Weiss how he told Yonah about Lunar Tears, but a sharp voice from behind him cut him off.

"Hands off the flowers!"

Nier pulled his hand back and whirled around to see a tall woman looming over him. While he was flustered by the anger on her face, he was absolutely astounded by her outfit.

"Uh, Weiss?" he said as he desperately looked for a place to safely rest his eyes. "Why is that lady in her underwear?"

"I fear we have greater issues to deal with," replied Weiss.

At Grimoire Weiss's prompting, Nier noticed a black haze surrounding the woman's tightly balled fist. There was a similar haze around her left leg, and patterns writhed across parts of her skin. The woman said nothing, instead breathing deeply, as if trying to intimidate them.

"Wait," said Nier. "Is she a *Shade*?!" He took a step backward despite himself. While the telltale haze of a Shade covered part of the woman's body, the rest of her appeared to be human. Since the Shades at the Lost Shrine had been statues, he wouldn't have been surprised to find one in the form of a person. And yet, he still found himself hesitant to do anything.

"What are you waiting for, fool?" cried Weiss. "Attack her!"

Weiss was right—Shades needed to die. With this thought in his mind, Nier readied himself and fired off a barrage of magic.

"Son of a bitch," muttered the woman-Shade. "I knew this would happen." She drew a pair of swords, holding the identical blades in each hand before swinging them with astonishing force.

"Your attack must be unrelenting!" Grimoire Weiss commanded. "This woman is clearly not to be trifled with!"

The sound of metal slicing air rang out as Nier dodged backward, putting distance between himself and his foe. He fired another barrage of magic as she attempted to pull her swords out of the ground where her forceful swing embedded them. A moment later, she was pressing the attack again. Although the woman-Shade was faster, her fighting style reminded him of the statues at the Lost Shrine. If that held true, it meant she was vulnerable while readying her next attack. Powerful blades such as hers were heavy and somewhat slow to maneuver, forcing defense to become an afterthought.

Nier deliberately opened himself up to her attack, then dodged the blow and let fly a with volley of magic. It connected with a boom, causing the woman-Shade to fly backward and land on her back.

"Did we get her?" asked Nier. As he asked the question, he realized she hadn't started to bleed black Shade blood, nor vanished in a puff of dust. Instead, she slowly rose to her feet, her left hand making strange movements as her breathing quickened.

"By my very pages!" gasped Weiss. "The girl wields magic!"

The odd movements had been her casting a spell. A red light quickly encircled the woman-Shade, exuding an aura many times more powerful than that of the Shades Nier had fought on the bridge earlier. A moment later, an intense burst of magic came flying at him—one that would mock the thought of his taking cover behind a crate.

If any of these hit me, I'm dead, he thought as he barely dived out of the way. He realized the woman-Shade's magic wasn't just offensive. A white barrier woven from arcane power had deflected Nier's own attack.

With his plan to attack from afar no longer viable, Nier knew his only choice was to run. Unfortunately, the woman-Shade seemed disinclined to allow a graceful retreat. He probably should have bolted before the fight even began, but now it was too late. His life was about to end in a mixture of cowardice and defeat.

This is the end for me.

The woman-Shade screeched to a halt. Though Nier knew he should run, he turned to see what had grabbed her attention and felt his heart drop.

Slithering down the face of the cliff was the biggest Shade he'd ever seen in his life.

The unspeakable thing resembled a lizard, albeit one the size of the library in his village. It had three fat legs, and a gnarled crustacean tail with what appeared to be fingers at the tip. Each time it moved, its black form shimmered as if covered in oil.

Caught between the woman-Shade and this new, horrific beast, Nier knew he was a dead man if they both decided to attack at the same time. But a moment later, he realized the woman-Shade was not moving to attack *him*, but instead was staring at the newcomer with pure hate in her eyes. A moment later, she drew her twin blades and leaped at the lizard, who responded by batting her away with one clawed arm.

"It would appear we are not the focus of her anger," noted Grimoire Weiss.

The woman-Shade began spouting a series of incredible profanities as she pressed the attack. Nier now realized she had been holding back when she fought him. If she'd come at him with even a fifth of her current anger, his life would already be over.

"We can figure out what's going on once the big one is defeated," Nier said as he readied himself for combat. If he hadn't run yet, he wasn't about to start doing so now.

"The scale of this one is like nothing you've encountered before! Ready your guard!"

Nier nodded and aimed his magic at the massive Shade's head before letting fly with the same lance that subdued the Shades on the bridge. While he wasn't hoping to get so lucky this time, he *also* didn't expect that the attack would make the creature focus its complete attention on him. Before he knew it, a clawed hand was racing at him—one he had no time to avoid. It was going to crush him, and he was going to die.

But death never came.

Instead, Nier felt himself flying through the air. By the time he realized he'd been kicked out of harm's way, he was already rolling on the ground; the Shade's claws sank deep into the earth where he had been standing not a moment before. For some reason, the woman-Shade had chosen to save his life, even if it was in the most violent way possible.

"Um, thanks?" he said.

"I told you to stay outta the way!" she spat as she readied her swords again. But before she could use them, the Shade's other hand came crashing down on her. She likely could have avoided the attack had she not gone out of her way to save Nier, but now she had been smashed to the ground by the fiercest of strikes.

Despite being struck by what should have been a killing blow, the woman-Shade managed to return fire with a volley of the same fearsome magic she'd launched at Nier earlier.

Though the attack was a sloppy, desperate thing, either luck or tenacity had managed to guide it right into the center of the lizard's eye. The massive Shade gave an eerie roar as its body shuddered and quaked. A moment later, it slithered back up the cliff wall with a speed that belied its incredible size.

"Get . . . back . . . here," croaked the woman-Shade. Her face twisting in anguish, she raised one trembling hand in the direction of her escaping prey before letting it fall weakly to the ground.

"The patterns are disappearing," Grimoire Weiss remarked. As he spoke, the black haze that had covered the left half of the woman's body receded like an ebbing tide, as did the patterns that accompanied it. A moment later, the clearing was once again draped in an eerie silence.

"Is she human?" Nier wondered aloud. Without the black patterns—and the knowledge of how fiercely she'd wielded her blades—he easily could have mistaken the woman collapsed on the ground for a resident of his own village.

"This one has been possessed by a Shade. She exists as neither fully human nor other." Grimoire Weiss went on to explain that though there *was* a Shade living inside the woman, she herself was still human, which made her completely human so far as Nier was concerned.

"I feel bad for treating her like one of those things," he said. He'd attacked her because he assumed she was nothing but a Shade, a thing he never would have done to another human being.

Son of a bitch. I knew this would happen.

Her voice had sounded so pained when she said that. Her words were likely borne of others previously seeing her as a Shade and attacking her for it. Still, she'd saved Nier from the massive Shade even *after* he treated her like one.

"We have to help her," he said. He picked her up, carried her into the ramshackle hut, and began tending her wounds. Once she regained consciousness, he intended to give her both proper thanks and a genuine apology. A few minutes later, the chance arrived when her dark eyelashes began to flutter.

"Hey there," he said.

The woman's perplexed eyes rested on Nier, then Weiss. She tried to sit up, but only managed to lift her head slightly. When she spoke, all that came from her lips was a sort of half-hearted muttering.

"I'm sorry we attacked you," began Nier. "We thought you were a Shade."

"Well, you're half right," she snapped. "Now get the hell out of here."

"Now, see here!" began a vexed Grimoire Weiss. "We made our apologies and came to your aid! The least you can do is grace us with your name."

"It's okay, Weiss. She's probably just exhausted." In truth, Nier wasn't sure that was the reason behind her anger at all—more likely she knew they'd been in the wrong and just wanted to be left alone.

"Let's just go," he continued as he made to leave the hut. But before he could move more than a few steps, a voice stopped him.

"My name's Kainé."

"The name we heard back in the village," Grimoire Weiss remarked. Nier shared the book's thought. Both of them remembered the vitriol in the voices of the people who uttered that name.

"Look, nothing good is gonna happen if you stick with me, so do like I said and go." Kainé paused a moment, looking between her two visitors with an icy, determined gaze. "Oh, and that monster back there? It's mine. Stay the hell away from it."

Once Nier and Grimoire Weiss left Kainé's hut, they hurried back to the village. Though Nier was worried about Yonah, the first thing he did upon arriving was to head to the library and find Popola. He briefly recounted The Aerie's chief kicking them out, then went on to tell her about the massive Shade. He left the part about Kainé out of the story, however. She had nothing to do with his mission, and he felt uncomfortable dragging her into it for some reason.

"I can't believe a Shade of that size was in The Aerie," said Popola when they finished.

"Yeah. It took everything we had just to chase it off."

Even though Kainé had told him to stay away from the thing, he had no intention of doing so. Grimoire Weiss had told him that he'd obtained a Sealed Verse when Kainé's magic bore into the massive Shade's eye. And even better, it wasn't the only one—he'd said he sensed others in there as well.

"I wish there was some way to strengthen my weapon."

Letting the giant Shade be wasn't an option. He needed to defeat it, find a Sealed Verse, and help Weiss learn more powerful magic. Yes, he could now summon a massive hand of dark energy that crushed everything around him, but it still wasn't enough. He needed more.

Popola thought for a moment, then looked up. "You know, there's a little shop at the entrance to the Junk Heap that might be able to help. If you bring them materials, they should be able to enhance your weapons."

Now that she mentioned it, Nier did recall seeing a place labeled "Junk Heap" on a map of the northern plains.

"Interesting," he said. "I'll check it out."

The map indicated it was even closer than The Aerie, so Nier decided to drop by the shop the following day.

3.

NIER ENDED UP having to postpone his trip to the Junk Heap by a day in order to earn enough money to upgrade his weapon. Thankfully work was plentiful, and he spent most of the day hunting sheep in the northern plains so he could sell the mutton. Chasing the flighty animals used to be rough work, but Grimoire Weiss's magic allowed him to attack from afar, making the entire process much easier.

Though the Junk Heap was closer than The Aerie, he still set out in the early morning. Yonah spent the night passing in and out of sleep, and she couldn't hold down more than a few mouthfuls of food. He knew he had to find a cure as soon as possible.

Cool morning dew wet his feet as he dashed across the northern plains. Following the map, he made his way over a large metal bridge in the northeast and soon found himself at the entrance to the Junk Heap. It was a fence of woven metal, beyond which was a series of off-kilter ladders and a maze of scaffolding seemingly without rhyme or reason.

"What manner of place is this?" asked Weiss as he curiously regarded their new surroundings.

"I guess there are ancient ruins buried here?" said Nier, who was equally confused as to why anyone would build such a place. Looking down, he was surprised to find two thin strips of metal and a grid of stone tiles like he'd seen at the entrance to The

Aerie. The track ran across the entire bridge before moving off into the depths of the Junk Heap maze.

That was the only similarity between the two locations. There were no weather vanes here, no tank-like homes. Instead, thick metal pipes belched smoke from the ground, while steel crates lay scattered across the landscape. The word *odd* didn't even begin to describe how he felt about the place.

"I can't believe there's a store around here," said Nier as he rubbed at his face. Something had been stinging his eyes and throat since he arrived—most likely related to the horrid-smelling smoke. The owner of the item shop back in the village once told him that natural rubber smelled rank when burned, so perhaps that was it.

Just when he was wishing he could ask someone for directions, he heard a child complaining about being hungry. "Hey, someone *is* here!" said an excited Nier. "Let's check it out."

Nier dashed toward the voice, keeping an eye out for any rusted pipes sprouting from the ground. Soon he came to another door made of wire netting. The child's voice was coming from behind it—a little boy calling for his brother.

"Hey there," Nier called as he opened the door.

"Welcome!" responded a pleasant voice. "Please come in. I'm Jakob, and this is my brother, Gideon."

The person greeting him was a boy around Nier's age. Sitting beside him was his little brother, the one who had whined about being hungry.

"What is this place?" Nier asked.

"It's my shop!" said the boy in his best imitation of a professional clerk. "I'm the finest smith in these parts—er, usually."

"Usually?"

"My brother and I build items from scrap we find in the Junk Heap, but we're a little low on supplies at the moment."

There was no doubt this was the place Popola had mentioned. Nier had imagined it would be a simple stall with a supply of items like they had in the village. It never occurred to him that the store might be located behind a mesh door without so much as a sign.

"Folks say the Heap used to be a military base," the boy continued. "I don't know about that, but there's lots of great stuff in there. It's not exactly the safest place in the world, but we gotta eat, you know?"

"It's just the two of you out here?"

"Yes. Our father died when Gideon was very young."

Just like ours, thought Nier, remembering how his and Yonah's father had died in a faraway town soon after she was born.

"And Mom is . . . She's out right now. Getting supplies."

"You mean scavenging for parts? I guess you did mention running low, huh?"

A little hand sprang out from the side of the counter, fingers going up one at a time as Gideon began to count.

". . . Five, six, SEVEN! Mom's been gone for SEVEN days!"

"That's a long time," Nier remarked. The little brother couldn't have been much older than Yonah, and that was still far too young to be apart from his mother for an entire week.

"It's getting harder to find good scrap," Jakob admitted. "She probably had to go deeper into the Heap."

Now Nier understood why Jakob had qualified his statements about being a smith with *usually*. As he mused on this, Gideon whined about how hungry he was again, which caused Nier to chuckle. It reminded him of Yonah . . . though she was better behaved.

"If you had the materials, would you be able to upgrade my weapon?"

"Well, yeah, but it's really dangerous in there."

"No problem. We'll go."

"You will?!"

As Nier watched the boy's eyes widen in shock, a thought came to him. He'd always had Devola, Popola, and all his kind neighbors in the village when times got hard, but Jakob had no one. It was a sobering realization.

A minute later, he and Weiss left the brothers' shop and made for the Junk Heap proper. Pillars snaked out of the ground here as well, but they also encountered metallic panels, bent poles, and a variety of other strange items poking out of the dirt.

Eventually they made their way into the Heap. While Jakob had warned them about how it used to be a military base, it resembled any other oversize building from the inside. Though there were no windows, the interior was bright. When Nier looked up, he saw lights affixed to the ceiling that were neither torches nor candles.

"Ruins from ancient times, patrolled for eons by unstoppable machines," murmured Weiss. "This place is hardly befitting one of my grand stature."

"You sure do like to complain, Weiss," replied Nier. Despite the quip, he understood how the tome felt. Not only did the place reek of rust, but there was also the constant scent of smoke, as if something was on fire. Additionally, the slippery floor made it difficult to walk, and the smell suggested it was oil.

Though there were no Shades here, the pair found themselves under regular assault from a series of boxlike machines. Nier had always thought machines stayed rooted in one place, but the ones in the Junk Heap zipped around with incredible speed. Thankfully, his recent sheep-hunting experience came in handy against the automatons—although he *was* surprised the first few times they exploded in flames instead of simply collapsing to the ground.

"It's pretty rough in here," admitted Nier at one point.

"Hardly suitable work for children," replied Weiss.

Nier figured it wouldn't be easy for a grown woman, either. Perhaps the boys' mother was remarkably strong, able to go toe-to-toe with these machines, weapon in hand—or perhaps she was the type to sneak about and pilfer materials when her enemy wasn't looking. Either way, the job was dangerous, and because she hadn't been back for an entire week . . .

Nier didn't want to focus on that. He cleared the thought from his mind and focused on the task of destroying machines.

4.

AFTER ACQUIRING THE necessary materials, Nier and Weiss returned to the shop. Gideon was crying for his mother, which caused Nier's heart to clench in his chest. The same impulses affected him after his own mother died, but he always managed to push the sadness down.

"Hello again!" said Jakob. He was all smiles, which only made the situation more painful.

"We got your materials," Nier informed him.

"Thank you so much. I'll get right to work on your weapon."

After collecting the materials and Nier's weapon, the boy vanished into the back room, his little brother close at his heels. While Nier didn't mean to eavesdrop, Gideon's cries were clearly audible between the sounds of metal being sharpened and hammered. He was insisting on going to look for their mother, and nothing Jakob said seemed able to soothe him.

"Sorry that took so long," said Jakob when he returned, trying his best to ignore his crying brother. "Normally I'd charge you, but you can have this one for free. All the materials you brought should keep us going for a while longer."

"Hey, so—" Nier began.

"I'm sorry. Gideon's just impatient for our mom to come back." He placed his hand on his sobbing brother's head to placate him, then knelt to look in his eyes. "We just need to wait, okay?"

But Nier had no intention of waiting any longer. "Weiss . . ."

"Yes, yes, I know. We're off to search for the misplaced mother, aren't we?"

Though Jakob was hesitant to accept their offer, an ecstatic Gideon urged them to set out as soon as possible. After receiving the activation code for an elevator that would take them deeper into the Heap, Nier and Grimoire Weiss found themselves heading back into the same danger they'd so recently left. Though it wasn't like Nier had known this would happen, he was still relieved they'd left the village early in the morning. Even with this latest detour, he thought they'd still be able to get home at a reasonable time.

"If I may ask," said Grimoire Weiss after a bit, "what is it that possesses you to meddle in the affairs of these children?"

"Yonah and I both know what it feels like to miss your mother."

In addition to the loneliness, Nier was also acutely aware of the weight of an older brother's worry—and that was *with* Devola, Popola, and a variety of neighbors helping out when they could. There was no such community here in the Junk Heap, and even meeting the occasional customer wasn't the same as greeting familiar faces day in and day out. There was no one here to lend Jakob a hand, and when Nier imagined the sheer depth of the boy's isolation, finding his mother seemed to be the least he could do. Also, unlike the brothers, he had the strength to see the task through.

As the pair went deeper into the Junk Heap, the machines grew more aggressive. If a sword wasn't enough to bring them down, Grimoire Weiss's magic was always there to finish the job. This helped Nier rest easy but also raised a rather troubling question: How did the boys' mother manage to make it this far without a powerful floating tome at her side? It was a question

Grimoire Weiss was clearly considering as well. After a long stretch of battling robots, he finally snapped.

"You can't possibly believe their mother managed to fight her way down here! Or, for that matter, that she has been collecting scrap metal for a solid week? Open your eyes, lad! The woman is clearly—"

"She's alive!"

Nier was unwilling to let his companion finish his sentence. Once he put the idea into words, there was a chance it could solidify in reality. That prospect terrified him because the boys needed their mother—and Gideon much more than Jakob.

Still, the depths of the Junk Heap smelled of oil, soot, and rust. There were no springs from which to drink, no cover to rest under. Was it even *possible* to wander lost in a place like this for a week?

Nier shook away the relentless questions that bubbled up in his mind. *She's alive*, he told himself. *She has to be.*

"Look, miracles don't happen if you don't believe in them, okay?"

"Miracles? Pah." With that, Grimoire Weiss said no more.

When they finally reached the first underground floor of the Junk Heap, they found a mess of passages so complicated that Nier was worried he'd get lost even with his map. Luckily, however, the brothers' mother did not work beyond that floor. She likely deliberately kept away from the more dangerous deeper levels. Thankfully, the elevator Jakob directed them to stopped on the first underground floor.

Though unexpected obstacles like mine carts and seemingly unbreakable barriers slowed their progress, they eventually traversed the entirety of the floor and found themselves at a massive circular room at the far end. It was labeled as a "testing area" in a faded, scrawled script on the map, and it was apparently the largest room on the floor. What had they been testing . . . and why was a familiar-looking mailbox sitting just outside?

"Maybe lots of people used to come here back in the day," mused Nier as he recalled Jakob saying this had been a military base. Still, he hadn't seen any sign of human beings around, so what happened to the people who once used the mailbox?

Popola once told him the metal bridge that led to the Junk Heap used to carry metal boxes filled with people. When he asked where they all went, Popola said she didn't know, and that it was unlikely anyone remembered. Sadly, this meant that the mystery of the mailbox's users would likely remain unsolved forever.

The sound of a door opening shocked Nier back to reality. As he stepped into the test site, he was amazed at how much bigger it was in real life when compared to the map. In fact, the ceiling was so high that it hurt his neck to look up at it.

A short bridge extended from the entrance to the circular platform in the middle. It was made from a kind of material Nier had never seen before, and his footsteps echoed loudly in the massive room as he crossed it.

According to the map, the only thing beyond the test site was an elevator hall. If the boys' mother wasn't in that room, there would be nowhere left to check on the floor. This thought—along with the sheer size of the room—made Nier uneasy. He soon abandoned walking and decided to dash straight across as fast as he could.

A horrible noise cascaded through the once-quiet chamber. There was a crackling sound like ripping paper, followed by a noise vaguely like speech. Despite having the form of language, the utterances were a sequence of sounds without meaning.

"What's going on?!" cried Nier.

"Mmm," remarked Grimoire Weiss. "This bodes ill."

"No! The bridge!"

As the speechlike noises continued and a red light began to strobe, the bridge they had just crossed fell away. There could be no turning back now—not that Nier had any intention of doing so. His original goal was the elevator hall beyond the room. So long as he had a path forward, he intended to take it.

But he now had to take something else into account: the enemy who was blocking the way to the exit. Though the creature resembled a random chunk of metal, it was apparently a machine with some sort of sentience or programming; like all the others that attempted to block their path, it moved and attacked of its own free will.

"Yeah, this might be a problem," Nier muttered.

"An enemy worth the trouble, however," Grimoire Weiss said.

"What do you mean?"

"I can sense the presence of a Sealed Verse."

"I guess Shades aren't the only ones with Sealed Verses."

The way forward was clear in his mind. He was going to take down the enormous machine and claim its Sealed Verse for himself.

"Here it comes!" cried Weiss as the battle began and Nier drew his sword.

After destroying the attacking machine and obtaining its Sealed Verse, Nier opened the door to the elevator hall. He was certain the answers he sought would be here one way or the other, and a single glance at the ground confirmed his suspicion in the most unfortunate way.

"It's a woman," said Nier. He didn't bother checking for signs of life; the body on the floor had clearly been dead for some time.

"I fear we have discovered the delinquent mother," Grimoire Weiss murmured. He floated over to a second corpse, which lay beside the dead woman, and examined it for a moment. "Hmm. This one is male."

The young man wore a gold chain around his neck with a cheap and gaudy air. His expression in death was horribly twisted, likely out of fear or pain. After seeing this, Nier and Weiss were able to piece things together easily enough. The pair had made their way to the test site—likely to access the elevator marked on the map—when they were attacked by the enormous machine. They made it that far through stealth and guile, but such skills would not have availed them against a foe that fired burning lasers and lightning-quick bullets. It was an enemy Nier couldn't have handled without Grimoire Weiss; the two poor souls on the ground never had a chance.

A large bag lay crumpled on the floor beside the woman. The clasp had come undone, spilling out a variety of brightly colored clothing. Nier began rummaging around, hoping to find proof that she was not the boys' mother, but he discovered only additional traveling clothes, makeup, and money.

"Why would she bring this stuff here?" he wondered.

"It would seem she abandoned her children to seek comfort in the arms of a swain," spat Grimoire Weiss. "So much for miracles. Instead, we have discovered the worst possible truth."

Nier was speechless. While he knew the chances of her being alive were likely nonexistent, he'd still hoped for a miracle to happen. But even with that being the case, it never occurred to him that she might be abandoning her children entirely. He assumed she wanted to come home and was unable to do so—instead, she'd stuffed her bag full of beautiful things with which to decorate herself, grabbed all the money she could find, and left her children without even a morsel of food to sustain themselves. But now her nice clothes were soiled with oil and rust, her perfume bottles were cracked, and her money was useless. The entire plan had been for naught.

"Let's go," said Nier. "There's nothing left for us here."

Since they only needed to take the elevator to the surface, Nier didn't have to do much walking. Despite that, his steps felt heavy as lead as he made his way back.

"What will you tell the children?" asked Grimoire Weiss.

That question was the reason for the weight in his legs. Gideon had pleaded for them to find his mother. It would be beyond cruel for him to learn what had taken place here. And yet, perhaps he deserved to know.

Nier pondered this question during the far-too-short ride to the surface. Should he tell Gideon a gentle truth and say his mother was now in heaven? Or should he lie and claim they were unable to find her despite a thorough search? No matter which answer he gave, tears were sure to follow.

The conversation went much as Nier suspected it would. The younger brother stared at him with anger in his eyes, spewing the most hateful things his limited vocabulary could muster before retreating into the back of the store. And though Jakob scolded his brother for his rude behavior and his nonstop crying, Gideon paid him no mind.

"I'm sorry," said Jakob. "I didn't mean for him to be so rude."

"It's fine," replied Nier. "You don't have to scold him."

As the little boy's wails continued in the back, the older brother dropped his voice and asked a single question: Did she die alone?

Nier's eyes went wide. It sounded as if the other boy knew someone had been with his mother in the end.

"It's okay," he confirmed a moment later. "I know all about it."

Thinking back, Nier realized the boy had been acting strange when he gave them the elevator code. He'd started to say something about their mother multiple times, but he ultimately never found the words. It turned out he'd suspected everything from the very start.

"Just tell me: Did she die with the one she loved?"

Nier couldn't find the words to reply, so Grimoire Weiss did so instead. "We found two bodies. It appears they left this life as one."

Jakob inhaled, then let it out in a long, slow breath. "Okay. That's okay. Mom was always so frustrated, you know? Torn between her duty to us and her heart . . . I think . . . I think maybe this is for the best."

The emptiness in his voice—and the way he simply stood and bore his pain—made Nier think his heart would break. With no idea what else to do, he reached into his bag and withdrew the mother's only unbroken bottle of perfume.

"Here," he said, handing it to Jakob. "We found this."

"This is Mom's perfume," he said. He turned the bottle over in his hands, then unscrewed the lid, causing the scent of roses to rise in the air. "It smells like her."

Tears began to well up in the boy's eyes, and he finally allowed himself to mourn for a moment. When he finished, the mild expression came back to his face, and he insisted on seeing Nier and Weiss off. Gideon also emerged from the back as they were making ready to depart and waved at them until they moved out of sight down the path.

Though a heavy weight lay on Nier's chest, he felt he had made the correct decision. He also swore to visit the brothers' shop again to get his weapon strengthened and enjoy a friendly chat, for he knew better than anyone how such things could bring relief and encouragement in dark times.

Though Nier ran across the northern plains as fast as he could, it was still evening when he reached the village. Not wanting to waste a second more without seeing Yonah, he gently pushed open the door to their house and climbed the stairs to her bed, praying she would look at least a little better.

"I'm home, Yonah," he said quietly. The blanket rustled, and he could tell she was awake.

"Yonah?"

Normally she would have replied by now, if not leaped out of bed with a happy *hello*. Even when she was feeling ill, she'd give him some sort of weak greeting. But this silence was new—and deeply disturbing.

"Yonah? What's wrong?"

A terrible feeling churned in his gut. As his hand peeled back the blanket, he felt his entire body grow cold.

"It hurts . . ." said his sister as greasy sweat poured from her forehead.

"I'll go get some medicine from Popola," Nier said as he wiped the sweat away as best he could. "Just hold on."

"Wait . . ." came her whisper of a voice. "Just . . . don't do anything dangerous."

"Stop worrying already."

He was touched that she might worry about him at a time like this. All he wanted in life was to free her from her pain as soon as possible, and he made this wish over and over in his mind as he raced off for the library.

REPORT 04

Nier's reaction to the records on Grimoires Weiss and Noir went far beyond what I anticipated. While I fully expected him to think the Black Scrawl and Grimoire Weiss were related in some way when I showed him my book, it never occurred to me that he might set out to collect all the Sealed Verses. Surprisingly, it was Grimoire Weiss who encouraged him in this endeavor. I thought luck was on our side when I realized the tome had lost his memory, but this proved a grim reminder of how such things can backfire.

While I fear Nier's haphazard search for massive Shades might cause more unexpected situations to arise, I still told them about The Aerie. Though things seemed calm enough in the moment, I'd heard and read ominous signs from the place of late, and thought it convenient to send them there. When they returned, I learned they had found Shades in the village proper, and even encountered a massive creature in possession of a Sealed Verse.

Though this news was disquieting, I still felt I had no choice but to tell them about the Junk Heap when Nier asked about strengthening his weapon. At present, I remain uncertain if this was the correct decision.

Nier is growing more powerful with an

improved weapon and repeated exposure to battle. This is an unprecedented situation, and one I believe we should keep a very close eye on.

Record written by Popola

The Boy 4

1.

NIER'S LEGS ALWAYS felt heavy when he went to Seafront. If it weren't for the Shades and the aggressive deer between here and there, he would have dragged his feet the entire way. Despite that, he now found himself running frantically in an attempt to shave minutes—or even seconds—off the once-painful journey.

All for Yonah, of course.

Although she was still taking her medicine, it was no longer keeping the pain at bay. Nier despaired that her condition had deteriorated to the point that the medicine no longer worked. He'd immediately gone to Popola to see if she had any ideas and was thrilled when she delivered once more. She explained how taking the medicine for an extended period of time could lessen the effectiveness, which meant it wasn't Yonah's illness growing untreatable after all. After thinking for a moment, she then proposed a new solution:

I guess we could try a shaman fish.

What's that?

It's a fish found near Seafront. Their livers contain a chemical that's said to dull even the strongest pain. Unfortunately, they don't keep very well. You'll need to go there and catch it yourself.

This was how Nier found himself once again leaving the village before the chicken-keeping couple was awake. All of his running across the plains was worth it when he rolled into Seafront before noon. If procuring the fish wasn't too much trouble, he was hopeful he might return home before the day was out.

"I doubt we'll have much luck blundering about blindly for this shaman fish," grumbled Grimoire Weiss as the pair moved through the town.

"So what should we do?" replied Nier. "I don't even know what one looks like, so if you've got a better idea, I'm all ears."

"Perhaps we could try asking some of the townspeople for advice?"

"Works for me. Heck, we might even find someplace that sells them."

The thought made Nier remember one of his first visits to Seafront, when he'd stumbled into a shop that sold fish near the beach. As he watched the kindly old shopkeeper wrap fish in oiled paper, she smiled at him and asked if it was his first time seeing such a creature. She then went on to point out each type she had in her stall, as well as their names. While he didn't remember a shaman fish being among them, fish hadn't been his overwhelming concern in those times, so it was possible she'd said the name and he simply didn't remember.

When he approached the shop, he found the same woman wiping down an empty display stand. "Sorry, dear," she said. "None of the boats have come in with their catches yet."

"I see. Thanks."

It seemed leaving the village early had backfired on him.

"Patience, lad. Our only option is to wait until this shaman fish graces the—"

Before Grimoire Weiss could finish his sentence, a young man passing by turned around. "You want a shaman fish?"

"That's right," replied Nier. "Are there any other shops that sell them?"

"Oh no. Nobody sells those."

"Why not?"

"Because they taste *terrible*! Good for what ails you, sure, but gross as can be and ugly as an old boot. If one ever turns up for sale, it's only because it ended up in the same net as a better fish."

That meant waiting patiently outside a shop was a fool's errand. Before Nier could even ask their next option, however, the young man pointed to the pier at the end of the street. "You should try asking the old man up by the quay."

"Why?"

"Because that old-timer can tell you everything you ever wanted to know about shaman fish, and plenty of stuff you didn't."

"That's great. Thank you."

Nier felt encouraged; if they couldn't simply purchase the fish at the shop, finding someone who understood the creatures was the next best thing. Why, some fisherman might even be reeling one in as they approached! If that happened, it would be a simple matter of negotiating a fee.

When they arrived at the quay, they found an old man looking out over the sea and muttering to himself. "We're a stone's throw from the ocean, and not a man around knows how to fish properly."

He finished this statement with an angry grunt that gave Nier pause. Still, approaching grumpy old men with questions wasn't a big deal here—unlike in The Aerie.

"Um, excuse me? I'm trying to get a shaman fish."

"Eh? Shaman fish? Oh sure, sure. They're a cinch—practically jump into the net, they do!"

Though the old man's speech was blunt, Nier found himself strangely at ease around him; clearly there was kindness buried beneath his gruff exterior.

"But I won't do it for ya," he continued. "Here! Take this pole and go fish one up yourself."

The old man thrust a fishing rod into Nier's hands. His movements were natural and without a hint of condescension, reinforcing Nier's suspicion that he was a good person at heart.

"Can't catch 'em here at the pier, so go dip yer line at the big beach on the west side of town."

Nier paused. "Er, but how do I fish?"

"How do ya *fish*? Is that a serious question?"

Despite the exasperation in his voice, the old fisherman took the time to give Nier a brief rundown on fishing protocol, then lent him a lure while he was at it. "Fishing is a test of wills 'tween man and beast!" he concluded. "Never give up the fight!"

With the old man's encouraging words in his ears, Nier headed toward the western beach. "You know, Weiss," he mused as he walked, "none of the people here seemed to be surprised to see you. Not even that old fisherman."

"They must already know of the great Grimoire Weiss. As they should."

"Heh. Maybe so."

Thanks to the unending stream of foreign ships that docked in Seafront, it was a town used to oddities. People were exposed to foods seasoned with strange spices, materials with no obvious uses, tools with bizarre mechanisms, and all manner of other things. A floating book with an arrogant attitude was likely par for the course.

Now that Nier was here, he found himself appreciating just how beautiful the city was. The pure, chalky white of the building walls made the blue of the sea shine that much brighter, and the uniform flagstone paths made walking easy on both the feet and the eyes. The people were free and open; no one was snarling at outsiders to leave. The only negative was the overriding smell of fish, which was something Nier thought he might never get used to.

The pair turned off the stall-lined main street onto a smaller path, passed through a cave, and exited onto the western beach. Seals lay sunning themselves on the wide sands, and the sight of children playing warmed Nier's heart. With the halcyon scene in the corner of his eye, Nier attached the lure to his fishing line and swung the pole forward as he had been taught.

"Careful, lad," Grimoire Weiss warned.

"Yeah, I know. I have to wait for the lure to bob."

Once the lure sank and the rod bent, Nier had to use his entire body to pull the rod in the opposite direction of the fish. He also kept in mind the old man's advice to speak as quietly as possible, since fish would swim away from loud noises. A few moments later, the fishing rod bowed, and a shaman fish appeared on the end of the line.

"Gotcha!" cried Nier as he reeled it in. Either the old man was an exceptional teacher, or he was just lucky, but either way the attempt had been a success. The fish was indeed an ugly thing, and far smaller than he was expecting. But considering he still had to make the return trip home, a lighter fish was something of a blessing in disguise.

A few hours later, the pair found themselves back in Nier's house, where he quickly began preparing the fish for Yonah. Though young children typically hated food with aggressive tastes, Yonah simply ate it without complaint, which told him exactly how unbearable her pain had become.

The effects were almost immediate. When Nier went to check on her later that night, he found her snoring softly. Her brows weren't knit in pain, nor was she gripping the blanket with an unusually tight fist. It was a sleep of deep and dreamless peace—and the next morning, he found her sitting up in bed with a hint of color in her cheeks.

"Hey, Yonah," he said. "How you feeling?"

"Better. It doesn't hurt anymore."

"That's great. That's . . . really great."

Nier decided then and there to find errands that would take him to Seafront so he could acquire more shaman fish. As he was planning out a way to do this, Yonah looked over his shoulder and widened her eyes.

"Hey! What's that book?"

Nier's confusion turned to realization when he remembered how Yonah had been unconscious the entire way back from the Lost Shrine and in bed ever since. Mindful of her condition, Grimoire Weiss had scarcely spoken when he'd been in the house. Though they'd shared a space multiple times already, this was Yonah's first chance to really look at him.

"Oh yeah," said Nier. "Guess I should introduce you."

"I am Grimoire Weiss, wielder of arcane—"

"Hi, Weissey!" interrupted Yonah.

"Now, see here! My name is—"

"Weiss has been worried about you," Nier told Yonah.

"Really? Aw, thanks, Weissey!"

Grimoire Weiss gave a deep, long sigh. "Pah. Oh, very well. Call me whatever you like."

"Sure thing, Weissey!"

"It appears impudence is the fruit of this family tree," muttered Weiss as an oblivious Yonah continued to look up at him with unbridled joy.

2.

SEVERAL DAYS AFTER his expedition to Seafront, Nier found himself delivering medicinal herbs to the library. "How have things been?" asked Popola after receiving them. "Is everything okay?"

"The shaman fish is really doing the trick," Nier replied.

"I wasn't just asking about Yonah. I'm also wondering about you."

"Me?"

"You've made a number of long trips lately. Are you sure you're not pushing yourself too hard?"

She was right. In fact, the day before last had seen Nier make another Junk Heap excursion to find materials for his weapon. The foes with Sealed Verses were powerful indeed, and his blade would need to be sharp if he wanted to take them down.

"I'm okay," he replied after a pause. "I can't just sit around all day while Yonah's sick, after all."

"If you say so."

"So then! Anything I can do for you?" Nier made sure to make his voice especially cheery; the last thing he wanted to do was worry Popola more than necessary.

"Well, I suppose there *is* one thing I could use a hand with. Have you heard about our plans to repair the canal?"

The village had a small dock on the canal. Though it wasn't in use now, someone in the village had told Nier about how boats once came and went all the time. They'd been planning to repair it so that could happen again, but nothing had come to pass yet.

"The work probably won't take place for a while," continued Popola, "but once it's done, we can use the canal for all kinds of things."

"And we wouldn't have to worry about being attacked by Shades on a boat," added Nier.

"Unfortunately, we're a bit behind schedule at the moment."

"Oh?"

"I hate to burden you, but if you're willing to help out, I'd really appreciate it."

"No problem! What do you need?" Since Popola was always the one taking care of Nier and Yonah, being of use was the least he could do to repay her.

"The man I originally asked to help on this project hasn't shown up for work in a few days," said Popola. "I'm starting to get a little worried, so maybe you can head over to Seafront and check up on him?"

"Sure thing. I was just thinking about catching more shaman fish, so this works out perfectly." Nier didn't mention how Yonah's brows had been furrowed slightly before she went to bed the night before, meaning the last fish's effects were likely wearing off.

Popola gave a sigh of relief. "Thank you," she said. "He always carries a red bag over his shoulder, so he should be easy enough to find. You can probably ask anyone in Seafront."

"Got it."

After Popola marked the location of the man with the red bag on his map, Nier set off on the long trip to Seafront. When he arrived, he made straight for the main street, where the man was said to live. Nier was thankful he had a clear location to shoot for in the maze of Seafront homes, and doubly happy when he saw the man with the red bag sitting in front of his house. But as Nier drew close, he could tell something was wrong; the man had his arms wrapped around his knees, and he was mumbling something with his head hanging low.

"Oh god, it's over . . . My life is over . . ."

What is he talking about?

"Surely you must realize nothing good can come of being involved with this particular endeavor," said Grimoire Weiss. He was obviously ready to turn around and leave before their mission had even begun, but after calming the tome, Nier turned back to the despondent man.

"Hey, you're the guy who's supposed to help repair the canal, right? Are you okay? What happened?"

"It's my wife," wailed the man. "She left home a week ago and hasn't come back! I've searched all over town for her and turned up nothing. I'm so worried I can't even focus on my work. Oh, my sweet dumpling! Where are you?!"

Nier suddenly understood why the man had been missing work—the search for a missing wife would take precedence over any kind of employment. "Would you like us to help you look for her?"

"Really?!" cried the man. "You'd do that for me?!"

Nier said he would, leaving out the part about how helping him would be the fastest way to make sure he went back to work. "Do you have any idea where we should start?"

After a moment of thought, the man looked up. "I can't say it's much of an idea, but she always used to enjoy drinking at the tavern with her friends."

"All right. We'll start with them."

"Thank you. This means the world to me. And by the way, my wife always carries a red bag just like mine. If you mention that, it might ring some bells."

"I've met some odd couples in my day, but none who felt the need to wander about flaunting matching luggage," observed a grumpy Grimoire Weiss.

"These bags are special. We bought them for our anniversary." As the man said this, the corners of his mouth suddenly drooped, making him look like Yonah right before she burst into tears. "But now my sweet dumpling is gone, and it's all my fault! Oh god . . ."

"Okay, okay!" cried Nier. "Just stay calm. We'll go look for her, all right? You sit tight."

Unfortunately, Nier's visit to the tavern revealed no clues as to the wife's whereabouts. Her supposed friends—the ones her husband said often accompanied her in revelry—had no idea where she was or even where she might be. All they told Nier was that she often gossiped with the wife of the man who owned the tackle stall.

The pair made their way to the tackle stall and spoke with the owner's wife. "Last time she came around, she mentioned something about leaving town," she said. "I figured it was just idle talk, you know? Er, but that was a little while ago."

If the missing woman had left the city, she could be anywhere by now. Vague information was better than none at all, so Nier felt he had no choice but to continue wandering and see what he could find.

"The husband seemed to know the reason his wife ran away from home," noted Weiss at one point.

"You got the same impression, huh?" replied Nier.

"However, the *whys* do not explain the *wheres*."

"Too bad it's not the other way around."

"That would be its own sort of trouble, my lad."

Speaking with people around town led them to one inescapable fact: the red-bag couple fought often and spectacularly.

In fact, the pair were so well-known to locals, everyone knew exactly who the phrase 'that married couple' was referring to. It seemed unlikely a man so torn up about his wife's absence could engage her in angry verbal spats, but that was clearly the case.

After searching the town entrance, Nier and Weiss left Seafront and made their way to the southern plains. The events of the Junk Heap replayed in Nier's mind. Had the missing woman been alone? He certainly did not want to go through *that* experience again.

The pair encountered several Shades along the way, the number and strength of which only grew the closer they got to the plains. The path was much too dangerous to venture down alone, which only made the awful feeling in the pit of Nier's stomach grow stronger.

He discovered his hunch was right when they reached the southern plains and found a Shade a step above the others in strength. Nier and Grimoire Weiss managed to take it down using the magic gained at The Aerie and the Junk Heap, but the battle ended in a sight neither wanted to see. When the dead Shade turned to dust and vanished, it left behind a bright red bag.

"This is identical to the red satchel carried by the man who sent us on this mad quest," said Grimoire Weiss. "Perhaps it belongs to his spouse."

"Oh no," replied Nier. The Shade had clearly killed the man's wife. Though they searched the area carefully, they found no corpse; she must have met her end somewhere else. "Well, this is terrible. What are we supposed to say?"

"However difficult it may be, we've no choice but to tell the man the truth."

If only this was some kind of mistake, Nier thought as he

returned to the man's house. *If only that bag belonged to some-one else.*

Unfortunately, the bag clearly belonged to his wife—and when Nier presented the item to the man and told him they found it on a Shade, his face went white.

"Oh god! How could this happen to her?!" He collapsed onto the floor and began sobbing like a child. "This is all my fault! All my fault!"

"If I may, my good man, why did your wife leave home in the first place?" Grimoire Weiss asked.

"C'mon, Weiss," Nier scolded. "I think we should give him some time to himself."

As he urged Grimoire Weiss to leave, a bright voice suddenly rang out from behind them:

"Honey! I'm hooo— Good heavens, you're a wreck! What's wrong?"

The man's eyes went wide as he scrambled to his feet. "Dumpling! You're not dead!"

"What in the *world* are you talking about?" asked his bewildered wife.

"Your bag! It was—"

"Oh! You found it? Thank you SO much. I can't believe I went and dropped it like that."

"This has all been a terrific waste of effort," muttered Grimoire Weiss.

As the man broke down again, he and his wife began explaining the entire situation. It turned out the woman had just gone to visit her parents—and she became enraged when she realized her husband had either forgotten that fact or never heard it in the first place.

"You never listen to what I have to say," she spat.

"And you lost our anniversary bag!" snarled the man. Soon

the two of them were verbally at each other's throats, causing Nier to take a step back lest he get drawn in.

"This must be what people were talking about," he mused as he watched. Finally, he managed an edgewise word about the waterway repairs and took his leave, as exhausted as if he had just finished a confrontation with a massive Shade.

3.

AFTER LEAVING THE arguing couple's house, Nier made his way to the western beach to catch a shaman fish. Once he had one in his pouch, he left the beach feeling as though a weight had been lifted from him. He doubted he would be running into much trouble after this—but that hope turned out to be short-lived.

"Hold it!"

Nier heard someone yelling near the path that led to the main thoroughfare. The tone was cranky—crankier even than that of the old man who had taught him to fish. But since he had no friends here, he did not think it was meant for him and continued walking.

"I said, hold it!" came the loud, impatient voice again. "Over here! How can you just ignore an old woman in need?! Oh, I weep for this generation! The children of this age are nothing but selfish, heartless cads!"

Nier came to a halt and looked around for the target of the elderly woman's rant, but the only things he saw were lazy seals and scampering children.

"Uh, is she talking about me?" he asked.

"Oh, ignore her!" responded Grimoire Weiss. "People like that are best left to their own devices."

Nier knew how the tome felt; he had a feeling this would only lead to trouble. That said, he couldn't ignore the woman when he was fully aware she was calling to him specifically. As he stood there thinking about these things, the woman began to wail.

"Ohhh! Ohhhhhh! The pain!"

"What's wrong? Is everything okay?!"

Thinking she might be hurt, Nier rushed to her side, at which point she directed a sharp stare toward Grimoire Weiss.

"My illness has returned! It must have been the shock of seeing this rude floating book!"

"Rude?" sputtered Weiss. "*Book?!* Now see here, madam! I'll have you know—"

"You! You did this! Oh, what a terrible thing you are!"

"Why, you insolent crone! How dare you address me like some common paperback!"

"Weiss! Knock it off!" barked Nier, pulling the tome back before he could fly at the old woman. He then attempted to flee, but before he could get more than a few steps, the woman began yelling again.

"You would truly abandon a pitiful old woman to this cruel world? Oh, to think lifting a single finger would bother you *that* much!"

"Our apologies, ma'am," said Nier sheepishly.

Grimoire Weiss exhaled one of the more impressive sighs Nier had ever heard. "I am at a loss as to what aid we could possibly give a woman who is so clearly able to talk her way into anything."

"I need you to go to the post office and tell them to deliver my mail," she replied sharply.

"I can't fathom why they haven't been here yet . . ."

The sentence had barely escaped Grimoire Weiss before the old lady began wailing in pain again. "Okay, okay!" Nier cried in an attempt to placate her. "We're going! Look at us go!"

It seemed this would be another day of chance meetings.

Somehow, Nier always seemed to find himself wrapped up in other peoples' business no matter what he did. Perhaps it would be best to just accept that fact and move on.

Thinking back, he recalled some of the villagers telling him to "beware the lighthouse lady" while making his way to the western beach. He cursed his past self for ignoring the warnings and not understanding what they meant. If he ever found himself in the face of another unknown, he swore to stop and question it in the future.

With that encounter complete, Nier made his way to the Seafront post office, which was conveniently located near the main street, town plaza, and docks. Nier's village had a mailbox, but no post office. If letters weren't coming, one had no choice but to wait for a mail carrier to drop by. This is why Nier had been astonished when the old woman demanded he go to the post office and collect her mail—he didn't even know that was an option.

"Afternoon!" called the postman when they walked in the door. He had a pleasant voice and an open, honest face, and Nier immediately felt bad for demanding mail from him.

"Hey, so there's some old lady who yelled at us to come here and check on her mail, and—" Nier began.

"Oh, you mean the lighthouse lady?"

"The very same," interjected Weiss, who clearly didn't share Nier's reticence to make demands of the kind postman. "Now could you please deliver her parcels and silence her flapping gums?"

The postman stared at them for a moment before lowering his head. "Sorry, but I injured my leg. I won't be delivering anything for a while."

Now Nier felt even *worse*; if the man was injured, he couldn't even do his everyday shopping, much less deliver mail. He immediately started racking his brain for ways they could help.

"Oh, that's too bad. Maybe we can—"

"A hurt leg?" cried a stunned Grimoire Weiss. "What about your sacred postman's oath?! 'Neither wind, nor sleet, nor terrible monsters of the night shall keep thee from'—"

Before his companion could complete his rant, Nier interrupted and offered to deliver the mail in the postman's stead.

"Oh, that would be a huge help! Er, just be careful, all right? That lady has a bit of a temper."

"You don't say?" said Grimoire Weiss, who seemed more than a bit sour about the entire affair.

"Actually, since you're here . . ." continued the postman. "You're from Popola's village, right?"

"Yes," said Nier. "How'd you know?"

"You're dressed differently, and you just have a certain . . . air about you, I guess. Anyway, would you mind taking this letter to Popola when you go back?"

"Sure!"

Nier knew delivering the letter meant the postman wouldn't have to cross the southern plains with a bad leg. And since he was going straight to Popola to tell her about the waterway, it seemed like an idea that worked for them both. Grimoire Weiss, however, was not so happy.

"Bah! We may as well take the postman's oath ourselves!"

Though the post office and lighthouse were close as the crow flies, the latter building needed its light to be seen for miles, meaning Nier had to climb a large hill to get there. Even worse, the old woman's personal residence was at the very top of the lighthouse, which entailed multiple sets of stairs. It was a laborious affair even for a young man of his age, and he could only imagine how difficult it would be for an old woman and a post-man with an injured leg.

"What do you want?" The old woman frowned when she saw the pair darken her doorway.

"We have retrieved your letter," Grimoire Weiss informed her.

"The postman hurt his leg," Nier began. "That's why he—"

The old woman's eyebrows shot up. "That's no excuse! It's his job to deliver the mail, no matter what! Didn't he take the postman's oath?!"

"He can barely walk," Nier insisted.

"Hmph! So you say."

"The thought that anyone would actually bother to write you a letter staggers the imagination," Grimoire Weiss remarked.

"Such a rude book!" she exclaimed. "I'll have you know, this is from someone very dear to me."

The way she cradled the letter in her hands made Nier feel like he was seeing a different person. The old woman who spewed such prickly insults seemed to melt away and be replaced by a dreamy-eyed young girl—although it was possible all the climbing had just addled his brain for a moment.

"Well, I suppose I should give you something for your trouble," she said finally. Her wrinkled hand shot out and firmly placed several coins into Nier's hand. Despite her grumpy demeanor and speech, her fingers were gentle, and Nier found himself thinking that she might not be such a bad person after all.

Upon exiting the lighthouse, he left Seafront and made the half day's journey back to his village. He made straight for the library when he arrived and found Popola writing away in her office despite the lateness of the hour.

"Hey," said Nier. "I brought a letter for you."

She took the letter with thanks and undid the seal. After reading for a moment, her brows began to furrow.

"What's wrong?" Nier asked.

"It's from the mayor of Seafront. He says a horde of Shades has appeared in The Aerie."

"I would sooner hurl myself into a bonfire than revisit that unsociable hellhole," Grimoire Weiss muttered. "Those people listen to neither logic nor reason and went to absurd lengths to see us shut out. If there is a worse location anywhere in this world, I do not know of it."

"I understand," said Popola quietly. "But there are still so many innocent people there."

"Don't worry," Nier reassured her. "I'll go take a look."

He had his own selfish reason for agreeing to the request. If a horde of Shades had appeared in the village, there was a good chance the massive one who looked like a lizard was among them—the one who was likely in possession of a Sealed Verse.

4.

AS SHE WRAPPED a new set of bandages around her left leg, Kainé found herself falling deep into thought.

Having entered the world in a body that was both male and female, she was used to being seen and mocked as an anomaly. And once a Shade came to occupy the entire left half of her body, she had also become used to being treated like a monster.

So when some kid showed up and started attacking her with magic, her only thought was a tired *Again?* She set about scaring him so he'd leave her alone—which was about the only kind of interaction she had with other people these days.

This boy turned out to be different. After the fight, he apologized for what he had done—and he seemed to be *genuinely* sorry. She couldn't remember the last time someone had done that—and in fact, she was fairly certain it had never happened before. Rather than providing comfort, this truth gave Kainé a horribly unsettled feeling in her stomach.

A ripple of goose bumps suddenly ran up the left side of her body as staticky laughter echoed in her ears. She would never get used to her Shade, Tyrann, speaking directly in her mind. It was more than uncomfortable—it was annoying.

"Sure are some weirdos out there, huh? Kid musta had a few screws loose to treat a monster like people. *I mean, unless he's the kind of idiot who thinks saying* let's be friends *is enough to keep him from being attacked! Kya ha ha!"*

"Shut up," replied Kainé. Though she didn't need to speak to the Shade aloud, the unpleasant feeling inside her could not be released in any other way.

"Aww, are you taking the idiot kid's side? Do you wanna be fwiends with him? How precious!"

The moment she realized Tyrann was just egging her on again, the jumbled mess of emotions in her heart went quiet.

"Whaaat, not gonna get angry at me this time?"

Tough titty for you, Kainé thought in response. The twisted Shade loved nothing more than to feed on the darkest, most horrible emotions; he would smack his lips and wait for wrath, hatred, and loathing to fill Kainé's entire being. Once she realized this, she also realized how stupid it was to get worked up over everything he said, which was why she would feed him no more crumbs today.

"See, this is what makes you such a terrific asshole."

You're old news. Get used to it.

Tyrann, no longer amused by the exchange, gave no reply. Yet he *was* old news to her and had been for a while. She'd stopped counting how many years it had been since he possessed her. Otherwise, the number would have been on her mind constantly. How many years since her grandmother died? How many years since her only living relative had been killed by a Shade? How many years since she had nearly died herself? How many years spent in this abominable body?

It wasn't as though her life before all that had been particularly peaceful. The other villagers had long shunned her for being intersex, despite the fact that she'd done nothing to any of them. They persecuted her family simply because she was different. The harassment proved too much for her parents, who both died when she was young. Even the elderly grandmother who took her in was forced to move their home beyond the bounds of the community. This experience taught Kainé that being different was reason enough to be attacked.

Still, the fact that those things were able to hurt her back then was testimony to how peaceful the days were, relatively speaking. For human violence and cruelty paled in comparison to what Shades wrought.

The Shade that killed her grandmother had been massive. Overpowering. Brutal. It enjoyed the terror and pain it brought and did not make quick work of the old woman. Instead, it watched her slowly perish beneath its massive claw, all the while delighting in Kainé's anguish.

Though her grandmother had been killed right in front of her, Kainé could do nothing about it. The kindly woman who had placed a white flower in her hair and said, "You're my granddaughter, and I don't give two shits what anyone says," had vanished into a dirty red stain beneath the filthy talon of a Shade.

Rage had overcome Kainé in that moment, and she leaped onto the creature and attempted to stab it to death. This wasn't just reckless; it was stupid. And only now—after all these years—did she finally understand why. She never could have killed such a beast with the puny knife she wielded. The end result when she nearly died, and the Shade escaped unharmed, should have been obvious to anyone.

Yet the reason she did not die was the oddity that attempted to take over her body at the moment of death—a sticky black *thing* slithered across her shattered left arm and into her missing left eye.

"*Give me that weird body of yours,*" it whispered in her mind. "*Give it to me! I wanna stand on the ground, feel the rain, taste the wind . . .*"

The creature was Tyrann, but his desires did not come to

fruition because Kainé's will to live stopped him. Her grandmother's dying wish had been for her to live, and she intended to
do so no matter what.

Having failed at overtaking Kainé, Tyrann repaired her body
and set up residence inside her. He was clearly intent on taking
over the moment she slipped up, and he now spent his days pro-
voking and abusing her for the sheer cruelty of it.

Kainé's musings on the past came to a halt as she raised her
head. She sensed a Shade. This was something she had been unable to do when she was human, but she now shared the senses of
the Shade who lived inside her.

Darkness spilled from the tunnel leading toward the village.
Blades in hand, she rushed to beat them back.

"There's more, Sunshine."

Tyrann didn't need to tell her twice; she sensed Shades coming from the village—dozens of them. Though she'd been feeling their presence strongly these past few days, it was still an
astonishing number.

"These fuckers really need to give it a rest already," she muttered to herself. Unlike the small Shades that cropped up around
the northern plains, the new ones reflected her magic back at her,
which meant she'd have to use her blades to cut them down indi-
vidually. It would take far longer than just mowing them down
with magic, a reality that annoyed her to no end.

Oh, but she would kill them—she would kill every last one
of them. After all, the Shade that murdered her grandmother
seemed relatively intelligent, so slaughtering its brethren might
cause it to show itself.

Ever since Tyrann's strength became her own, Kainé had
gained the ability to wield massive blades that would have been
impossible for her to lift previously. Her legs had also grown into
mighty things that could close the distance between her and a

Shade in a single stride. Her half-possession by a Shade may have earned her the renewed loathing of The Aerie, but it had proved indispensable in her quest to avenge her grandmother.

"Look out! We got company!"

Though her Shade perception was sharper now, she was less aware of the presence of people, and it was Tyrann who first noticed someone else leaping into the horde of Shades with his sword held high. When Kainé whirled around to identify the new arrival, she was shocked to see the boy who'd apologized to her, with his floating book companion.

"The hell are you doing here?" she growled.

"We thought you could use a hand!" he called in response.

Okay, WHAT?! First you apologize, and now you're here to help *me? This is some high fucking comedy.*

"Yes, and I do believe a heartfelt thank-you is in order, hmmm?" interjected the book when she made no move to reply.

"Yeah, that's not happening!" yelled Kainé. But the book seemed disinterested in her wrathful reply, which only made her angrier. Rather than dwell on it, she turned her attention back to killing Shades.

As they fought, the number of Shades began to fall rapidly. Though the boy appeared to be barely a teenager, he was mowing down Shades at roughly the same rate as Kainé—and that was *without* the advantages Tyrann provided. He'd clearly grown a lot since the last time he came out this way.

"Well, well, wellll! I didn't know you were capable of being in-terested in other people."

"Cram it," she muttered. Tyrann's unnecessary scrutiny irritated her, and she put all of her strength into her next swing. The clump of Shades before her flew backward and disintegrated into dust.

"What could have caused these Shades to appear in such

force?" mused the talking book, whom Kainé found to be incredibly creepy. Though the design of a mask on the cover served as a face, he lacked any kind of functioning eyes, nose, or mouth—and yet somehow was perfectly capable of speech.

"I don't know," she replied. "But they're all over the village too."

"Then we need to go help!" cried the boy, who immediately dashed off with his floating companion hot on his heels.

"Well, Sunshine? Now what? You're not actually thinking of HELPING those morons in the village, are you?"

She began forming an argument in her mind—a way to justify inserting herself into the fray without admitting she was aiding the villagers—but a sudden ripple through her flesh brought everything to a halt.

"Oh boy, Sunshine! Heeee's heeere!"

"Oh, I know."

Kainé broke into a run and caught up with the boy near the far end of the tunnel, where the sensation only grew stronger. As they burst into the light and began to cross the narrow rope bridge that spanned The Aerie, a deep rumble shook the boards beneath them. Seconds later, a shiny mass slithered up the cliff from the depths of the ravine. The massive Shade leaped over Kainé and the boy and landed in the wide space on the bridge, almost as though it wanted to block their way. For a brief moment, Kainé felt like it was looking straight at her.

"Rot in hell, asshole!" she cried. She leaped forward, her upper body twisting in impossible positions as she closed the distance between herself and her prey. Her blades flew out and slammed into the creature with as much force as she could muster, but only bounced harmlessly off its thick skin. Landing, she whirled around, adjusted her grip, and prepared to go again. If all she could deal were scratches, she'd kill the thing with a thousand cuts.

"Keep your guard raised!" the book called out to the boy, who was doing his best to help.

"As if there were any other choice!" he called back.

Kainé ignored their conversation, focusing on firing her magic and swinging her swords. As she did so, a thought suddenly came to her:

If I can't kill this thing alone, maybe I can do it with the kid.

The idea caused her mind to reel. Why did she think that, and why did it cause her such consternation? She didn't know, and the lack of understanding made her ill. The only way to fight the sensation was to let it out through her swords, so she launched herself back at the Shade and attempted to clear her mind of everything but revenge.

After several attacks, the Shade jerked to a sudden, unnatural halt. Looking down, Kainé saw that a giant black hand had appeared from the book and was now lifting the Shade into the air by its tail.

"Never seen magic that color before," muttered Kainé.

The hand slammed the massive Shade against the cliff, creating an impact that shook nearby tanks free from their holdings. But the Shade was too powerful to be rendered immobile for long; it slipped free and clambered to a spot farther in the village, then began vomiting smaller Shades out of its mouth.

"I'll take care of the big one!" cried Kainé to her two unexpected allies. "You worry about the rest!"

Kainé leaped across the village and over the tiny Shades pooling below. As she flew through the air, she could hear the residents' horrid jeers coming from the tanks:

"Get out, half-breed!"

"You disgust me! You disgust us all!"

"You summoned these Shades here!"

"*Would've made the whole revenge thing a lot easier if you actually could summon Shades, eh, Sunshine?*"

It sure as shit would have.

Kainé had spent every moment since her grandmother's death waiting for this damned Shade to show up, and the fact that it managed to escape her wrath the other day caused her physical pain. She'd figured it would be months—or even years—before the thing dared show its face again.

And yet, today was the day.

The massive Shade was on the move again. Tired of Kainé's relentless sword strikes and magical attacks, it leaped onto a cliff wall even out of the impressive reach of her half-Shade body.

"Shit!" she yelled in frustration.

"Kainé!" called the boy. "I'll drive him to you! Get up there and wait for him!"

She hadn't even thought of trying to pincer the thing until the boy brought it up. Having fought alone all her life, the idea of working with others was something she still needed to explore.

"Watch yourself," she said before leaping from the pathway to the bridge, then onto another path. Lacking wings, the massive lizard could only run so many places—and the boy's prediction turned out to be spot-on when an earth-shaking howl signaled her foe's approach.

"*Here we go!*" cackled a delighted Tyrann. The idea that one Shade could be so pleased at the impending death of another was something Kainé would never understand.

"*Kya ha ha! Look at the thing! It's in trouble now!*"

That black hand wasn't the only magic pummeling the massive Shade. There was also a spear, as well as the occasional hail of bullets. Each time one struck its shimmering body, Tyrann chimed in with gleeful, nonstop narration:

"Oh boy, it ain't doin' so hot. That kid's not half-bad! Didn't think he had brains or brawn, but there ya go. Oooh, nice one! Kill it! Kill it, kill it, KIIIILL IIIIT!"

Tyrann's bloodlust resonated with Kainé's own, causing it to swell. She wasn't going to let this thing get away again. She would slice it into a thousand pieces, cut and hack and slash until it was an unrecognizable pile of blood and gore. When she was done, the thing would look exactly like her final image of her grandmother.

No longer having the energy to cling to the cliff, the Shade dropped to the plaza below. There was a dullness to its movements, and Kainé recognized the perfect opportunity to finish her work. She leaped toward her foe, raising her blades high above her head. She thought it would be her final attack, but the Shade suddenly opened its mouth and flooded her with a strange white mist. Her hand whipped up to cover her nose and mouth, but it was too late. One taste of the mist caused her mind to spin and her vision to blur. Somewhere far away, she heard wind blowing up from the depths of the ravine. The boy was calling for her, but it sounded as if he was at the end of a miles-long tunnel.

"Kainé."

A new voice—not the boy. Yet it was familiar somehow, a person she had heard long, long ago.

"Kainé . . . It's me . . . Grandma . . ."

Kainé's breath caught in her throat. How was this possible? Her grandmother was *dead*.

"Oh, how you've grown."

She thought she would have given anything to hear this voice again, but she never expected it to hurt so much.

"How long has it been?"

"Grand . . . ma . . . ?" croaked Kainé as the old woman's face shimmered into view before her. She always suspected she'd start bawling like a baby if she ever saw her grandmother again, but shock prevented even a single tear from falling.

"It gladdens my heart to finally see you again."

Memories of her grandmother that Kainé had kept locked away in the depths of her heart began bubbling to the surface: teaching Kainé to chop wood and build a fire, throwing rocks at village bullies to keep them away, cackling with delight at Kainé's spectacularly terrible attempt to draw her.

"Come, Kainé. Come to your Grandma's side."

If only she could live with her grandmother like she used to all those years ago. They weren't well-off by any means, but they were happy.

"You've been lonely for so, so long. So much pain. So much despair. Why go on living anymore?"

The moment the voice said this, the mist fogging Kainé's mind parted, making everything perfectly clear.

". . . Kainé?"

"Is that it?"

A hue of dismay colored the face before her—the one that looked so infuriatingly like her deceased grandmother.

"Are you finished?"

"Don't speak to your Grandma like—"

"You're going to stop talking RIGHT NOW!" cried Kainé as she leaped at the creature. She was concerned her strength might fail after inhaling the strange mist, but rage was more than enough to overcome the loss.

"My grandmother would never say that!"

Her vision cleared. Her body shook. An anger so large it couldn't possibly be contained raced through her system in a desperate search for an outlet.

"She'd never tell me to give up on life! Never!"

She felt her blade smash deep into the Shade's body, but she had no idea where. Her vision had gone from white to red to a perfect black—and she had no idea if it was the color of the Shade or that of her own fury.

"I've spent my entire life searching for a way to avenge her death! She gave me the strength to deal with this goddamn mutant body!"

Blade struck flesh, tearing it apart.

"Do you know how long I've been like this? How much I loathe myself?!"

Another jump. She poured her strength into her swords as she aimed for the Shade's head. Suddenly, she heard an ear-piercing howl, as well as a voice yelling, "Now!" A moment later, a black hand lifted the Shade into the air and slammed it back to the ground, causing her to become weightless as her helpless body was sent soaring through the air.

As heaven and earth flipped, she spied the Shade being skewered on a jagged pillar out of the corner of one eye. As its limbs and tail began to sag in death, Kainé finally allowed herself to let go.

I'm done, Grandma. I'm . . . tired.

Something began absorbing her consciousness as she fell into a deep, dark pit without end.

I finally killed that fucking Shade. I avenged you. There's nothing left to do now. It's over. It's all over.

I can come join you now. Right?

Kainé received no response. Her grandmother's voice was silent. But in a way, this made her happy. This wasn't some illusion being forced upon her. Instead, it was reality. Her quest was complete, her grandmother was avenged.

The darkness became all-consuming. She loosened her grip on consciousness and gave herself over to the abyss.

"Kainé!"

It was the boy, his voice accompanied by a ray of light.

"Don't give up! You're stronger than that!"

Give up? On what?

"Don't you dare give up now!"

Why does this voice sound so . . . comforting?

As a warmth began to filter through her, she reached out, unable to help herself.

"This woman is more trouble than she's worth," came another voice.

That's the talking book, Kainé thought. The second she did so, her vision flooded with light.

"You're going to live, Kainé!"

The sky was so bright. Her vision took on the color of cliff rock, and she realized she was being lifted up. A moment later, the boy's face was directly in front of her own.

You're going to live repeated over and over in her head as she recalled the warm, bright light.

"Live? What for?"

"What?" asked the boy, who was clearly not expecting her response. She suddenly found herself annoyed that she'd asked the kid a question only she could answer and went on to clarify.

"I had my revenge. Now it's over."

Vengeance was her entire reason for living. Without it driving her forward, what point was there in going on? How was she supposed to exist in the world without a purpose?

"Oh, now, see here!" the talking book snorted. "This is rich! We help you in some mad quest for vengeance, and now you think to bid us adieu?"

The boy shouted the book's name in an attempt to scold or shame him, but talking was clearly something he was very skilled at, and he continued his rant without so much as a pause.

"How can a fighter so skilled be cursed with such a thick head?!"

Goddamn, this book seems pissed . . . Wait, is he pissed at me?!

"A true warrior would fight! They would give all in service of their friends!"

Though Kainé had zero idea what the book was going on about, the word *friends* struck a sudden chord in her heart.

"He's right!" yelled the boy. His voice was bright, warm, and filled with joy—almost like light itself. "We're friends now!"

"See here!" the book retorted. "That was hardly the point!"

"Then what *is* the point?"

"Er . . ."

After causing the book to fall silent, the boy looked back at

Kainé. His eyes were free of falsehood or affectation, just like when he apologized. No one in her life had ever done something like that before, and all she'd felt at the time was bewilderment. But the moment he uttered the word *friends*, she suddenly understood where her confusion came from. Her whole life had been a never-ending stream of abuse and shunning, so when a boy showed up and cheerfully accepted her for who she was, the strangeness of it threatened to break her brain.

"We need your help," continued the boy. "Will you fight with us?"

"Fool!" the book interjected again. "You cannot simply ask her outright! There is a proper order to these matters! One must ease into the topic with carefully considered words before commencing negotiations to—"

As Kainé listened to the boy and book converse, a strange feeling overcame her: a smile that was gently tugging at the corner of her mouth.

"Cram it, book," she said.

"BOOK?! How dare you! I am Grimoire Weiss, wielder of arcane—"

"Weiss, then."

"Do not abbreviate my name!"

Kainé was secretly delighted at how she'd managed to piss the book off so completely. And while she knew Tyrann wouldn't be happy with the whole *friends* development, he was staying quiet for the moment, which only amused her further.

"You're an ass—but you're right. I can't just live for revenge."

Kainé stood. Her footing was unsteady, but the sensation felt refreshing. New. The part of her that had lived solely for revenge had died, and a different Kainé was rising in its place.

"So you'll come with us?" asked the boy.

Rather than answering his cautious question, she reached out to the blades on the ground beside her. Now that her swords had fulfilled their role as tools of revenge, she wasn't sure what kind of weapons they would become. But . . .

"These swords of mine need a true home," she said. "But you'll do for now."

Indistinct as it was, Kainé was finally starting to see where her path might take her.

REPORT 05

Nier has started to visit Seafront frequently to procure shaman fish. Due to the incident code-named Red and Black, Popola hoped we might be able to avoid telling him about that option, but Yonah's condition had other plans.

Happily, Popola's fears turned out to be groundless—in fact, Nier seems to be having the time of his life. He apparently found himself in the middle of a marital spat, and also had to navigate around the lighthouse lady, who can be a tough old bird. Regardless, he told us these stories with a smile.

Oh, and he seemed equally happy when he explained how an old man taught him the "secrets of fishing." Weiss didn't care much for that and huffed about how the old man was "simply using him."

And hey, what can I say? The book is right. Fishing doesn't require absurdly long training runs or sit-ups, and I also suspect the old man is simply selling whatever fish Nier catches in the name of this "training." (Five bream would be *expensive* at a shop!) But it's not bad for him to get better at fishing, and better still that we can offer him a wider range of jobs because of it. Collecting ingredients is *much* less dangerous than hunting Shades, so I'll try to find tasks that put his fishing to use in the future.

Sadly, while Seafront sounds peaceful enough, chaos has come to The Aerie. Popola had been concerned about the trends of the village for a while now, and while I thought she'd been overthinking it, it turns out the worrywart was right. Though the problems are caused by a small portion of villagers, I'm still worried it might spark something bigger. Still, so long as they stay locked up in those tanks not interacting with the outside world—or even their neighbors—I doubt anything too terrible will come of it.

Unfortunately, the fact people rarely come and go from The Aerie also makes it difficult to collect any information. And since mail carriers are loath to go inside due to its terrain, our only choice is to go ourselves or send someone—although at least the chief is good about writing letters on a fairly consistent basis. All that is to say, we're urgently increasing surveillance of The Aerie and plan to offer jobs to Nier that take him out that way.

I know this is another report that turned out a little on the long side, but I think we're done now.

Record written by Devola

The Boy 5

1.

TO REACH THE desert, Nier had to leave his village via the eastern gate and walk in the opposite direction of the Lost Shrine. He knew the desert was a land covered in sand as far as the eye could see; he'd heard as much from traveling merchants, and vaguely recalled Popola telling him the same. But today was the first time he'd actually *walked* on sand, and he found it an altogether unpleasant experience. His feet sank deep with each step, and small grains lodged themselves in his shoes with alarming regularity. Also, he had to keep his eyes nearly shut, lest regular gusts of wind fill them with grit.

"There is sand between my pages! *Pth! Pth!*"

Nier wondered if Grimoire Weiss could even expel sand by spitting but decided not to push it. He had plenty of his own grains to deal with, and he didn't want to exacerbate the issue by talking.

In total disregard of her companions' struggles, Kainé marched ahead with measured, practiced steps. It was clear she'd made the crossing several times before.

"Hey, Kainé?" asked Nier. "What's Facade like?"

The party was in the desert on her suggestion. Once Nier revealed that Yonah had fallen ill with the Black Scrawl, Kainé told them of a king who had contracted the same disease. His kingdom, called Facade, lay deep within the desert and was frantically working on a cure. With all of their resources devoted to the search, it was possible they might have found something. And even if they were still searching, a hint of an idea was better than none.

"Good question," replied Kainé as she shortened her stride and looked back. It could have been a sign she was concerned about Nier falling behind, but he knew she'd deny it if he brought it up. "It's strange," she continued. "Let's just leave it at that."

"Stranger than a boorish young woman who battles monsters in her undergarments?"

Grimoire Weiss now saw fit to bring up Kainé's dress—or lack thereof—at almost every turn. Even after Nier admonished him for his behavior, the book continued on as if he simply hadn't heard. Kainé, however, seemed untroubled, claiming she didn't care how Weiss spoke to her. She also gave as good as she got, calling Grimoire Weiss things such as, "a waste of perfectly good paper." So Nier decided their nicknames for each other were their own business.

"Hmm?" said Nier suddenly. "What's that over there?"

Dark figures were moving in the swirling dust. Moments later, the howl of a beast rang out—one that sounded much like the baying of a dog. Suddenly, the figures began racing toward them, catching Nier completely off guard.

"Look out!" cried Grimoire Weiss.

Kainé leaped into action. The black mass of figures turned out to be a wolf pack, and as she dived into the middle of the fray with her twin blades swinging, Nier began firing off magical bullets.

The wolves were fast and tough. Though many of the party's attacks connected, it didn't even slow the animals down. As Nier began considering unleashing the black-hand spell, another howl rose on the wind that caused the pack to immediately change course.

"They're leaving," he said. He looked in the direction of the howl and saw another dark figure on top of a rock. It was clearly the pack leader; even from a distance, Nier could see how much larger it was than the others.

The wolves retreated as abruptly as they had appeared. The party strained their ears in an attempt to pick up any stray howls but heard only the lonely sound of the wind. Satisfied no further attacks were coming, they set off once again into the depths of the desert.

"Well, that was a surprise!" Nier sighed. "I wasn't expecting to be attacked by wolves, of all things."

Mind you, wild animals, on the whole, attacked people— sheep, goats, deer, and even boar often turned their ire on humans. Though not as bad as Shades, they were still enough of a threat to make people wary.

Kainé lifted an eyebrow. "Yeah, wolves in the desert? That's weird."

"It is?"

"Wolves live in the forest. I've never heard of them in the desert before. Hell, there's not even anything for them to eat out here. I bet they got chased out of the forest for some reason or another."

"What kind of reason?"

"Meh. Who knows?" Kainé stomped off, whatever interest she may have had in the lives of wolves apparently exhausted.

Finally, they arrived at a long stone leaning against a rock face, beyond which was a wall of human construction. This had to be Facade. Nier had heard an adult could reach the city in half a day if they moved at speed, and was pleased to see that estimation had been correct.

From a distance, the gates looked like the ones in Nier's village, but they turned out to be much larger up close. Stairs led up to them, and there was a guard on either side armed with a spear. It was impossible to tell how old they were or their genders. Both of their faces were covered by strange masks that resembled black plates straight from the dinner table.

"I guess the name Facade refers to the fact everyone here wears a mask?" Nier asked.

"It certainly appears that way," Grimoire Weiss replied.

A commotion suddenly broke out between the guards. It was impossible to hear what they were saying, which Nier attributed to the strong winds. All his ears could pick up was a single word: *Kainé.*

"You know these guys, Kainé?" Nier asked.

"Not exactly." She raised her hand and waved at them, at which point they turned to yell something to an unseen person beyond the wall. "A while back, I saved a local kid from a pack of wolves. Ever since, this town's welcomed me with open arms. Gotta be a pretty screwed-up place if they let me in, huh?"

As the gates swung open with a loud scraping sound, the guards rushed toward them, every step accompanied by the jingling of bells sewn into the hems of their clothes. Apparently masks weren't the only odd thing about the city's denizens.

"*Kitu warera onginda!*" cried a guard.

"What?" replied Nier. He originally thought the wind was making it difficult to hear the guards, but he now realized he couldn't understand a thing they said even when standing next to them.

"Yeah, the language they use here is pretty crazy," said Kainé. "I got no idea what they're saying."

"Oh. Okay. Can you understand them, Weiss?"

"I would be delighted to tell you that I am able to comprehend even the most complex of languages in all my great power! Er, but no. I cannot."

Nier discerned that the guards were showing Kainé some sort of gratitude, but that was all he could surmise. He felt a twinge of unease that they might not be able to tell him anything about a Black Scrawl cure, and that he couldn't understand them even if they did.

They stepped through the gates and into a city the color of sand. The whole of it seemed to be made up of stairs; the outer walls were at the highest point, with the levels gradually getting lower the closer they came to the center.

"The king lives in the big building. Figure out the rest for yourself." Having said this, Kainé leaned up against a pillar by the entrance and closed her eyes.

"What about you?" Nier asked.

"I'll stay here. I hate crap like this."

As Nier looked out over the mess of passageways that led into the city, he could certainly see why.

"I don't know whether to thank you or wish you ill," Grimoire Weiss muttered.

Regardless, Nier and his floating companion ventured into the city to get the lay of the land. When he took a closer look, he noticed the straight paths stood out more than the curved ones. Waterwheels dotted the landscape in the central and lower parts of the city, carrying what at first seemed to be a steady stream of brown water.

"Is that sand?" wondered Nier. He'd first thought it was water muddied by sand, but when he rubbed his eyes to get a better look, he realized the sand *itself* was flowing like water. Additionally, large rivers of sand carried people to and fro on square boats.

"I suppose that big building serves as the king's manor," said Grimoire Weiss as he indicated a structure at the far end of the city.

Now that they had a location, the only question was how

to get there. The lower central part of the city made it easy to look across the entire town, but the river of sand cut off roads in certain places, and the narrow slopes and stairs made for a complicated tangle of possible routes. Though it was an entirely different structure than The Aerie, the two towns shared a confusing navigational sensibility.

Even if they did suss out the correct path, there were no roads leading through the center of town. This meant they'd be forced to make their way around the edge of the city to reach the king's manor instead of plowing right through—a not-insignificant detour.

Looking away from possible paths for a moment, Nier noticed three children playing near the entrance. Unlike the plate masks the guards wore, theirs were triangular in shape. Nier glanced around and saw the other adults also wore pyramid masks; apparently plates were reserved for guards alone.

He greeted the children and they responded enthusiastically, but he still had no idea what they were saying. He said hello to another passing woman and was equally befuddled, but the kindness in her tone told him she at least gave a favorable response.

"Come on, Weiss. Help me out. I feel bad that I can't understand them."

"I am a brilliant book of unspeakable value, not some dog-eared travel guide."

Finally, they gave up trying to understand what people were saying and made their way to the king's manor. Turning right at the entrance, they followed the outer wall and exited onto a ledge above what looked like a store. Merchandise was lined up neatly on display next to a shopkeeper, which reminded Nier of the village weapon shop. This store, however, did not sell weapons. Instead, it carried a wide assortment of odds and ends, including large boards in the shape of leaves, metal discs bigger and heavier than the guards' masks, and containers filled with unknown contents.

"That's some weird stuff," said Nier. He knew the comment could be construed as impolite, but it wasn't as if the townsfolk could understand him.

The pair continued on. Each time their path came to a river of sand, they would go down a nearby flight of stairs or leap over the river as best they could. Once they lost their way, they would climb back to the outer rim to get a better look, then repeat the process. After struggling in this way for what seemed like forever, they finally arrived at the king's manor.

"We made it!" cried an exhausted Nier.

"We would have been here in no time at all if we could understand the locals," muttered Weiss.

Nier looked back to see the city entrance beyond the depressed central area. Grimoire Weiss was right—if they knew the way, it likely wouldn't take much time at all to move between here and there.

"I find this town odd," Grimoire Weiss remarked. "We are clearly outsiders, yet they seem completely unconcerned with our presence."

When Nier greeted the people in a language unfamiliar to them, they returned the favor in a nonchalant, almost relaxed manner. No one they passed remained silent in response, and not once did they come across an utterance that exuded any malice.

"Well, it's better than being thrown out for being different," said Nier. Indeed, just taking a few steps into town proved the people of Facade were friendly and kind. Unfamiliar, yes, but certainly nothing off-putting. The language barrier, however, was another matter entirely.

"*Aratate site tas oik,*" said a guard at the entrance to the king's manor.

"I wonder what that's supposed to mean," muttered Nier.

"Aratate site tas oik."

Apparently the guards had nothing else to say. Of course, they had no idea why Nier and Weiss were even here, which meant they lacked a way to help.

"This is pointless," huffed Grimoire Weiss. "Let us go back."

Even though it had taken them so long to reach the manor, Nier's only option was to do as the book suggested.

2.

NIER SUSPECTED IT wouldn't take much time to traverse the city once they understood it, and his point was proven right as he and Weiss made good time back to the entrance. But moving at a good clip did little to quell his disappointment with how things were going; if anything, it only served to make him more depressed.

As he walked with his head hung low, he happened upon some fruit scattered in the dirt. Lifting his gaze, he saw a girl lying facedown on the ground. She'd clearly tripped; her basket was empty, and everything she'd been carrying was now strewn around her. Nier hurriedly began collecting her goods as best he could, then extended a hand as the girl moved to stand.

"Are you . . ." he began before remembering she couldn't understand him. To his surprise, she began making grand gestures with her hands and body. It was different from how the other villagers communicated and seemed to be an attempt to tell him something.

"Oh, ho!" cackled Grimoire Weiss. "This one lacks the power of speech! Perhaps she can communicate through gesture."

Nier suddenly realized why the girl was waving her arms around—and now that he knew, he was delighted at how easy she was to understand. He could tell she was trying to thank him, as well as assure him she was unharmed. She also seemed to have a basic grasp of what Nier and Grimoire Weiss were saying—perhaps she'd lived somewhere besides Facade.

Grimoire Weiss stared as she repeated the same gesture over and over, trying to figure out her message. "'Thank . . . you . . . Do you . . . need . . . help?'"

"Yes, we do!" cried Nier, which caused the girl to break out into a new series of gestures.

"'I . . . can . . . guide . . . you'? Oh, she will act as our guide! How fortuitous!"

"Thank you very much," said Nier. "Could you take us to your—"

"Hold, lad," said Weiss, who was attempting to interpret a new round of translation. "'But . . . first . . . I must . . . explain . . . this city.'"

"Uh, but must you? We really just need to see the king."

"'No. There are . . . rules to follow.'"

Rules? Nier would have appreciated clarification on this point, but the girl stopped gesturing.

"'Follow . . . me,'" finished Weiss. "Well, there you have it."

With that, the girl ran off. Her short legs didn't carry her very quickly, so Nier found he could keep pace by moving at a brisk walk.

"What rules is she talking about?" he asked Weiss as they moved.

"I haven't the slightest. All I know for certain is that whatever they are, they will be a right pain in the index."

As the two whispered to each other, the girl came to a sudden halt and began gesturing anew, sending Weiss into another round of translation.

"'This . . . is . . . an item shop.'"

"I understood that!" exclaimed Nier.

The girl nodded happily and continued with different gestures.

"'All shops and houses . . . in this city . . . must abide by the following rule . . .'"

Nier had a hard time keeping up once her gestures started stringing together so many words, so Weiss's translation was genuinely impressive. Perhaps he really was worthy of calling himself the culmination of humanity's wisdom.

"'Rule 106: Do not . . . live on level ground.' Is this rule the reason for your labyrinthine system of staircases?"

"That doesn't sound very convenient," noted Nier. His legs hurt just remembering what it took to get to the king's manor. What must it be like for people who had to go up and down stairs and ramps every day?

The girl ignored his utterance and took off again. Their next destination was not a store, but a dock, where they learned the square boats that traveled the city were called sand-skiffs.

"'Rule 115,017: You must view the town by ship . . . before purchasing any items.'"

Nier understood "view the town by ship," but he didn't understand the significance of the rule, nor why they had to ride in the boat before buying anything. Either way, they followed instructions and hopped on board. The square rafts were surprisingly comfortable and glided smoothly over the river of sand. At this speed, they would reach the king's manor in no time.

Indeed, when they stepped off the skiff, a large board in the shape of a leaf came into view; they were at the same shop where Nier had rudely expressed how odd the contents were.

"'This is . . . a strange-thing store,'" said Weiss as the girl began signing again. Nier was surprised to learn his observation was not rude, but instead entirely accurate.

After that, the trio hopped on and off the skiff as the girl explained different shops and rules. Once they'd made a complete loop, Nier felt he had a good understanding of where things generally were—and more important, what the locals were saying. He also learned that their guide's name was Fyra.

Once the tour ended, Fyra took Nier and Grimoire Weiss to the largest building in town. *This is the king's manor,* she signed.

Nier didn't even need Weiss to translate for him anymore. He'd thought making outsiders like himself learn the rules of the city was a pain at first, but he now understood why it was done.

However, we have no king now.

Nier and Grimoire Weiss exchanged unwitting glances. How was that possible?

Our king was stricken with a foul, black illness, and so passed away. His son, the prince, now rules this land.

"The Black Scrawl," Grimoire Weiss murmured. It seemed an entire kingdom's research efforts were not enough to save their liege.

A man who was not a guard had emerged from the manor during their discussion and was now looking at them. Fyra glanced over, then signed, *This is the prince's royal advisor. He would know far more about these things than I.*

"Thank you," Grimoire Weiss began. "All of this touring has been helpful for understanding your language. I believe I will be able to speak with this advisor myself."

Though Nier only had a handle on a few words, Grimoire Weiss was now apparently able to have whole conversations.

"We need to talk to the prince," began Nier. A moment later, Grimoire Weiss kindly interpreted the statement into the city's local tongue.

"I'm afraid the prince is not taking outside visitors at present," the advisor explained. *"Aratate site tas oik. I would appreciate it if you could come back another day."*

At last they understood what the guards had been repeating

at them when they first came to the manor: *Aratate site tas oik.* Yet while it was nice to know what it meant, with the king passed on and the prince unavailable, they were no closer to their goal of helping Yonah.

I'm sorry, signed Fyra. She bowed her head, clearly sensing Nier's disappointment.

"It's not your fault, Fyra," Nier reassured her. "Let's go back to Kainé for now."

They hopped on another sand-skiff and returned to the entrance with Fyra in tow. Though they'd only asked to be taken to the manor, she was apparently intent on seeing them off as well.

After alighting from the skiff, they rushed up the stairs. A good deal of time had passed since they first arrived in the city, and Kainé was likely *very* sick of waiting.

"We're back!" said Nier.

Kainé, who had been leaning up against a pillar with her arms crossed, opened her eyes. "Finish your business?" she asked as she stretched.

"Sort of. Thankfully we met a girl who helped us get around."

"A girl?"

"Yeah. She's right over . . ."

He glanced over his shoulder and saw Fyra rushing toward them, making exaggerated gestures all the while. She was either surprised or panicked—the speed at which her arms and legs moved made it impossible to tell.

"Slow down!" cried Grimoire Weiss, who was having trouble keeping up. "'The person . . . who saved me'?"

Fyra nodded enthusiastically.

"Wait, Kainé helped you?" asked Nier. "Huh. I guess she did mention saving a kid from wolves, but I had no idea it was you."

"*Kainé* helped you?!" Grimoire Weiss exclaimed. "*This* foul-mouthed hussy?!"

Though Weiss was again crossing multiple lines when it came to Kainé, she only snorted in response. "Piss off, book. You guys done or what?"

At that moment, a guard in a plate mask ran by in a panic. Nier turned to look and saw there were more soldiers by the gate, and he now knew enough of the language to follow the conversation.

"*The prince is missing!*"

"*What?!*"

"*According to Rule 83,348, we have to start looking for him right away!*"

"*No, you don't get it! The prince went missing in the Barren Temple!*"

"*But Rule 50,527 states that only nobility may enter the temple! That means we* can't *go look for him!*"

"*But what about Rule 83,348?*"

"*But what about Rule 50,527?!*"

Nier knew from the way Fyra spoke how important rules were to the people of Facade. As of this month, they had over 124,000 and were still making more. It only made sense that there would be some contradictory elements among such a vast number of precepts.

"I don't get why they made a bunch of rules that contradict each other," Nier said.

"This is their way and their system of laws," replied Weiss. "As outsiders, we have no say in the matter. Now come. We should be off."

"But . . ."

Should they just go home, though? The soldiers seemed genuinely concerned; they were looking at one another with arms crossed, hemming and hawing among themselves. When Nier and Weiss had been outsiders who didn't understand the language, the townsfolk had still treated them kindly—and now that they could communicate, that compassion was only magnified. The idea of pretending not to understand and walking away gnawed at Nier's conscience.

As he debated, Fyra stepped before one of the soldiers, gesturing wildly. *I'm going to save the prince!*

The guards gasped beneath their masks, then shook their heads.

"*You can't!*" said one.

"*Have you forgotten about Rule 50,527?*" said another.

Oh, screw the rules! signed Fyra. Nier could tell she was ready to run off at any moment, so he quickly positioned himself between her and the guards.

"That rule only forbids *your* people from entering the temple, right?" asked Nier.

"Oh, and what luck! We just happen to have an outsider who can't stop meddling in the affairs of others right here!" Though clearly annoyed, Weiss asked Nier's question anyway, but the guards kept their arms folded. Though the idea didn't appear to conflict with any rule, they were hesitant to leave the prince's rescue to an outsider.

"Real sticklers for the rules," Kainé muttered. "Well, I'm going too."

The soldiers' heads whipped around in shock.

"Rule 1,024," she continued. "You know that one, right? You must honor the request of any outsider owed a debt. That's how it goes, right?"

Kainé looked at Fyra as she spoke, causing Nier to chuckle inside. Despite her continued insistence that helping people was stupid, he'd never seen Kainé ignore someone in danger. It was a trait he'd experienced firsthand when she saved him from the massive Shade in The Aerie.

"Why did I ever agree to travel with such a pack of do-gooders?" moaned Weiss. But though it sounded like he had a laundry list of complaints to raise about the subject, he surprisingly let it drop.

3.

FYRA VOLUNTEERED TO escort the group to the Barren Temple, claiming that only those who knew how to navigate a sandstorm could reach it. But as they neared the temple, she stopped and turned to them, saying, *This is as far as I can go.*

A stone entrance was carved into the base of a mountain. At a glance, it seemed like a slightly prettied-up cave, but Fyra claimed the Barren Temple lay just beyond.

"Thanks for your help," said Nier. "We wouldn't have gotten past the sandstorm without you."

Please save the prince.

"We'll find him. I promise."

As Fyra bowed deeply, the others turned and walked into the temple. There was no door on the entrance, so they managed to cross the threshold with alarming ease. Once they did, a magical barrier went up that sealed them inside—a trick designed to punish scoundrels who were hoping to plunder the ruins for treasure.

That turned out not to be the only magic in effect inside the temple. Every door inside was sealed with the same sort of barrier.

They managed to find one that was open, but upon entering, it, too, sealed itself behind them. They found themselves in a vast room as wide as it was tall, dotted with boxes that spat out magical bullets, making even walking across the floor an exercise in frustration. The solution was to dodge their way through the bullets and destroy a shining box to undo the seal, but there were also *rules* to deal with . . .

"I wonder what this prince is like," Nier said aloud after finally destroying the shining box. The temple was clearly not safe even for royalty, and he doubted the prince had come here because he *wanted* to. What was he after—and for that matter, what kind of person was he?

"The man is tasked to protect his people, and yet he's made them toil to save him," said Weiss. "I think that tells us he is naught but an incompetent fool."

"*What did you say?!*" cried a strange voice in the language of the Masked People.

"Did you just hear someone, Weiss?"

Before his question could be answered, a child leaped out of the nearby darkness. "*How dare you insult me! Bow down and beg forgiveness!*"

Skinny legs jutted out from the wide hem of his clothes; his bare arms were equally scrawny. His clothing was similar to that worn in Facade, but his mask was fixed to the side, leaving his face visible. Nier had guessed by his physique that the person was younger than himself, and now he could see it was the face of a child.

"Where did you come from, boy?" Grimoire Weiss asked.

The newcomer went red in the face. "*I am no boy! I am the 93rd prince of Facade!*"

Nier looked at him, confused. "Wait, really? But you're just a kid."

"*You're one to talk! You're hardly any older than—*"

The prince's yelling reverberated off the high ceiling, seemingly triggering a giant box to appear out of nowhere—one the same size and shape as those which had been spitting magic bullets earlier. As the prince spoke, it moved toward him before stopping above his head and emitting a white beam of light that enveloped the young ruler.

"Argh! What is this thing?!"

The box then floated merrily away, taking the prince with it.

Nier was stunned. They'd come to the temple to find the prince, and just when he thought they might be able to pull something off with a bit of ease for once, their goal had been whisked away.

"Come on!" Nier exclaimed. "We have to help him!"

"Or we could simply pretend we didn't see him instead," Grimoire Weiss muttered.

They ran back to a nearby corridor and found that a previously secured door was now open. It seemed another long stretch of rooms and mechanisms and rules awaited them if they were to rescue the prince.

"Here we go again," Grimoire Weiss said with a sigh.

As they entered the next room, it sealed tight behind them. Just as it had in the first room, a disembodied voice then began echoing throughout the area:

"The following actions are prohibited in this room . . ."

It was the voice of the rules—yet another mechanism that kicked into place once the seal went over the door.

"'Stationary owls' are forbidden?" muttered Nier. "Does that mean we can't stop moving?"

In the first room, it was *leaping rabbits* that were forbidden. Any time Nier ended up putting too much space between himself and the ground, he would be shunted back to the entrance via some kind of magic. Even worse, any boxes he destroyed were then reset to their original state.

"Goddammit!" cried an enraged Kainé. "This shit's starting to piss me off!" She then came to a complete halt in order to fire off some magic.

Oh no, thought Nier—but it was already too late. The same box that had stolen the prince away appeared again and enveloped Kainé in its soft white light.

"What in the . . ." she muttered as it began lifting her off the ground. "Oh, are you fucking *kidding* me? Lemme go! Lemme—"

The box floated to the ceiling with Kainé dangling below before flying away. When Nier had broken the rules, the most he'd suffered was being thrown back to the entrance; apparently shouting or throwing a fit warranted being carried away.

"I assume we'll have to find her as well?" Grimoire Weiss remarked dryly.

"Yep."

Knowing there was nothing for it but to solve the puzzle and move on, Nier made his way to the glowing box while breaking others that fired magic bullets. He never slowed his pace all the while, and after a number of nail-biting moments, they were finally free.

When they moved on, they found rooms that forbade things called *racing wolf* and *magic-spewing bat*, meaning Nier had to dodge enemies and destroy boxes without running or using magic, respectively.

"This madcap barrage of rules shows no signs of slowing!" cried an infuriated Weiss.

"We need to be quiet, or we're gonna mess this up again!" scolded Nier. There was no way he'd ever be able to solve these puzzles if his companion was whisked away too. Thankfully, Weiss seemed to understand this and fell into a begrudging silence.

They progressed in this way for some time. Solve a puzzle. Open a room. Solve a puzzle. Open a room. By the time a door leading to an outside corridor finally opened, Nier and Weiss were exhausted both physically and mentally.

"These Masked folk certainly enjoy their bizarre customs," Grimoire Weiss remarked.

"Yeah, but they didn't have to make their rules *this* bizarre . . ."

"Fyra claims they serve a higher purpose, but I am finding it difficult to agree with that proposition."

Nier knew exactly what he was talking about. When Fyra was leading the two of them through the city, she'd overhead them grumbling about the rules and turned to face them.

Someone once told me that rules do not exist to bind you, she'd said. *They exist so you may know your freedoms.*

Nier agreed with Grimoire Weiss. He felt unbound and free as he walked down the lawless corridor they were now in, though perhaps that was just because there was no ceiling above him, but an open sky.

The outdoor passageway was hewn from sturdy rock and neatly packed stone, unlike the wooden pathways in the Lost Shrine. But there were also cracks and breakage throughout the passage; since no stonecutters or masons were allowed inside, the place had been ravaged by the elements.

Nier ran as fast as he could through the rule-free corridor. When he passed through the door at the end, he found himself in a room several times larger than the ones he'd traversed earlier. The walls had crumbled in places, and the center contained a large hole in the floor as well as the ceiling. It was as if something massive had fallen from the sky and left proof of its existence behind.

"Well, this doesn't look suspicious at all," said Grimoire Weiss. The moment he spoke those words, the door slammed shut behind them—and in a tighter way than the others in the temple. It seemed this room was special.

"Hey, look!" cried Nier. He pointed to the ceiling, where a

floating box was holding the prince of Facade in a familiar beam of light.

"It's the mewling child!" Grimoire Weiss exclaimed.

The box slowly lowered into the abyss. Nier rushed to the edge in an attempt to save the prince but came to an abrupt stop as a staggering number of boxes began to fly out of the pit—the same kind that had been firing magic bullets in previous rooms. The boxes came together in a series of rings before starting to spin at a frightening speed.

"We have to kill this thing to save the prince!" Nier said.

"Without any rules to bind us, we are free to unleash the entirety of our powers!"

"It's about time!"

The voice that had lectured them on all the bothersome rules earlier—no running, no stopping, no magic, no swords—was not present, meaning Nier could attack and defend as he liked. In that moment, he could sincerely feel how rules existed so he might know his freedoms.

Taking a moment, Nier noticed that some boxes were glowing inside the spinning rings—an obvious sign that he had to destroy them in order to solve the puzzle of the room. He began firing magical bullets and spears, shattering the boxes one at a time. It wasn't much different from the other rooms he'd passed through, save for the fact that there were more boxes, and their attacks were slightly ramped up.

"How mindless," commented Grimoire Weiss.

Finally, Nier managed to hit the last of the glowing boxes, which caused the others to vanish. But the door didn't budge, so he gripped his sword tightly and waited to see what was to come.

He didn't have to wait long. A moment later, another cluster of boxes flew out from the depths of the abyss. But rather than forming rings, they came together in the shape of a human, one tall enough to punch straight through the ceiling.

"The guardian of this temple is a curious sight indeed!" Grimoire Weiss exclaimed.

"Says the talking book!"

Nier was more blasé about things like a cluster of semisentient boxes because of the very existence of his companion. But the cluster quickly proved it shouldn't be underestimated when it slammed one of its glowing fists into the ground, cracking the flagstone and sending fragments flying.

Nier was immediately concerned; if the giant was strong enough to shatter stone, it would likely be a pain to destroy. And, indeed, no matter how many times he attacked with magic, the giant continued to swing its fists without so much as a flinch. Soon Nier found himself abandoning his offense to focus on rolling out of the way in order to preserve his life. But then . . .

"There you are, you bastard!"

Even if the voice hadn't been familiar, there was only one person Nier knew who would have announced her presence with such an insult.

"I'm gonna kill the *shit* out of you!" continued Kainé. "Now hold still and die already!"

She was standing in a large gap near the ceiling, swords and voice both raised. Since the room had no rules, she could curse as much as she liked without repercussion. This seemed to delight her, because she suddenly leaped onto the giant's shoulder and unleashed a flurry of superhuman attacks. Each time one landed, dozens of boxes shook free and fell to the ground.

The giant turned away from Nier and Weiss to focus on Kainé. As the young man shouted a warning, she leaped into the air again, dodged a massive incoming fist, and landed elegantly beside him.

"How did you find us?" asked a stunned Nier.

"Beats me. I just kicked a buncha ass and wound up here."

"And without even bothering to get dressed!" Grimoire Weiss exclaimed.

"Fuck off, book!"

It wasn't surprising that Kainé took the unsubtle approach, but Nier was still surprised she'd managed to meet up with them while somehow remaining unharmed. It made him wonder if her way of doing things warranted a closer look on his own part.

"The glowing cubes take priority!" yelled Weiss as the battle continued. "This temple's mechanisms cease operation upon their destruction!"

"Screw your priorities! I'm gonna kill this thing *my* way!"

As if to demonstrate her resolve, Kainé's blades sent several boxes flying. Nier followed up with a barrage of magical bullets and spears, even though the results weren't nearly as exciting.

The twin attacks were enough, however, to make the cluster of boxes lose its human shape, at which point it counterattacked with an endless barrage of magical spheres. The humanoid Shades in The Aerie had used a similar attack, but never so many at a time, and never ones that moved with such speed. Nier used a new Sealed Verse to absorb them, then spit the energy back. It was a skill he'd picked up at the Junk Heap and was very effective against enemies that attacked with magic.

But that newfound spell was only the beginning; the team found themselves using every tool in their arsenal during the fight. While Nier and Weiss fought with magic and blades, Kainé darted around the room slicing whichever boxes she could. When the last of them finally dropped into the pit, a deep silence fell over the room.

"Right," said Nier. "Time to save the prince. I hope he isn't hurt."

The box that captured the prince had lowered into the abyss, and Nier knew they needed to save him as fast as possible. But as Nier rushed to the hole, the prince suddenly appeared at the edge, having somehow climbed his way to freedom.

"There you are!" said Nier. "Now let's head back before—"

"*There it is!*" cried the prince. He rushed to a corner of the room, then proudly scooped up a mask with long ears from a mound of debris.

4.

WITH THE GIANT defeated, all the traps, locks, and puzzles throughout the temple were released, allowing them to walk out the front door without any muss or fuss. The prince remained silent as they walked, not bothering to explain why he had come to such a dangerous place. Nier assumed it had something to do with the long-eared mask, but that was as much as he'd been able to figure out.

When they returned to town, they found the masked advisor waiting for them outside the manor, along with a number of soldiers. Even with their faces hidden, the relief they all felt was palpable.

"My liege, have you any idea of the trouble we've been through?!" scolded the advisor, who also appeared to act as a de facto caretaker. The lecture ground to a halt, however, when he saw what his young charge was holding.

"Ah! The Royal Mask!"

Excited murmurs rippled through the nearby soldiers. Nier figured anything called a Royal Mask had to be somewhat important, but he'd clearly underestimated just how vital an item it was.

"Our people have suffered since the king's death," the prince began. *"I was too young to bridge the gap between them and other civilizations. Trade has come to a halt. We lack food and water, and the people despair for it."*

This was the first Nier had heard of the Masked People's lives being difficult. None of them had complained during his time in the city, nor had he caught anyone moping on the sidelines. All he'd seen were people living peaceful, diligent lives. But it's easy to assume the best of someone when they are hidden behind a mask, and the prince clearly understood that his people no longer smiled—which was why he had risked his life to see them happy once more.

"*This mask is an emblem of the king,*" the prince continued. "*With it, I can project a strong image to other lands, and our people can be prosperous once more.*"

"*My prince . . .*" the advisor replied in a breathy voice.

"*And now that I have this mask, I believe I can ascend to the throne. Is this correct?*"

"*Of course! Hail! All hail the new king!*"

The advisor knelt before his new ruler, and the soldiers did the same. With the Royal Mask now in his possession, the prince had proved he had the courage and mental fortitude to lead his people. His face shone proudly as he looked out over his grateful people, for he understood that a new king had finally been born.

Yet, while the city now bubbled with joy, Nier remained unsatisfied. He had come all this way to find a cure for Yonah and was no closer to that goal than when he first arrived. Further conversations with various people revealed they had done all they could for the sickly former king, including trying medicine and remedies from far-off lands. Yet, despite their diligence, the Black Scrawl had taken their leader's life in the end.

But it was not all bad news: Nier had managed to obtain a Sealed Verse from the box giant, which represented at least a small step forward. If he didn't know how to cure the Black Scrawl by normal means, he would just keep collecting Verses until they were rid of it for good.

As the party made ready to depart, everyone saw them off, including the new king, his advisor, Fyra, and all the soldiers. Though Nier hadn't spent much time in the city, he'd truly come to enjoy and appreciate the kindness of its people.

"*One moment, please!*" called a small voice as they stepped onto the sand-skiff. "*Can I ask you to visit us again? To return as friends?*"

Though it was the new king asking the question, the request was made with the fervor and joy of any normal boy.

"Of course!" Nier replied with a bright smile that caused the king to beam.

One day, he thought, *when Yonah's better, I want to bring her here.*

5.

A DREAM.

There was a boy. A stranger. How lovely his silver hair that danced in the wind was. How beautiful his crystalline eyes were.

There came the sound of wind. Of singing birds. Yet the boy's voice was lost. His lips kept moving; he wanted to say something.

Concentrate. What is he saying? What is he trying to tell me?

The first sound is S. The second is E. Then A. Then L.

S-E-A-L-E-D

V-E-R-S-E

Sealed Verse.

Something about the boy's movements changed.

He spoke: "Dream."

He spoke again: "Forest of Myth."

Forest of Myth?

Nier awoke with a start. Though the grasp of sleep dissipated in an instant, the dream remained fresh in his mind. There had been a boy he didn't recognize, as well as the words *Sealed Verse* and something called the *Forest of Myth*.

Nier could understand why he was dreaming about Sealed Verses, since his mind was always in a panic about finding the next one. But he had no idea who the boy was, much less where to find this Forest of Myth.

"What's wrong?" asked Yonah. "Are you feeling sick too?"

Nier shook his head, trying to clear his thousand-yard stare.

He'd been apprehensive about Yonah's symptoms upon returning from Facade, but they'd calmed for the time being. They weren't gone, of course, but the pain-killing shaman fish was working its magic once more. She felt good enough to take meals with him at the table instead of in her bed, and to begin worrying about him. It made him happy to see her feeling better, and he felt a smile creeping around the edge of his mouth at her question.

"I'm fine, Yonah," he said. "I just had a strange dream."

"What about?"

"Nothing. Don't worry about it."

"'Cause I had a dream too!"

"What kind of dream?"

"I was playing a game!"

Nier tilted his head slightly. "Oh yeah? With who?"

"A boy! It was called Guess The Words. . . . I think he made it up, because I never heard of it before."

"How did it work?"

"The boy would move his mouth, but no words would come out. Then I had to guess what he was trying to say. It was hard."

"So what *did* he say?"

"I dunno. All I could figure out was 'dream' and 'Forest of Myth.'"

Nier's heart leaped into his throat; somehow he and his sister had experienced the exact same dream.

"I didn't know the rest," Yonah went on. "But don't worry! I'm gonna study hard so that next time I can figure out everything. You and me should play a game together sometime too!"

Nier was lost in thought by the time she finished and found himself making a vague noise of agreement without knowing what she'd said. Whatever it was, it could wait; there were more important issues at play now.

As the morning progressed, Nier found himself obsessed with

the dream—and the more he thought about it, the weirder it became. What did it mean for him and Yonah to have the same dream? Would Popola perhaps have some kind of insight, or would she brush it off with a smile?

Still unsure if he should ask, he eventually made his way to the library, where he found a frowning Popola sitting at her desk.

"What's up, Popola?" he asked. Though he'd been sure to knock and wait before opening the door, she still seemed startled when he greeted her. Clearly something was on her mind.

"I just got a strange letter in the mail." She unfolded a piece of paper and turned it around on her desk to show Nier. It read:

> I hope this letter finds you well.
>
> I am writing in hopes of bringing to your attention a certain dream issue of concern regarding recent events in dream the village. I was hoping I might be dream able to get your advice dream on the matter.
>
> Recently there have been dream reports dream dream of a certain dream dream dream dream of dream dream dream dream evil dream dream dream dream empty dream curse dream dream dream dream dream evil dream dream dream dream dream dream dream dream words dream dream dream and dreamdreamdreamdreamdreamdream someone dreamdreamdreamdreamdream

Nier thought it was a bunch of nonsense, but Grimoire Weiss flew backward with a start after giving it a single glance, almost as if he didn't want to look at it.

"That is certainly a bizarre piece of writing," muttered the book—a position with which Nier wholeheartedly agreed.

"It came from the mayor of a small northern village in the Forest of Myth," said Popola.

"The Forest of Myth?!" cried Nier, who was surprised on multiple levels. He couldn't believe it was an actual place, nor could he have imagined that Popola would bring it up before he had a chance to ask about it. And then there was the letter itself, and the fact that it was filled with the same word the silver-haired boy had said to him and Yonah the night before.

"They're usually a bright and cheerful group of people," said Popola, frowning. "Something like this is very out of character for them. I have a bad feeling about this."

"I'll check it out," Nier offered.

"Er, you will? But—"

"It's fine. Don't worry about it. I've got business there anyway."

"Oh. Well, all right."

He opted not to tell her about his dream; she would only worry more if he did, and perhaps even try to stop him.

"How do you get there exactly?" asked Nier.

"It's just after you cross the small wooden bridge in the northern plains."

She jotted the location down on Nier's map before thanking him for his assistance. He gave a brief word of reassurance like always, yet there was a part of him that silently regretted not telling her about the dream.

6.

THE FOREST OF Myth was located beyond a passageway flanked by stone cliffs. As Nier moved down the path, the sky was replaced by leafy branches that blocked out the sun. Though it wasn't foggy, there was a definite sensation of cool, dank air that reminded him of being surrounded by Shades in the mist.

"You want to wait outside, Kainé?" Nier asked.

"Yep. I'll meet you here."

Kainé never wanted to go into any settlement—be it Nier's village or Seafront. The only place she ventured into was Facade, but even there she was content to wait at the entrance. Nier wished she'd come inside on occasion so he could invite her into his home, treat her to a meal, and introduce her to Yonah, but Grimoire Weiss had warned him not to force the issue.

"Okay," he said. "See you later."

Kainé replied with a short grunt as she leaned against a tree. That small act was enough to cause the branches to shiver.

"It sure is quiet here," Nier remarked as he moved forward. He'd expected to find tweeting birds or humming insects, but all he could hear was the rustling of leaves. Well, that wasn't entirely true—he *did* hear the occasional animal noise, but it was strangely muffled each time.

"Such silence bodes ill," noted Weiss. "There's trouble on the way—I'm certain of it."

In a fluster, Nier put a finger to his lips. While his footsteps were painfully loud in the quiet, Grimoire Weiss's voice boomed out to every corner of the village.

"Keep your voice down, Weiss," Nier said. The last thing he wanted was to earn the ire of the people they were about to visit. He'd had enough of that kind of thing at The Aerie.

Thankfully, no one was screaming at them to leave—or even whispering, for that matter. The village was dim; even the glowing insects floated by without a sound. Soon Nier found himself walking lightly in an attempt to smother his own footsteps.

The village was filled with large trees, each of which had a door in the trunk. While the people of The Aerie lived in tanks, those in the Forest of Myth apparently preferred the hollows of trees. There were no obvious paths, but scattered throughout were places where the grass had been trampled short or worn away entirely to reveal bare earth beneath. With no one out and about, the makeshift paths took on an eerie air.

Finally, they came upon a woman standing before an open door in one of the trees. Her expression was blank, and though her eyes were open, she gave no reaction whatsoever when Nier approached.

"Hi there!" he said, a greeting that earned only silence in response.

"Uh, hello?" he tried again. Still no response.

"Look!" interrupted Weiss. "There is yet another villager over there."

Nier turned and saw a young man. But just like the woman, he made no reply to any query or greeting.

"Real 'bright and cheerful,' Popola," muttered Nier, remembering how she'd described the villagers.

"I say, is that the mayor?" asked Weiss, his attention drawn to an old man on a tree stump. When the pair approached, they seemed to detect a slight glimmer in his eye—a reaction different from any of the other villagers' so far.

"Um, hello?" asked Nier. In a surprising twist, the old man's mouth slowly began to move.

"Be . . . ware . . . Be . . . ware . . . the words . . ."

"The words? What do you mean?" Despite the man's mostly blank expression, Nier could tell he was trying desperately to communicate something.

"Contagious . . . words . . . Those . . . who . . . dream . . ."

"Those who dream? What does that mean?"

The moment Nier said that, something changed. It was an odd feeling—one he had never experienced before.

"Hold a moment," said Weiss. "There is a strange new sensation in my mind."

GRIMOIRE WEISS's voice rises in a quizzical way.

GRIMOIRE WEISS
It is NOT quizzical!

NIER
What's going on? Why's my voice turning into words?!

The villager's body shudders as he slowly opens his eyes.

GRIMOIRE WEISS
Perhaps we should attempt to aid this poor fellow.

NIER
Oh, weird! What you say is turning into words, too, Weiss!

MAYOR

Wh—who are you?

NIER

Hey, he was the mayor after all! (pause, then to MAYOR)

We heard something happened to this village, so we came to see if we could help.

MAYOR

If you can speak to me, I must have caught you in my dream.

NIER

How's that again?

The villager explains: in the past weeks, a mysterious disease called the Deathdream has spread across the Forest of Myth. Those who catch it are cursed to fall asleep and live forever within the world of their own dreams. The village mayor determined the Deathdream is spread from person to person by spoken words, but before he could learn more, the disease took him as well.

GRIMOIRE WEISS

Are you saying that we have been absorbed into your dream?

MAYOR

Um, well . . . yes. I think you have.

GRIMOIRE WEISS

*Ridiculous! Preposterous! Completely
unfathomable on every conceivable level! I
don't even recall falling asleep!*

MAYOR

*That's just how the Deathdream works. Did
you converse with anyone in the village?
Something must have caused you to enter my
dream. A certain conversation, a specific
word. Something!*

    NIER and GRIMOIRE WEISS rack their brains
    but find no solutions. There are simply
    too many words to consider, too much
    random chatter, too many meaningless
    conversations.

GRIMOIRE WEISS

*Grimoire Weiss does not engage in
meaningless conversations!*

    The mere suggestion that GRIMOIRE WEISS
    chooses his words carelessly seems to
    sting his pride.

GRIMOIRE WEISS (CONT'D)

*It does not seem to sting my pride, you
bloated gasbag of a narrator! It has
demolished it utterly!*

NIER

Wait. Contagious?

GRIMOIRE WEISS

What now?

NIER

(to MAYOR) *You told us to watch out for contagious words, right?*

MAYOR

What was it? Some specific combination of words?

NIER

It was about dreaming, or something that dreams, or . . . Oh, what the heck was it? (pause) I remember! Those who dream!

The MAYOR produces a thick sheaf of papers from his pocket.

He flips through them a few times before nodding his approval.

MAYOR

That sounds right. My notes also mention something about that.

I bet it was the last thing you heard before you fell asleep.

The MAYOR shakes his head, his worn pencil stub tracing lines across a lone piece of paper.

MAYOR (CONT'D)

For the last month, I've done nothing but study this disease. But I never expected a couple of outsiders to start entering people's dreams.

GRIMOIRE WEISS
I applaud the force of will it takes to
research a disease in your dreams, but
perhaps we should bend your efforts to
escaping this place instead.

MAYOR
I've tried to escape. I mean, this is my
dream, so if there was an exit, I'd know
about it. But I've looked in every nook and
cranny and found nothing. What else can I
do besides take notes? Nothing!

NIER nods in agreement as the desperate
MAYOR looks on.

NIER
Huh? Wait a second, I didn't nod.

NIER smiles as he offers to help.

NIER
Now hold on! I did not just offer to help!

GRIMOIRE WEISS
Silence!

GRIMOIRE WEISS looks from NIER to the
MAYOR and back again, his face filling
with confidence.

GRIMOIRE WEISS
Grimoire Weiss's face is always confident,
thank you very much! Now, see here, Mayor.
You think that nothing can exist in this

dream *without your knowing it, yet you seemed surprised to see us when we first arrived, yes?*

MAYOR

Oh my god. You're right. You're right! I had no idea you were coming!

GRIMOIRE WEISS

The human imagination is a limitless engine, and dreams are the fuel. If you can imagine an exit, then it must be so.

With your permission, we shall search it out.

MAYOR

Thank you! I don't know how I can repay you!

GRIMOIRE WEISS

Payment is not required.

We are as eager as you to be done with this place.

As NIER and GRIMOIRE WEISS venture into the misty forest, the MAYOR is struck by a sense of déjà vu. He feels as though he's seen them somewhere before but can't pinpoint where.

Meanwhile, NIER's steps grow heavy as he trudges through the forest. The mist makes it hard to see more than a foot in any direction, and moss-covered rocks seem determined to twist his ankle. It feels as though the forest is closing in around him.

NIER
This sure is a deep forest.

As he speaks, a cacophony of insects springs to life. Every imaginable form of buzz, click, *and* hiss *roars out at a volume that rattles the teeth. NIER slaps his hands over his ears.*

NIER
Weiss! What's going on?!

GRIMOIRE WEISS's mouth moves, but NIER can't hear him.

The insects scream.

NIER
Wait. Are these . . . words?

NIER realizes the insects' cries are forming words.

Listening, he hears a different sound amidst the writing.

The screaming changes to letters, which then create words.

ON-SCREEN TEXT
One with it is lacking. Two with it is ideal. Three with it is dangerous. What is it?

GRIMOIRE WEISS
By my pages! Is this a riddle?

NIER

*I guess so? I mean, it feels sorta forced,
but maybe it's the key to getting out of
this place.*

*GRIMOIRE WEISS nudges NIER, who gives an
answer.*

NIER

*One with it is lacking, two with it is ideal,
and three is dangerous. It's a secret.*

*The sound of insects stops. The forest
undergrowth parts before them, opening
a new path. They proceed down it to find
themselves facing a clear forest spring.*

NIER

Everything looks normal here.

*Smiling, NIER picks up a small rock and
sends it skipping across the surface
of the water. GRIMOIRE WEISS exclaims
in surprise. Each time the rock strikes
the surface of the water, a musical note
rings out. The ripples left behind come
together to form words.*

ON-SCREEN TEXT

I enter through the window, but break no glass.
When night falls, I vanish. What am I?

GRIMOIRE WEISS

Not this again.

NIER

Sunlight!

> A plume of water suddenly bursts from the
> spring. Sunlight filters through the trees
> and reflects off the droplets to create a
> shimmering rainbow.

GRIMOIRE WEISS

In all my years I have never seen such a
sight.

NIER

Hey, Weiss! Look!

> NIER points to a small cottage. He walks
> over and pounds on the door, which cracks
> open to reveal a small MAN. He is cloaked
> from neck to toe in a large black cape,
> his face obscured.

> NIER opens his mouth to speak, but the
> MAN holds up a hand.

MAN

I have four legs in the morning and two at
noon, but end the night with three. What
am I?

> NIER attempts to ask more questions, but
> the MAN only repeats his own.

GRIMOIRE WEISS

If we wish to engage this man in conversation,
it seems we must answer his riddle.

> **NIER**

At least it's an easy one. Four legs, two, and then three, right? It's a man.

The mist parts.

The MAN's lips, just barely visible, curl into a smile.

> **MAN**

Correct.

He flings his garment aside.

> **NIER**

You're the mayor!

The MAN shakes his head.

> **MAN**

I am not the mayor you know. Now listen to my words:

Long ago, I saw a version of you that was not yourself.

> **NIER**

What's that mean?

> **MAN**

It will make sense in time. At present, I simply congratulate you on cracking the seal of the Deathdream.

Now you must go to the person at the forest entrance.

The MAN turns on his heel and slams the door behind him. As NIER watches, mist seeps up from the ground to envelop the cottage. Like the insects and fountain, NIER knows he will never see it again, even if he does somehow find his way back into the woods.

MAYOR
Good gravy! You made it! You actually made it back!

The MAYOR is leaning against a tree at the forest entrance.

NIER
We broke the Deathdream's seal. At least, I think we did.

The MAYOR smiles.

Then they all lie down on the ground and fall asleep.

NIER
Okay, hang on a second.
Why would we just lie down and go to sleep?!

GRIMOIRE WEISS
Cease your endless prattle and go to sleep, fool!
Fighting against the rules of this place is futility itself.

NIER and the MAYOR obediently recline atop the grassy earth.

GRIMOIRE WEISS (CONT'D)
Have you forgotten? It is words that control the Deathdream, words that allow us to move from place to place.

No matter how unnatural they seem, the words are absolute.

Therefore, if the words tell us to sleep, then sleep we shall.

The three find their eyes growing heavy. Their breath slows.

MAYOR
This is the first time . . . I have felt tired . . . since I was imprisoned . . . here . . .

They might have slept for an hour or a year. When they wake, things feel more real. The mist is thicker, the leaves greener. It's clear they have awakened from their prison.

NIER
Good news! I think we made it.

MAYOR
Oh wow. We did. I'm back.

You have no idea how much this means. Now I must pray to save the villagers still trapped in the Deathdream.

The MAYOR starts praying to the Divine Tree in the center of the village.

NIER
You're praying to a tree?

MAYOR
This is a holy tree. We pray to protect ourselves from disaster. It's the guardian of our village's history—and memories.

GRIMOIRE WEISS
Superstition will only make our mission harder.

We should not put our faith in the gods.

MAYOR
Not the gods—the words. Legend says that our tree is home to a powerful magic known as a Sealed Verse.

NIER and GRIMOIRE WEISS cannot contain their surprise.

Their goal has been found in the most unexpected of places.

GRIMOIRE WEISS
I say, this is certainly a stroke of luck.

As they say their goodbyes, NIER mentions the MAN who gave them the third riddle and the mysterious words he left them with.

MAYOR

You know, this is going to sound odd, but I had a feeling I'd seen you before too.

NIER

What?

MAYOR

Déjà vu, right? Anyway, I figure it's just some kind of illusion created by the Deathdream. It probably doesn't mean anything.

NIER gives the mayor a nod and a smile, but inwardly, his thoughts are racing.

NIER (V.O.)

There's something wrong about the mayor and his words.

And what exactly is going on here?

That riddle will prove to be the most difficult one of all.

After waking from the dream for real, Nier and Weiss found they had obtained a Sealed Verse that summoned deadly spears out of the ground.

"Oh, thank you so much!" said the grateful mayor from his position on his stump. "Now I can finally return to a normal life."

"This is one of the most bizarre diseases I have ever encountered," Grimoire Weiss said.

Nier agreed wholeheartedly; a disease spread through words that also acted as the cure was a most peculiar ailment indeed.

"Still," he said, "we got a Sealed Verse, and it didn't even take much effort."

Indeed, the previous Verses had only been earned after taking down powerful Shades or battling massive machines. It wasn't even that long ago that they'd fought the box giant. In comparison, this one was obtained simply by entering another person's dreams and solving some riddles. Yet if the previous Verses were taken from powerful foes, where did this one come from? Could it possibly have been the holy tree in the center of the village? That idea snapped Nier from his thoughts.

"Yes," Grimoire Weiss began, suspicion palpable in his voice. "All a touch too easy, if you ask me. It's almost as if someone was guiding us to this village."

"Don't overthink it, Weiss. Let's just focus on saving the other villagers."

Now that they knew why the other villagers were unresponsive, it was simply a matter of entering their dreams and curing them with words. By the time they were done, Nier and Weiss were thoroughly worn out, and they scarcely had the energy to trudge back to the entrance.

"So how was the village?" asked Kainé when they approached. She seemed to be in a relatively good mood, despite how long they'd made her wait.

"Oh, it was truly magnificent," said Weiss. "There are no words, really."

Hearing his response, one would have thought Grimoire Weiss had been the one who was made to wait for twelve hours.

REPORT 06

As of late, the range of Nier's activities has rap-idly broadened. In fact, not long ago he began regular visits to Facade. The city is closed to outsiders and home to a vastly different lan-guage and culture, yet he is now heavily in-volved with their affairs. It's . . . unexpected. Also, a new king has apparently assumed the throne there, so we will be keeping a close eye on that going forward.

In other news, a strange disease called the Deathdream recently swept through the For-est of Myth. Victims find themselves unable to wake from dreams, and a majority of residents in the affected district were said to have been infected.

Luckily, Nier was able to survive with the aid of Grimoire Weiss. When he told me the details, it seemed the matter was much more serious than our previous estimation; no such phenomenon has ever been observed in the Forest of Myth before, and there are no prob-lematic villagers there (as opposed to The Aerie). Considering the location's importance, we should carry out a thorough investigation.

Finally, I believe we should scout out and recommend suitable equipment for anyone we dispatch to troubled spots in the future. This would, of course, include Nier.

Record written by Popola

The Boy 6

1.

THE LOST SHRINE. The Junk Heap. The Aerie. Facade. The Forest of Myth.

Slowly but surely, Nier was collecting Sealed Verses. And while this task required him to battle powerful foes (save for the Forest of Myth), from great trials come ever greater rewards. Between fights, he'd also gone to Seafront to secure shaman fish, as well as run errands across the land whenever his neighbors asked for help.

Yes, it had been a busy time for Nier.

As promised, he visited the king of Facade from time to time as a friend. But the new ruler often left his manor with little warning, giving his advisor many headaches. "I suppose people do not change so easily," Grimoire Weiss had mused with a grimace.

In fact, the king's wandering ways were the original reason Nier had met Fyra. When she was new to the city—a place far from her hometown—the king (then a prince) ended up becoming her good friend. After Nier learned that, he thought it was all right that people don't change so easily, and it helped him enjoy the relaxing times spent with the king and Fyra all the more.

But with good came bad, including news that the ornery lighthouse lady had perished from the Black Scrawl. This happened shortly after Nier learned the supposed letters from her beloved had been written by the postman. Her love had actually been dead for many a year, but the people of Seafront continued sending false letters to hide the truth.

When Nier learned of this, he recalled how the lighthouse lady held the letter with a wistful look on her face, and it threatened to break his heart. But the postman told him she'd died at home with a smile on her face, which helped dull the pain. So far as Nier could tell, the postman took the old woman's death harder than anyone.

He knew this because he'd been crossing paths with the postman more and more of late. He attributed their frequent meetings to his constant Seafront trips, including many to purchase bulbs and seedlings for the flower-shop owner in his village. But the postman had begun coming to Nier's village more often as well—and he learned why one day from the most surprising conversation.

"I need a favor," Yonah had said, her expression uncharacteristically serious. She sat stock-still, trying and failing to find the right words.

"I can't help if you don't tell me, Sis," said Nier.

"Okay. I'm gonna say it. Ready?" She inhaled briefly, paused, then let it out in a torrent. "I need you to help my friend!"

"Your . . . friend?"

Nier had never heard her use the word *friend* before. Could it be someone from the village? Yonah didn't often venture outside to play, so she and the rest of the children had always been a bit distant.

"Yep! We've been writing each other letters."

"A pen pal?" said Grimoire Weiss. "How delightful."

Nier finally realized why the postman had been coming around so often: Yonah had been writing and receiving letters.

"So who is this friend?" he said.

"Um, well, he's kinda—"

"It's a *guy*?!"

Nier realized his voice had just cracked. *Okay, calm down*, he told himself. *Take it easy.*

"Yes, and he's sick and in a whole lot of trouble! And I know that you and Weissey are the only ones who can help him!"

"Tell me about this guy."

"He lives in this really big house down south, and he's super nice, and he's my friend."

This is bad. I can barely think. What is she even saying?

Yonah looked up at her brother, her face the very picture of sincerity. "So you have to help him. Please?"

Nier found himself flustered when he saw her eyes wavering under a layer of tears, but still tried to resist. "I don't know. Right now your sickness is more important, and I'd rather work to make you better instead of . . ."

Nier's voice faltered, as did his will. When Yonah clasped her hands together and pleaded with him again, any resistance he may have had disintegrated. She rarely asked for things from him like this, after all.

"Fine," he said. "I'll see what I can do."

"Yaaay! Thank you!"

A smile bloomed across her face—one he would do anything for. In truth, he wished he could make all her dreams come true, although this particular situation felt like one beyond his control.

Some time later, Nier found himself leaning against the front door and staring blankly at the sky, his mind awhirl.

"Yonah has a pen pal . . . A boy who's a friend . . . A boyfriend . . ."

"Is something amiss, lad?" asked Weiss. "Your voice is trembling."

"N-no it isn't! Shut up!" Nier tried his best to put on a brave face and keep his reeling mind hidden. "Anyway, let's head for this big house in the south."

He knew of a place that might be what she was talking about: a large manor on a hill near the edge of the southern plains. The front gates were always closed, and he'd never seen anyone coming or going, so he'd always assumed the place to be abandoned.

"We would learn the precise location of this manor were we to look at one of the letters from this pen pal," noted Weiss.

It was a good idea, but Nier felt it was too much trouble to go back and get one of the letters now. Also, he couldn't bear to look at letters from a boy to his sister . . . though he *was* curious what was in them.

2.

THE MANOR WAS a large, sturdy stone building, but terribly worn down. Its elaborate design made its age stand out all the more; the paint on the metal gate was peeling, and there was a faint presence of rust.

When Nier pushed on the gate, he was surprised to find it unlocked. The last time he'd wandered up here, the gate had been locked tight.

"Maybe they knew we were coming and opened it for us?" he mused. He pushed the gate open wide enough for them to pass and waited for someone to yell, but nothing came. Before he knew it, they were moving up the path to the manor, where a tall man was waiting for them—presumably a resident of the place.

Nier began moving toward the man, then stopped as a strange sensation overcame him. He felt an odd sense of unease similar to when he entered the Forest of Myth—and just like in that case, he couldn't put a finger on why. There was a chill in the air, and while he'd been sweaty after running across the southern plains, his perspiration evaporated the moment he stepped through the gate. Nier knew the climate couldn't change so drastically simply by crossing from one outside area to another, yet he couldn't explain why the air suddenly felt so cool on his skin.

The other thing that made him uneasy was the man standing in front of the manor, although that part was at least easy to put a reason to. Though he was well-dressed and of middling physique and height, he was perfectly emotionless. He showed no reaction to their presence at all when Nier, Weiss, and Kainé stepped through the gate. And a man who would not greet guests was also unlikely to turn away intruders, a prospect that gave Nier an eerie chill. Part of him wondered if the man might actually be some kind of statue instead of a human.

"We have been waiting for you, sirs," said the man suddenly.

"Whoa!" cried Nier, who was shocked to learn the man was human after all. Yet despite how Nier's face twisted in shock, the man showed no reaction. Most people would have at least raised an eyebrow in his direction.

"Please," he continued, "right this way."

As they were led inside, Nier began to regret coming. This was partly because the man could be planning to harm them, and partly because the manor was in a *terrible* state. The moment they stepped through the front entrance, they were greeted by the sight of a collapsed staircase. Candelabras lay fallen on their sides. Passageways were blocked by crossbeams and pillars. The windows were so clouded with grime, it was impossible to make out anything beyond one's immediate surroundings; Nier had no idea when they had last been cleaned.

"Well, we've come this far. I suppose we can't turn back now." Grimoire Weiss spoke in an unusually hushed tone, making it clear they should keep their guards high.

"Right," Nier replied. "We need to meet this friend of Yonah's."

Ahead, the man came to a stop. Though he said nothing, it was clear he was waiting for them to catch up by how he turned back to examine them. The situation suggested he was being considerate of their pace, yet his lack of expression suggested anything but.

As Nier jogged to catch up, another sense of unease overcame him, just like when he'd stepped through the gate. And like that moment, he still couldn't pinpoint where it was coming from.

The party ultimately found themselves escorted into a large dining room. The table was long enough to seat six people and was topped with serving platters, glasses, and multiple large bottles of drink.

"Please wait here," the man said. "I shall fetch the master."

The man left the room, the hinges on the door screeching behind him. What he said made him sound like a servant. His fine dress had Nier assuming he was lord of the manor and the father of Yonah's friend, but that assumption was clearly wrong.

"Waiting's a bitch. Just lemme know if any Shades show up, okay?" This said, Kainé yawned, lay down on a nearby bench, and immediately fell asleep.

"Kainé sure is something, huh?" Nier remarked.

"She must have nerves of pure steel," Grimoire Weiss replied. The astonishment was clear in his voice. Looking at her snoring, Nier thought her nerves were equaled only by her resolve to nap whenever possible.

He, however, did not have the courage to fall asleep in such an enigmatic place. There was something odd about this dining room: despite the blazing fire in the grand fireplace, the room retained an icy chill.

"Should we maybe walk around? I mean, Kainé's asleep, and it's kind of boring here." Nier wasn't *bored*, exactly, but the idea of staying in the room one moment longer filled him with unease.

"A splendid idea!" said Grimoire Weiss, who apparently felt the same.

The pair quickly located an unlocked door on the far side of the dining room. Nier pushed it open to find a wide hallway filled with the same chill as the room they'd just left. There was another door opposite, but as Nier went to open it, a flustered Grimoire Weiss flew between his hand and the handle.

"Hold, lad! We mustn't go opening doors willy-nilly!"

"I'm just going to take a peek."

The door, however, was locked tight. Nier casually glanced at the keyhole and saw it was located under the word *DARK*.

"What's this supposed to be?" he wondered aloud.

Grimoire Weiss peered from behind and yelped, causing Nier to spin around. "What's wrong, Weiss?"

"Nothing. It is just . . ."

"Just what?"

"That is a foreboding word."

"You think so?"

It was true that Shades liked the dark, but that didn't exactly make the word *foreboding*.

"Maybe we should try the other doors," he suggested. He took a few steps down the hall and encountered a large painting hanging on the wall. It showed an armored man holding a spear; the thick wooden frame surrounding it was darkened with age.

"I do not like this one bit!" said Grimoire Weiss in a quivering voice that caused Nier to chuckle.

"What's the matter? Scared?"

"N-not at all! But humans of the distant past considered certain things cursed, and I have seen much in this house that matches those descriptors! Not to mention the ominous writing, and . . . and . . ."

Grimoire Weiss faltered and fell silent. Surprised to learn how much of a scaredy-book his companion was, Nier moved to investigate another door. It was locked as well, with the word *MOON* engraved over the keyhole.

"*Moon* shouldn't be a bad sign, right?" said Nier, pondering.

The words above the keyholes had to mean *something*, a thought that led him to begin moving down the hallway in search of yet more doors. But when a clearly startled Weiss suggested they turn back, Nier relented. He didn't want to make the tome any more frightened than he already was, so Nier decided to return to the dining room.

He was surprised to find the dining room empty. Not only had the servant and his master failed to arrive, but Kainé was gone as well. When Nier wondered aloud where she could have gone, Weiss flew into a tizzy.

"I knew this was a terrible idea! Haunted manors and the like . . . Oh, why does no one ever listen to me?!"

"C'mon. This place isn't haunted."

Despite how deeply Kainé had been sleeping, she could have easily woken up while they were out and found herself bored out of her mind. She'd probably just taken her own walk as they had done—or perhaps she'd even been worried about her companions and gone looking for them.

"We just missed each other," Nier reassured Weiss. "We'll find her."

They retraced their steps from the dining room back to the main entrance, but Kainé was nowhere to be found. They even tried the front door in case she'd gone outside, but found it locked tight.

"Oh, woe!" cried Weiss. "We're trapped! Doors that lock of their own accord is a quintessential element of a haunted manor. Of course the brave protagonists would be locked in—that's the beauty of the drama!"

"OR this door is just really old and got stuck. We'll have to tell that weird guy it needs fixing."

They returned to the empty dining room and passed through

the door at the far end. Nier wanted to check out the doors they had yet to explore, but when they entered the hall, Grimoire Weiss gave another yelp.

"The painting has changed!"

"Has it?" Nier looked up and began examining the painting. The man was still armored and still holding a spear. It appeared to be the same—and yet, *something* was off.

"Now that you mention it, I think it has," agreed Nier.

"I knew it!"

"But can you even tell what's different?"

"I, er . . ."

"You can't, can you? It's hard to remember all those details."

"But moving subjects within portraits and the composition of the painting itself changing are sure signs of a haunted—"

"I think you're imagining it. Er, maybe."

Grimoire Weiss began to protest but stopped. After a moment of thought he said, "Well, I suppose we shall leave it at that."

"Yeah. We should focus on looking for Kainé, anyway."

Nier still felt bad for leaving her in the dining room, even though she had been asleep. While she was about as far from a coward as one could imagine, it still couldn't have been nice to wake up there all alone.

"How far did we go last time?" wondered Nier. After checking a locked door and moving on to the next one, he heard Grimoire Weiss clear his throat, most likely to suggest turning back once more. But before he could, the pair stumbled upon another door, one with no writing above the keyhole.

Nier turned the knob and found it unlocked. When he pushed it open, sunlight poured out and caused his vision to turn pure white. This door led to the inner courtyard, and his eyes weren't ready for that kind of glare after spending so long in the dark interior of the manor.

The courtyard was enclosed by a circular hedge. A long-dry fountain sat in the center, surrounded by several life-size statues of men and women. The moss growing on them told of how long they'd been standing sentry.

"They look like they're in pain. It's kind of scary."

Nier hadn't seen a lot of statues in his life, but he assumed they were usually created with calm, composed faces. These, however, were twisted in distress and pain—or perhaps fear.

"Come now!" said Grimoire Weiss. "Brave faces! Onward and upward, eh?"

He was right: the statues weren't things they should sit and observe for an extended period of time. Leaving them behind, Nier and Weiss cut quickly through the courtyard and opened a door that led to another wing of the manor. But though it seemed like a spacious structure from the outside, all it contained was a short hallway with one measly door.

Nier opened the door, not expecting much, and was greeted by an unexpected treat: a key with the word *MOON* engraved on it resting atop a small sink.

"This must go with that other door!" he cried. Grabbing it, they rushed out of the room and retraced their steps to the moon door. After putting the key into the lock, he turned it and felt a satisfying click. Seconds later, the door swung open to reveal a narrow corridor. Though there were small spots of light throughout, it was generally a dim and gloomy place.

"Did you hear that?" Nier asked suddenly after taking a couple steps inside.

"Someone screamed!" replied Weiss.

"That was a scream?" Nier had heard what sounded like a man's voice, but the way Grimoire Weiss was twisting violently from side to side convinced him it was a serious matter.

"It was a cry for help, lad! I'm certain of it!"

"Was it really?"

"It asked to be let out! There's no doubt about this, it must be a gho—"

"A servant, Weiss. Just a servant. I really think someone needs to oil the doors in this house."

While Grimoire Weiss didn't seem to agree with this assessment, he didn't argue further. Just then, Nier heard something. It wasn't a voice this time, but a sound. He strained his ears and picked up the unmistakable tone of a musical instrument—not the stringed one Devola played, but a piano.

Nier immediately cheered up; if someone was playing the piano, it meant there was life here. As he gently pushed a new door open, the creaking of the hinges caused the sounds of the piano to come to a halt.

The boy sitting at the piano stood up. His skin was pale and smooth as porcelain, his hair soft, and his lips the color of spring blossoms. Strangely enough, there were bandages across his eyes that served as a blindfold.

"You're a male . . ." the boy said in a halting voice. "Young . . . Not even 20 . . ."

"You figured that out from my footsteps?" asked a stunned Nier. It seemed impossible the boy could do such a thing, and yet there it was.

"It's not hard, once you know how," said the boy, his voice and expression both surprisingly bright.

"Then I suppose I should tell you about my friend Weiss."

"I . . . I only heard one set of footsteps."

"Grimoire Weiss does not strut about like a common land mammal!"

When Grimoire Weiss spoke, the boy squealed in shock—an understandable reaction to the sudden presence of another voice.

"Sorry. He didn't mean to scare you like that." After apologizing in Weiss's stead, Nier went on to introduce himself.

"But enough of this introductory chatter," Grimoire Weiss interjected. "Let us hear your tale." He showed no remorse whatsoever for scaring the boy, choosing instead to spur the conversation onward.

"My name is Emil," began the boy. "I'm the master of this manor."

"So you're the one that quiet man referred to earlier. I take it you sent the letters?"

Emil only tilted his head. "Letters? What are you talking about?"

Grimoire Weiss sighed. "Of course you don't know. Such a thing would be far too simple."

After going on to explain the situation, Nier took a step toward Emil, who immediately stumbled away and demanded that Nier stay back.

"I'm sorry," he said after a moment. "It's my eyes. Anything I look at gets turned to stone." He brought his hands up to the bandages on his eyes, as though reinforcing his statement. "That's why I live with this blindfold."

"What a remarkable skill!" Grimoire Weiss said. "I've never heard of such a thing."

The power reminded Nier of the statues in the courtyard, the ones whose terrified expressions seemed too lifelike to have been carved by human hands. Deciding he didn't want to think about it, he quickly directed his attention elsewhere.

"Anyway," Emil continued, "I suppose my butler might know more about the letters you received. This key here can unlock any door in the manor, so if you'd like my assistance—"

"Don't trouble yourself," Nier interrupted. "We can get around on our own so long as you let us borrow the key." He knew it wasn't safe to walk around blindfolded; they'd be in huge trouble if the boy tripped and injured himself.

"Then let me give you this as well," said Emil as he produced a piece of paper from his pocket. "It's a map. I don't want you getting lost."

"Thanks."

"The butler's quarters are at the far end of the manor."

As they left the room, the thought of Kainé suddenly entered Nier's mind. They'd been so preoccupied by their chance encounter with the manor's master that they'd stopped looking for her. Yet despite the regret Nier felt, Grimoire Weiss seemed quite comfortable with the decision.

"Leave her!" he exclaimed. "That woman is capable enough on her own."

It was a heartless reply, but Nier felt he had no choice but to agree and proceed to the butler's quarters. All of his concentration was dedicated to making sure they didn't get lost, and he quickly realized why Emil had given them a map. The building was such a tangled mess of halls and rooms that Nier started to wonder if it had been built for the sole purpose of disorienting guests.

Additionally, they began to encounter Shades in the corridors. They were medium in build, and though they didn't use magic, they were relatively strong and attacked in numbers. Though Nier wondered at first why they were there, he quickly realized the manor hallways were lit by candles, not sunlight. The people living here likely had no choice but to leave them be once they managed to find their way inside.

After they dispatched the Shades and found their way to the section which contained the butler's quarters, they faced another problem: The area was covered in a series of identical doors.

"I wish they would mark these somehow," muttered Nier.

Each time he opened a door, he found a narrow room that was both dark and cold. Just as he was starting to get annoyed, another loud sound rang out.

"More screams!" Grimoire Weiss exclaimed. It had been a woman's voice this time—one Nier heard loud and clear. He immediately rushed out of the room and slammed the door behind him.

"Let's just pretend we didn't hear that," he said.

"Indeed," agreed Weiss.

They still had a butler to find. Nier opened the door opposite to find a room as dark as all the others. He thought about leaving right away, but then spotted water dripping from a sink; whoever was here last didn't completely shut off the faucet.

Nier approached the sink, hand extended to close the tap. But before he could so much as touch the faucet, liquid began to gush out.

"Aaaaaah!" screamed Nier.

"Yaaaaaahhh!" agreed Weiss.

The stuff coming out of the faucet wasn't water—even in the dark, Nier could recognize the color of blood. In a panic, he leaped out of the room and slammed the door.

"What the hell was that?!" he cried.

"I know not, nor do I *wish* to know. I told you this blasted place was haunted!"

Nier wanted to believe it was just rusted water from old pipes. But the scent of the liquid had been overpowering; there could be no doubt as to what it actually was.

"This house isn't haunted, Weiss," insisted Nier. If anything, it was just a series of sick pranks. After recomposing himself, he gathered his courage and opened the next door.

"Hey! He's here!"

Standing in the dark was the man from earlier—the butler,

apparently. His expression was blank, and despite Nier's less-than-polite exclamation regarding his existence, the butler seemed unfazed. In fact, he did not seem to be much of anything at all.

"Excuse me?" said Nier. "Hellooo?"

Though he spoke in something close to a yell, he received no reaction. He then waved his hand in front of the man's face and was similarly ignored. In desperation, he poked the butler's cheeks, but received only a dull *thunk* in response.

"What's going on?" he said.

"It seems to be a remarkable likeness of a butler," replied Weiss.

"Does it really need to be *this* lifelike?"

It was so well done, Nier half expected it to suddenly apologize for keeping them waiting. The authentic nature of the thing only made it all the eerier.

"I knew this was a trap," Grimoire Weiss said as they exited the room. "Curse my brilliant intuition." It was a thought Nier found himself having as well. Either they were caught in some kind of nightmare, or the entire place really was haunted or cursed just like the people of the distant past had thought.

Either way, there was only one door left. Nier took a deep breath, wondering what sort of prank was waiting in this last room, and pushed it open.

"This again?" he said and let out a sigh.

They found themselves facing another lifelike replica of the butler; it seemed whoever set this up thought they could get away with the same trick twice.

You can't scare me again, thought Nier. *I'm not afraid.*

After all, it was just a statue. It stood stiffly, its expression blank. He wished he could flick it on the forehead, but he wasn't tall enough to do so. Figuring pinching it on the cheek would be good enough, he reached up . . .

At which point the statue moved.

"Aaaah!" cried Nier.

"Blaaargh!" sputtered Weiss.

The statue's arm began to shudder, as if preparing to leap at them. Nier's feet began to move, but before he could even think about running, Grimoire Weiss was already at the door. When said door was flung open to reveal a bewildered Emil, Weiss let out another panicked scream.

"What's going on here?" asked Emil.

"Sir?" replied a human voice.

Weiss began to stammer. "Wh-what *is* this?!"

"Oh," Emil replied casually. "This is my butler. He helps me out around the manor."

The way the butler lowered his head made him seem less like a statue and more like a person—even if the movements *were* rather awkward by human standards.

"He's a good man at heart, but a bit . . . inflexible. Almost like a statue."

"Yes, and I do apologize for that, Master Emil."

He's not a bit *inflexible, and he's not* almost *like a statue. He is extremely both of those things.*

"We're here because my sister received some letters from this manor," began Nier.

"Mmmm, yes," the butler replied. "I wrote those letters. Please forgive my impertinence."

"But why?"

"As you may know, Master Emil, deeply pained by his eyes, has shut himself away from the world. He suffers greatly behind that blindfold, and I feel it is my duty to help however I can."

Though the butler's movements were unnatural and his expression lacking as always, the concern he held for his master was clear.

"I heard tales of the exploits of an emerging hero," he continued, "and so sent a letter to you under Master Emil's name. However, I received a response from one Miss Yonah instead."

"So *you're* Yonah's pen pal?"

"I am, sir."

Relief filled Nier's heart; this guy friend of hers being a butler wasn't nearly the problem it could have been.

"My letters merely requested that you come to the manor. I meant no ill intent."

"It sounds like Yonah misunderstood the situation."

"Yes. However, I am quite pleased to see you here. Long have I dreamed of the day we might be able to do something about Master Emil's eyes."

Though Yonah had interpreted the exchange differently, it seemed the butler had done the same. Nier didn't feel like a hero, nor did he have any idea how to cure eyes that could turn things to stone.

Naturally, Grimoire Weiss sought to extricate them from the situation as quickly as possible. "Yes, well, I am afraid we—or at least this lad beside me—is neither hero nor physician, so if you'll excuse us—"

The butler shook his head furiously, cutting the tome off. "Please! We're so close! The cure for Master Emil's condition is located in this very manor!"

"Then why don't you go get it?" asked a confused Nier.

For the first time, the scarcest hint of an expression crossed the butler's face. "Alas, the location of the cure has become a den for those abominable Shades, and I lack the skill to combat them."

Nier recalled the Shades they had fought in the hallway; he'd been right to assume Emil and his butler didn't have the time or manpower to rid themselves of them.

"I beg of you," the butler continued, "defeat the Shades and restore Master Emil's sight!"

"You know this is an impossible task!" scolded Emil. "Why would you ask it of our guests?"

He turned to Nier and Weiss with an apologetic nod. "I'm sorry. My butler cares so much for me, but for him to make such outlandish requests . . ."

Though Emil seemed ashamed, Nier understood how the butler felt; anyone with another person under their care would. If there was a way to get help—a way to save that person—a caregiver would do anything to make it so.

"We'll do it," said Nier.

"See here, lad! This is no time to play the hero!"

"People need to look out for each other, Weiss. Plus, we have to find Kainé anyway."

The butler bowed his head deeply. "I owe you a debt that can never be repaid. A thousand thanks to all of you."

His perfect, precise bow almost made Nier feel bad.

3.

EMIL ACCOMPANIED THEM to the library, which was said to house the cure for his ailment. Nier had been worried about the boy tripping and hurting himself, but he soon realized such concerns were misplaced. In fact, it was the visitors who needed Emil's help in the end; they encountered spiders of grotesque sizes in the corridors, and Nier could only imagine how much time it would have taken to dispatch the creatures alone.

"I'm happy to guide you! This is my house, after all, and I know it like the back of my hand." Emil walked ahead of the others as he spoke, petrifying Shades and spiders the moment they leaped out.

"Wow, you can kill Shades faster than magic can," marveled Nier. "But wait a second."

"Yes?"

"If everything you look at turns to stone, why doesn't your blindfold petrify?"

It was a good question, for the bandages wrapped across his eyes still retained their white fabric nature.

"I can only petrify living things. I guess that makes Shades living things? Things that have their own will, at least. Things that feel fear."

"So anything that isn't alive can't be turned to stone."

"Yes, which is why I can read books and play the piano. So long as others stay away from me, I mean."

There was more than a hint of melancholy in Emil's tone. As Nier watched him speak, he started to understand why the butler wanted to cure his master so badly.

As they chatted, they eventually came to the library. Nier pushed the door open to find it much brighter than any of the other rooms they had visited. Or to be more precise, it helped him realize the rest of the manor was too dark for the number of lights that burned there. That said, the brightness in the library didn't come from the sun, which meant it was a place where Shades could live.

"Look at all these books," Nier said, marveling as he scanned the library. Though it was nowhere near as big as the one in his village, it was still a sizable collection; every wall in the room was a shelf that extended to the ceiling.

"I know they used to do some kind of research here a long time ago," said Emil. "Most probably come from that time."

"What kind of research?"

"I don't know. It was a *really* long time ago."

Nier had already assumed the building was old, but if what Emil said was accurate, it could have been built centuries before their own time.

"We should find the cure nearby," said Emil. He reached for a shelf as he spoke, and Nier thought he saw it shudder. Suddenly, a book flew out from the shelf as though pulled by an invisible hand. It had a deep crimson cover and seemed to glower at them as it floated in midair.

"This book's kinda like you, Weiss," said Nier as he noted the face on the cover. But the new tome didn't start monologuing like Grimoire Weiss, instead emitting a harsh cackling laugh that grated on Nier's ears. Somewhere in the middle, there was even a kind of introduction:

I am Grimoire Rubrum.

"Ho, aren't we clever!" Grimoire Weiss replied, his voice dripping with sarcasm. "As if any mere tome could compare to the wonderment that is Grimoire Weiss!"

Indifferent to Weiss's indignation, Grimoire Rubrum began flying about the room with terrifying speed, scattering paper everywhere. Settling in the center of the room, it swelled up as though to intimidate them, then flung its pages wide. They were the same deep crimson as the cover, and as Nier and Weiss watched, sheets detached themselves from the tome and flew toward them like daggers.

"They are sharp as knives!" Grimoire Weiss cried.

"Guess you never learned that trick, huh?" Nier quipped.

Grimoire Weiss remained silent—a clear sign the answer was no.

"Stay behind me!" Emil shouted.

As the battle began in earnest, Nier and Weiss distanced themselves from Rubrum and moved behind Emil. The boy shifted his blindfold as he had done with the Shades and spiders, then turned his gaze to the book. The crimson pages fell to the ground, becoming stone slabs that shattered upon impact.

"Petrification is a fearsome power indeed," Grimoire Weiss remarked.

More pages flew out of Grimoire Rubrum. Yet no matter how many Nier cut apart with his blade or Emil turned to stone, there was no end in sight.

"I can't petrify it!" cried a desperate Emil. And indeed, there was a faint red mist enveloping Grimoire Rubrum—a defensive barrier. Nier recalled the statues at the Lost Shrine using a similar defensive strategy. No matter how hard he hacked at the barrier or how much magic he unleashed, he'd been unable to even dent the things. Making matters worse, the stone statues could only keep up their barrier while standing still, whereas Grimoire Rubrum was flying around without a care in the world.

They were so busy trying to avoid its attacks, they had no time to go on the offensive. At one point, the tome slammed against Nier—barrier and all—and his sword nearly flew from his hand. He would be done for if that hit landed again.

As the red book approached him again, a shrill noise cut through the chaos. Familiar twin blades clashed against the barrier and Grimoire Rubrum, sending both flying.

"Kainé!"

"And where have you been, hmmm?" demanded Grimoire Weiss, who couldn't be bothered to thank her for the assistance.

"Lost. Where've you been?"

"Getting stomped by this thing!" Nier shouted. "Help!"

The Shade's signature black mist had enveloped Kainé's left hand, an indication she had power greater than any normal human. Grimoire Rubrum seemed to notice this, because it suddenly turned its aggression against her.

"This foe's strength is beyond measure!" Grimoire Weiss yelled. It could have been either a warning or advice, but Kainé ignored him completely and thrust her swords into their enemy. Yet Grimoire Rubrum was on its guard now, and the attack only bounced harmlessly away.

"What do we do?!" Nier cried, flustered.

"I am an arcane text, not a manual of combat," Grimoire Weiss replied, defeat unusually prominent in his voice. "You are supposed to deal with such matters."

"You guys run!" Emil called as he stepped toward the other book. "I'll hold it off while you escape!"

"Who's this kid?" Kainé grunted as she tried and failed to eliminate the barrier once more.

"That's Emil! He's the one who runs this—"

"Fuck! This book is a real asshole!"

Kainé didn't listen to a word Nier said and had clearly thrown strategy out the window in favor of pure rage. Unfortunately, Grimoire Rubrum's attacks were growing more intense. It was hard to say how intelligent the tome was, but it was at least smart enough to start choosing attacks that matched, if not surpassed, the ones it was receiving.

"You guys go!" Emil called again. "This is my fight. I can't ask you to die for me!"

"Bold words," Grimoire Weiss remarked. "And yet I fear that would be a foolish course of action at this juncture."

"Besides—" Nier began, but before he could finish his sentence, Kainé flew across the room with a single leg extended into a kick that would have smashed his nose in if he'd been leaning any farther forward.

"Would you all please shut the hell up?!" she cried. "Seriously, if you bastards wanna have a goddamn civilized discussion on the merits of bravery and sacrifice, we can do it *later*!"

Emil's mouth fell open, his mind reeling at how many bad words he'd just learned in the span of a few seconds.

But the kick did the trick—the barrier shattered upon impact. The moment it did, Nier launched an attack of his own, but Grimoire Rubrum immediately began reconstituting its defense.

"It's just her way of encouraging us," Nier explained to Emil, who was still standing there dumbfounded.

"Have we truly sunk to motivational speeches from a woman in her undergarments?" Grimoire Weiss asked dubiously.

"Guess so!" Nier replied, slamming his blade into Grimoire Rubrum. His physical sword was more effective than magic while the barrier was up—or at least that seemed to be the case based on Kainé's messy attacks.

As he doled out strike after strike, he noticed Grimoire

Rubrum's movements slowed at certain times; keeping the barrier up while moving seemed to require a great deal of effort.

"There!" Grimoire Weiss exclaimed. "Strike the book as soon as it stops!"

Nier put all his power into his attacks, waiting for the barrier to rip open. Almost . . . *Almost* . . .

"Now!"

Nier slammed his sword into the tome at Kainé's command. Grimoire Rubrum shuddered, its energy depleted. But Nier took no chances; he struck their foe again, then fired off a continual stream of magic. This was enough: Grimoire Rubrum flew into the air with a groan before shattering into a million pieces. As its scattered pages fluttered to the ground, Nier spotted one that contained the word *petrification* and reached for it.

"Weiss! This is it!"

"Research Report on Petrification . . . Well, well!"

Since Grimoire Weiss contained all of humanity's wisdom, Nier had suspected Grimoire Rubrum must contain special knowledge as well. It was nice to see that assumption proven correct.

"Oh no," said Emil as he glanced at the page. "This passage is written in some sort of code. We went through all this trouble to find it, and . . . Oh, I'm so sorry."

It made sense that the thing would be written in code, considering whoever wrote it down went to the trouble of hiding it in such a dangerous tome.

"It's not your fault," replied Nier.

"Oh, look," said a deadpan Kainé from the corner of the room. "Jeeves is back."

"Jeeves?"

Kainé jerked her chin to gesture at the butler, who was crossing the room in a series of perfect strides. "Please allow me to handle this, Master Emil. I shall put all of my efforts into deconstructing this cipher. No matter how long it takes, I will not fail."

"Sebastian . . ."

"Ah, so the servant has a name after all," Grimoire Weiss murmured in surprise. Emil had only ever referred to him as the butler, so everyone had forgotten that a name was even a possibility.

"I'm glad this was worth the effort," Nier said.

"And we've reaped great benefits for ourselves as well," boasted Grimoire Weiss.

"Wait, does that mean what I think it means?"

"Indeed it does, lad! We've obtained a Sealed Verse—and I believe this is the last one."

Nier's eyes went wide. "The last one?"

"Yes. We have all of them now."

Their mission was coming to an end. Having collected the Sealed Verses, all that was left was to vanquish Grimoire Noir and purge calamity from the world. The day of Yonah's salvation was very close now.

"Soon . . ." whispered Nier as his hands trembled with joy. "It won't be much longer now."

REPORT 07

I was shocked when Nier told me that he, Grimoire Weiss, and the Shade woman had gone
to the haunted mansion near Seafront. Apparently the butler there had been sending letters
to Yonah—although they didn't understand the
full story until they arrived. Once there, they
ended up fighting a tome that looked like Grimoire Weiss, then becoming friends with the
master of the manor. The whole story was so
confusing it made my eyes spin around like
little jackpots, but Grimoire Weiss thankfully
filled me in on the details later.

According to Nier, the manor was dark even
during the day, full of strange tricks, and was
a generally unpleasant place all around. Grimoire Weiss also apparently made a big deal
about hauntings and ghosts the entire time.
(That much is apparent based on how unhappy
the tome seemed when I brought the topic up.)
It's no big shocker that the manor isn't normal
considering what happened there, but that's
not something Nier needs to know about.

What *is* strange is Grimoire Rubrum's presence. I thought its jurisdiction was elsewhere,
but . . . No, never mind. It's not a topic important enough to share, and I'm just getting
sidetracked.

Either way, the whole matter was settled

by the time Nier told me about it—an ex post facto report, if you will. He's been doing that a lot lately, and I wish he'd talk to me before going off and causing trouble, even if there's only so much Popola and I can do.

I did tell him I was excited to learn more about this Emil character. I claimed it was because I wanted to meet a fellow musician, but in reality, I want to know *exactly* what he and Nier spoke about, and what sort of information Emil might have let slip. It represents another irregularity, one which might have an influence on the next generation.

This was another long one, but we're done now. End of report.

Record written by Devola

The Seal

1.

NIER PUT THE flower in a little cup and placed it by Yonah's pillow. Though rather wilted, the blossom still retained its floral scent.

"That smells nice," Yonah murmured.

"I picked it on the way back from the southern plains. Emil told me about it."

"How's my friend? Is he okay?"

"Yeah. He says hi."

Sebastian the butler continued writing letters to Yonah even after obtaining the petrification documents from Grimoire Rubrum. He clearly felt bad for the housebound girl, and likely saw a similarity between her situation and that of his master. When Nier dropped by the house to thank him for the continued letters, he found the manor grounds enveloped in their usual frigid air. Of course, poor Grimoire Weiss had been on edge the entire time.

"It won't be much longer, Yonah," Nier said as he placed a hand on Yonah's forehead. "I have all the Sealed Verses. Now I just need to find Grimoire Noir."

But therein lay the problem: Nier didn't know where to begin looking for Grimoire Noir. He wasn't even sure if the tome was under someone's care or sealed away like Grimoire Weiss had been. Emil had offered to check his library for records, but that was a long shot at best. Sadly, Yonah didn't have much time left—and whenever that thought crossed Nier's mind, he found himself overwhelmed by panic.

"That sounds dangerous," said Yonah, pulling her brother's thoughts back to the present. Her eyes were glassy with fever, her voice weak. "Will you be okay?"

"Of course. I'll be fine."

"Are you su—"

Her question was cut off by yet another coughing fit. It was the cold, dry cough of the Black Scrawl, one that seemed especially bad today. Worried, Nier told Yonah to lie on her side and began rubbing her back.

"Is your plan . . . gonna make me better?" she asked between coughs.

"Of course. That's why you need to rest."

Nier needed to find Grimoire Noir as soon as possible. He would turn over any stone and examine any lead, no matter how slight. Anything so Yonah didn't have to feel pain anymore.

"You're not gonna hate me because of this, right?" she asked suddenly.

"What are you talking about?"

"It's just . . . I don't want you to hate me because of this terrible disease."

"I could never hate you!" he cried, his voice much louder than he intended. "Sorry. Look, I'm gonna go see if Popola has more medicine, okay? I'll be right back."

Nier dashed out of the room and down the stairs. He felt so terrible for Yonah that he could barely look at her. *If only I could take her place*, he thought for what must have been the thousandth time.

The sun was bright when he went outside. No clouds crossed the sky; the shadows on the ground were dark. The leaves and grass were almost unbearably green; the birds and insects screeched loudly in his ear. The world was so full of vibrant, thriving life, and yet . . .

"Yonah's looking weaker every day," he said sadly.

"Do not lose heart, lad," Grimoire Weiss replied. "You are the girl's last hope."

The book was right: This was no time to mope. They had all the Sealed Verses, and so long as the tome was by his side, they would find Grimoire Noir. He was certain of it.

Heartened slightly, Nier ran to the library, burst into Popola's office, and told her he needed more medicine. Normally, she would have stood up and brought him something to ease Yonah's symptoms, but this time she remained seated at her desk with a furrowed brow.

"The thing is, I actually just ran out. But I can make some for you if you gather the materials."

"Of course."

"I need vapor moss. You'll find it growing near the southern gate."

The village's general rule was that medicinal plants were to be harvested from different spots at different times of the year. That way, if someone needed a lot all at once, they would already be growing back somewhere else. It seemed the best place to find vapor moss today was by the southern gate.

"I'll be right back," said Nier. He bolted out of the office and ran for the southern gate. Popola's cough suppressant worked well, and he wanted to get it to Yonah as soon as possible.

As Popola had said, there was a thick cluster of vapor moss growing by the southern gate. He hurriedly grabbed handfuls and stuffed them into his bag, filling it almost to the brim. Having done this countless times before, the harvesting didn't take long.

"We need to get back to P—"

"Over there, lad!" Grimoire Weiss exclaimed suddenly.

"Emil?!"

The boy should have been in the manor, yet he was currently staggering toward Nier and Weiss. Thankfully, his blindfold was on, so there was no risk of petrification. Though Nier continued calling out, Emil just kept stumbling forward. When he got close, Nier realized he was breathing far too heavily to manage even a meager response.

When he was nearly at their position, Emil collapsed to the ground. As Nier rushed forward to help him, he realized the boy's forehead was damp with sweat; he'd likely run all the way here from his manor.

"—rry . . ." whispered Emil.

"What?"

"H-hurry . . ."

With that, Emil fell unconscious. Nier immediately slung him over his shoulders and ran back to the library, where Popola directed him to lay the boy on a bench and loosen his clothes.

"He doesn't seem to be sick," Popola said after looking him over. "Still, I can't imagine how hard it must have been to run all this way without sight. We should just let him rest; he's strained himself both physically and in spirit."

"Thanks, Popola," said a relieved Nier, who was still amazed Emil had managed to make it all the way across the southern plains from the manor. Even though he could use his petrification powers on the Shades, it couldn't have been an easy—or safe—journey.

"Still, why did he do something so . . ."

Reckless, is what Nier was going to say, but instead he fell silent. He'd heard a loud, deep sound in the distance, something that was neither thunder nor earthquake.

As he listened, Emil moaned, then stirred. "Are you all right, Emil?!" Nier asked.

Emil didn't answer, but the corners of his mouth twisted in pain. "I can . . . see it," he said, reaching out as if trying to grasp something.

"Hey, whoa. Just take it easy, okay?"

Emil shook his head. "The air . . . It's vibrating . . . I can feel it behind my eyes . . . Get out."

"Get out from where?"

Emil opened his mouth, but the deep sound of an impact interrupted him—a sound more terrifying than any Nier had heard in his entire life.

2.

THE SKY IS *a weird color,* Kaïné mused as she gazed up. The sun was shining; the shadows at her feet were a deep black. The sky should have been clear and blue, yet instead it was a sulfurous white. It was a color she saw in the northern plains about once a year.

Thick clouds began to blanket the odd-colored sky. As gray hid the sun from view, the shadows on the ground faded. It looked like it was going to rain, yet the air was dry. It was perfect Shade weather.

A wave of goose bumps traveled up the left half of Kaïné's body as Tyrann sprang to life.

"Here it comes, Sunshine!"

She didn't need him to tell her that; she already knew *something* was on the way. Every pore in her body began dripping sweat, an indication some great and terrible power was approaching.

"Oh man, I think it's coming toward—"

Nier's village.

Kaïné ran the moment she felt the ground rumble, as fast and as hard as she ever had in her life. She could hear the sound even without Tyrann's help—the sound of destruction and slaughter.

"Aw, you wanna help? How altruistic! I'm cryin' over here!"

A wry smile crossed her face. She owed nothing to those people and had no intention of helping them. All she cared about was destroying the Shades she expected to find attacking the village.

While her journey for vengeance ended when she felled the monster that killed her grandmother, she continued to hunt Shades because of Nier. He'd called her a friend, and since he was hunting Shades to collect Sealed Verses (and sometimes to help people), she decided to aid him as a friend would.

And now that Nier's village was being targeted by a Shade a magnitude more powerful than any they'd faced before, there was only one thing to do.

Kainé already had a grasp on the situation when she reached the path leading to the northern gate. Screams and the smell of burning struck her like a slap. She sensed Shades—a hodgepodge assortment in all shapes and sizes—and one intensely powerful presence that stood out from the rest.

When she reached the gate, she found it shut tight; the Shades must have chosen a different entrance. Cursing softly, she whirled on her heel. She didn't have time to take the long way around to the eastern gate, which meant her only choice was to scramble up the stone walls surrounding the village. It was a task beyond any normal human, but the power granted to her by Tyrann made it very doable. Yet as she scanned the area for climbing surfaces, she suddenly froze.

There was a mountain beyond the wall—and it was *moving*.

A moment later she realized it was no mountain, but a Shade—a black mass of death that towered impossibly over the village. This was the incredible presence she'd sensed earlier, the one that nearly blotted out all the others.

Her plan to find an easily climbable surface went by the wayside; she had to reach the big Shade's blind spot, and she had to do it *now*. One reckless leap later, she'd hooked a foot into the wall and begun clambering up.

The massive Shade didn't seem to notice the woman rushing toward it with the intent of harm. Still, Kainé knew that approaching in its blind spot wasn't a fail-safe plan. Shades could sense one another, and that included Tyrann.

Of course, there were other options at play. Perhaps the creature had noticed her and just didn't give a damn. A Shade's power was generally proportionate to its size, which meant Tyrann held as much importance as a fly. Or maybe it was misjudging her, thinking it was impossible that one of its own kind would attack. Either way, things were temporarily working in her favor.

Once she cleared the wall, Kainé planted a foot on the ground, gave thanks once more for her superhuman strength, and launched herself at the back of the Shade's head with swords raised high.

"*Yeee-haw!*" screamed Tyrann in her mind. "*Now, THIS is fun!*"

"Hell yeah it is."

"*Kill it! Kill it; kill it; KILL IT!*"

As Kainé let gravity bring her swords down with even more force, a massive shock coursed up her arms. She leaped away and landed on the ground as the Shade collapsed behind her in a cloud of dust. It was almost *too* easy.

"You guys havin' a good time?" she cried at a startled Nier and Weiss. Nier's eyes immediately went wide, and Kainé figured he was just impressed she'd managed to bring the thing down in a single hit. But that wasn't what he was thinking at all.

"*It didn't work, Sunshine! It didn't do a goddamn thing!*"

There was no need to turn around and look; she could sense the creature behind her. Despite putting all of her strength and all of her being into the attack, the thing hadn't even been weakened.

"Keep hitting it!" she cried. "At some point, it's gotta start working!"

"Is she trying to raise our morale, or is she honestly that insane?"

Of course Weiss had an opinion on the subject. He really did use an infuriating number of words for a book—or maybe he just couldn't help himself because, you know. Book. But before she could ask the floating magazine who the fuck he thought cared about his opinion, Nier spoke up: "Either one works for me. Let's go!"

After that, Kainé's world became a whirling, bloody battle. She sliced and she sliced and she sliced, putting her swords to the test as never before. But not only was her foe bigger than any respectable Shade, it regenerated at an *unbelievable* rate. When she chopped off an arm, a new one was growing in its place. When she managed to remove a leg, flesh was covering the wound before the limb hit the ground.

By the time the titan finally lay still, Kainé's sword arms were numb; had she and Nier not been working together, they would never have brought it down. Her shoulders heaved with ragged breaths as she watched its massive black limbs lose definition and melt away. Looking up, she saw deeply gouged earth and an entire village in ruin. And while she wanted to take cheer from the fact they'd managed to stop the Shade when they did, she also felt regret for permitting it to sow such destruction.

Her time mulling over profound thoughts ended with an ear-shattering scream from somewhere behind her. Whirling around, she saw it was coming from a large brick building—the library, apparently. Nier immediately screamed his sister's name and took off running.

"Ya see? That big lug wasn't the only Shade here. You feel it, don't ya? You hear *it, can't ya? Their words—"*

Shut up, Tyrann! I don't need a goddamn play-by-play! I'm

gonna grab every last one of those bastards and tear their eyeballs out through their assholes!

Kainé rushed up the hill and burst into the building. She'd been in rooms that served as libraries before—including the one in Emil's manor—but never an entire *building*. But even though this was her first time in a real library, she instantly knew something was wrong, because this many Shades shouldn't be squirming around in *any* building.

Mind you, the library in Emil's manor had had Shades in it, but not this many. And really, those shouldn't have been there either.

Suddenly, Nier called out Emil's name, causing the boy in question to stop what he was doing and whirl around.

The hell? Kainé wondered. *He doesn't live here. He should be back in his crappy-ass house trying to decipher that code.*

Emil was busy fighting the Shades, trying desperately to protect the people who'd sought refuge in the library. But since he was still blindfolded, his steps were wild and uncertain.

"You can't keep fighting like this!" Nier cried as he swiped at the Shades swarming Emil. This caused the boy to stagger again, and Kainé suddenly realized he was moving that way not because he couldn't see, but because he was seriously hurt.

Kainé knew Emil's hearing was incredible and his instincts sharp, but the kid had clearly pushed himself beyond his limits. He couldn't fight off all these Shades in the best of conditions, much less when he was clearly unwell. He needed to be extracted from the situation pronto.

"Get out of here, Emil!" she cried. But before she could say any more, Emil cut her off.

"No! I won't abandon these people!" Emil's voice grew louder as he spoke. "You once told me that my eyes had value, and that

I shouldn't be ashamed of them! You told me that even a life like mine had purpose!"

Emil's words pierced her heart like an arrow. From the moment they'd first met—no, the very *second*—she could tell he was shunning his own power. In the battle they'd fought together, the moment he'd shouted, "You guys go! This is my fight!" reminded Kainé of the version of herself from long ago—the version from before she met Nier and learned what friendship was.

That was why, as they parted, she'd brushed her fingers over Emil's blindfold and said:

Your eyes are not a sin.

There were people in this world who would lash out at what was different without a second thought—a truth Kainé knew from a lifetime of experience. People rejected her and held her in contempt, and before long, she assumed they were right and it was all her fault. It was her grandmother who'd finally righted that misconception, and she'd wanted to do the same for Emil.

Don't ever be ashamed of them. They're a vital part of you.

She had taken Emil's hand and placed it on the left side of her arm—the portion where Tyrann squirmed beneath her skin. *You're not the only one* is what she'd wanted to tell him. *You are not alone.*

This arm is an accursed weapon.

Emil had gasped when she'd said that. He must have understood that what he was touching was inhuman.

I thought I would only need it until I earned my revenge.

And earn it she had. She'd been ready to die at that point, but once she'd gained friends, the option of a meaningless death was no longer one she was willing to consider.

But now I use it to keep my friends safe.

Kainé . . .

There's a reason I'm alive—that my arm is alive. And there's a reason for your eyes too.

A reason to live. A future. A future every child should have a chance to seize, one where a horrible power did not mean you had to surrender everything that mattered.

Keep going—always. Never give up. You'll find your answers. Those words—the last she'd spoken to Emil until seeing him again in the village library—had encouraged him to act as he did.

"I can't stop now!" cried Emil, snapping Kainé back to reality. "I won't just sit around and let you fight while I stay behind! I want to use this power to protect my friends!"

I can't hold him back any more than this, Kainé thought, especially since she'd do the same thing in his place. She knew better than anyone how much force was behind the desire to protect what mattered.

"Just don't die on me," she said finally. Emil was clearly forgoing his own safety to take on the enemy, but those five words were the best she could come up with to hold him back somewhat.

"I won't, Kainé! Now let's take care of these shit-hogs!"

His word choice mimicked one Kainé had made earlier and was so out of character that she burst into laughter.

"Right on," she cried. "I like it!"

Emil turned to the Shades and let fly a volley of magic. A spray of reddish-black liquid came pouring out of them as they fell dead to the ground. The boy not only possessed petrification powers, but offensive and restorative magic as well. Though his appearance was that of a helpless child, he was a reliable ally on the battlefield.

Meanwhile, Kainé swiped through a group of Shades and felt a satisfying weight against her blades as they went flying.

"Does this mean you're done with buddy-buddy time?"

Kainé ignored Tyrann's mocking voice and kicked another set

of nearby Shades aside. The creature inside her was screaming, a high-pitched wail of utter delight. He didn't care that his fellow Shades were being slaughtered—if anything, he *enjoyed* it. He pleaded with her to continue killing, to slaughter the Shades, to let him bathe in the blood. So unspeakable was his glee that it made Kainé want to cover her ears.

This was made worse by the fact that Kainé could hear what the Shades were saying. Tyrann's Shade senses had become part of her own, which gave her the ability to understand their language. Most of the time, their utterances were meaningless strings of individual words, but they sometimes resembled actual phrases. Yet she knew their talk sounded like random noises to Nier and Emil, because it had sounded like that to her before she was possessed.

Finally, the cries for help and death screams came to an end. The library was free of Shades. Nier and Emil stared at her, relief washing over their faces. Weiss was also looking at her, and though his face never changed, she figured he felt the same emotions inside.

"We can't let any more Shades in here," said Emil. "Let's bar the do—"

Before he could say more, the door burst open and sent him flying across the room. As Nier called out to their friend, Kainé readjusted the grip on her swords, readying herself for a new Shade.

But the black mass that had sent Emil flying wasn't new at all; it was the head of the massive Shade they'd supposedly killed. Though they'd watched its limbs melt into nothingness, they'd left, distracted by the screams coming from the library, before making sure the rest of it had done the same.

"Is there no way to kill this infernal thing?!" Grimoire Weiss yelled.

"Shit," muttered Kainé. They should have made sure the

entire body crumbled to dust—or at the very least *she* should have stayed behind. But it was too late for regrets now.

If I have time to mope, I have time to fight. If we didn't kill it outside, we'll just kill it in here.

Kainé ran to the head and slammed her blades across it, watching the gaping wound close in an instant. Nier hacked and slashed. Emil fired volley after volley of magic. But aside from causing the occasional spray of black liquid, their attacks did nothing whatsoever.

"It's healing too quickly!" Grimoire Weiss exclaimed.

It was the first time Kainé had heard the book yell like that— it almost sounded like a scream. His panic spoke to how stupefyingly fast the Shade was healing. On top of that, losing its limbs didn't seem to affect it at all. If anything, it only made the damn thing faster.

"Please tell me somebody has an idea!" cried Nier.

Kainé swung her blades with even more fervor, trying to drown out his desperate voice. When needed, Emil cast recovery magic. Kainé couldn't do that. And though she was loath to admit it, Weiss's wisdom was another useful trait she lacked. Swinging with all her might was the only action she could take to fulfill her role as a friend.

"Perhaps we could chase it to the basement and seal it there," Grimoire Weiss offered. "Those walls are thick rock; I doubt even this beast could break them."

It was as if the book had read her mind and decided to demonstrate said wisdom. "Great!" Kainé exclaimed. "I love basements!"

Unfortunately, the concept was better in theory than in practice. Because the Shade was now nothing but a head, it moved at an unbelievable speed, and guiding it to the basement was an exercise in frustration. The only thing the companions could do was continue their assault, block off escape routes, and slowly—*very* slowly—push it toward the back of the room.

Each slice of Kainé's blades was met with a spray of reddish black and a terribly unpleasant smell. The liquid that pooled on the floor was starting to look a lot like blood and made the battlefield slippery to boot.

Despite that, they had no choice but to push on in their onslaught. They hacked and slashed and sliced and diced, but the massive Shade's head showed no signs of weakening. After a while, Kainé started to wonder if they would run out of energy before the basement ever became an option.

Just as her hands were going completely numb, she heard Weiss cry out. The door to the basement was now open—either Nier or Emil had managed it during the chaos.

"Do it!" cried Weiss. "Knock it down the basement!"

As Nier pushed the head through the door, Kainé threw it shut and slammed her back against it. "Gimme the key!" she yelled. "Hurry!"

She extended a hand as Nier rushed over with the key in hand. The door was solid—it could surely hold the monstrosity back long enough for them to lock it in.

But then, Nier froze. The key flew from his hand. His eyes widened in disbelief as what looked to be a giant black thorn suddenly exploded out of his shoulder.

Kainé couldn't comprehend what she was looking at. A black thorn had erupted from one of the pools of liquid on the ground. But how was that even *possible*?

The thorn suddenly retracted into the pool, causing Nier to collapse. Liquid the same color as that on the floor gushed from his wound. As Kainé watched in horror, the pools swelled and undulated before forming into the shadowy figure of a man—one who either had wings sprouting from his back or preferred to wear *very* ugly cloaks.

The shadow-man moved. His wings unfurled as he began soaring across the library. Kainé had thought the Shade-head was fast, but it was nothing compared to this. Books scattered with each pass the shadow form made around the room, causing hundreds of tomes to explode in the air. Scraps of paper rained down in a white blizzard, leaving Kainé with no idea where her new and terrifying enemy had gone.

"*Whoa,*" murmured an astonished Tyrann. "*This is a piece of bad news. I mean, you know who this guy is, right? C'mon, you GOTTA know!*"

Sure. He was the same as the creatures that had covered this entire floor not moments ago, the same as the massive head held in place behind her by a single wooden door. He was a Shade.

And yet, he was somehow *so* much more than that; his presence was thicker and more foreboding than any Shade she'd ever encountered. A piece of bad news indeed, but as to Tyrann's question, she had no idea *who* he actually was.

The wind came to a sudden stop. The shadowy man stopped in his tracks, which caused thousands of fluttering pages to begin the long journey to the floor below.

"YONAH!" cried Nier.

The shadow held Nier's sister in his arms. Her eyes were closed, her body perfectly still. Though he seemed to have been flying around haphazardly, it turned out he had been looking for Nier's sister the entire time.

Shades of varying sizes began emerging from the pool on the floor. They staggered toward the shadow, then came to their knees before him, almost as though . . .

"Is that the leader of these creatures?" Grimoire Weiss murmured, echoing the thought that had just entered Kainé's mind.

The leader turned to Weiss and extended a hand, at which point another tome floated up beside him. It looked similar to Grimoire Weiss, both because of the face on the cover and the size. Could this be the one Nier had been so desperately searching for?

Before Kainé could think more on that, a strange light suddenly erupted in midair. Nier's face twisted in pain from his position on the floor, while Grimoire Weiss groaned as though he had been attacked.

"No! Stay back, Kainé!"

Nier's voice halted Kainé in her tracks; she'd started moving before she even realized it. She likely would have dashed forward in an attempt to save her friends, completely forgetting about the danger behind her, had he not stopped her.

"You have to seal the door!"

Kainé was trapped. She couldn't move from her spot, and yet the strange attacks were still ravaging Grimoire Weiss. At this rate, both he and Nier would meet their ends before long.

"Yeah, this looks bad, all right! You got the Shadowlord himself in front of you and Mr. Massive Head behind you. Looks like you and your little friends are screwed from all directions!"

No, we're not!

"Aw, really? C'mon, just give in already. Gimme your body. Not like you have any reason to keep living once your pwecious widdle fwiends are dead, right? Riiiight?"

Wrong! This isn't over! Nier and Weiss and Emil are still alive!

"Not for much longer! Hell, that book's writing his last will and testament while you and I sit here and gab!"

Though pain still colored Nier's face, Weiss had fallen silent. It was almost as if he'd been cut off from the rest of them just before some unknowable force stole him away for good.

"Our . . . ultimate goal . . ." intoned Grimoire Weiss, "fuse . . . Shadowlord . . . Become one . . ."

As the incomprehensible string of words spilled from Gri-moire Weiss's mouth, Tyrann began cackling with glee.

"Now THOSE are some last words if I've ever heard 'em! Hell, you remember what it was like with a special someone else, right, Sunshine? You and your precious grandmama?"

Shut the fuck up! This isn't the same, and those are NOT his last words!

A sudden rage enveloped Kainé, lending her voice a strength she didn't know it possessed until she began to scream.

"Weiss, you *dumbass*! Start making sense, you rotten book, or you're gonna be sorry! Maybe I'll rip your pages out, one-by-one! Or maybe I'll put you in the goddamn furnace! How can someone with such a big smart brain get hypnotized like a little bitch, huh? Oh, Shadowlord! I love you, Shadowlord! Come over here and give Weiss a big sloppy kiss, Shadowlord! Now pull your head out of your goddamn ass and *start fucking helping us!*"

Amazingly, this caused no response at all; Weiss simply continued floating toward the black book, repeating nonsensical words like *paradise* and *unite* in a monotone voice.

"Dammit!" Kainé yelled again. "If we don't do something, that black book will absorb Weiss!"

Nier stood, blood spilling from the wound in his shoulder, and managed to wheeze out the name of his companion.

"Ha! Keep trying, kiddos, but it ain't gonna work! You're all gonna die! You're done! Finito!"

Keep running your mouth, pal. We're not gonna lose!

"Yes!" cried the black book suddenly. "Now we shall unite in common purpose!" Its laugh echoed through the library, its voice dripping with malice. The face on the cover, the haughty attitude—Kainé hated it all. There was no doubt this was Gri-moire Noir, the creature of myth that brought plague to all.

"Now the world can finally bear witness to our true power!" it declared pompously as it neared Grimoire Weiss.

"Weiss!" cried Nier again. "WEISS!"

The tome shuddered as though rejecting Nier's call. The shuddering grew in intensity until shock waves began rolling off him. A sudden flash of light exploded, forcing Kainé to close her eyes. A moment later, a high-pitched whine nearly shattered her eardrums.

"For the last time . . ."

Kainé was stunned. Never had an utterance so arrogant sounded so reassuring. As if waiting for the rest of the sentence, the world became perfectly still.

"My name is Grimoire Weiss, and it is NOT to be abbreviated!"

Relief stole the strength in Kainé's legs, but she could not let them buckle with the massive Shade still slamming against the door behind her. Instead, she gritted her teeth and planted her feet firmly on the ground.

"Good to see you, Kainé," Grimoire Weiss said as he turned to her. "Although I don't think anyone has ever accused me of being a little bitch before."

She could feel Tyrann sulking, upset he'd been off the mark.

Nier staggered toward his companion. "Weiss . . . You okay?"

"I believe I could ask you the same question right now."

Grimoire Weiss was back to his usual self—a sarcastic, endless fount of needless lectures, yet also a busybody and worrywart. Just as it truly sank in that Weiss was back on their side, Grimoire Noir muttered a single word:

"Impossible!"

The relief Kainé and the rest of her friends felt was cause for an outcry from the black book. "We must unite!" it cried. "We must become as one!"

"I don't like you . . . And I want nothing to do with you,"

spat Grimoire Weiss. "Besides, I have my companions. Of course, they're weak, and they whine when I leave . . . It's almost too much trouble . . . But they are my friends! I shall fight by their side. Now . . . and forever!"

As he said that, strength returned to Nier's unsteady steps. Kainé wanted to grab one of her swords and immediately join the fight, but she had to keep the door shut lest the force behind it suddenly be unleashed into the room.

"Weiss?" said Nier suddenly. "What's wrong?"

"I can't use my magic! That fiend has stolen the Sealed Verses!"

"I'll get them back!"

Nier dashed toward Grimoire Noir with Emil hot on his heels. Shades began bubbling up around them again, but Nier shoved them aside and focused a relentless attack on Grimoire Noir. He moved so swiftly, so powerfully, that Kainé almost forgot he was severely injured. She hated that she could do nothing but watch.

"We have reclaimed my powers!" Grimoire Weiss declared suddenly.

"Damn you!" Grimoire Noir yelled. "Our true memories are still there! How dare you ignore them?!"

"Perhaps you should have scribbled them in my margins, hmm?"

Kainé had heard that Grimoire Weiss had lost his memory. Were those the true memories Grimoire Noir spoke of?

That was all the time she had to leisurely wonder about such things before the hinges on the door against her back began to creak ominously. Slowly, she lifted her head to look at them. Every time the massive head slammed against the door, the screws holding the hinges in place came out a fraction of a millimeter.

She immediately cursed. They'd been confident the door was sturdy enough to keep the creature in place, but the thickest door in the world didn't mean squat if the goddamn *hinges* couldn't hold.

Nier and Weiss's assault on Grimoire Noir was unfolding before her. They had eliminated all the Shades and appeared to have the upper hand, but the Shadowlord hadn't moved once the entire time, which worried Kainé.

With a snap, one of the hinges flew loose and skittered across the floor. How long could the remaining one last?

Kainé poured more strength into her arms and planted her heels into the ground. One of the remaining screws fell at her feet as if mocking her. She couldn't keep this up for long. Even if they managed to defeat Grimoire Noir and the Shadowlord, could they subdue the head on top of it?

No. They couldn't. In fact, it was precisely *because* the head was unbeatable that they'd decided to lock it in the basement.

Suddenly, Grimoire Noir began casting a spell. The book's outline melted away and took the form of a pitch-black sphere. Then that changed as well, and by the time Kainé realized it was the same shape as the thorn that had sprung from the puddle, the projectile was rocketing straight for Grimoire Weiss. Before she could cry a warning, Nier threw himself in front of it.

"No!" cried Weiss.

He was right. No. It was impossible. It could not be.

The thorn had pierced Nier's chest.

What had he even been *thinking*?! Nothing, most likely. The thorn was threatening Weiss, so he jumped in the way. He didn't think about himself; his only concern had been to protect his friend.

"You will understand in time," Grimoire Noir said as Nier

slumped to the floor. "No matter how things unfold, it all returns to us. All of it."

As if on cue, the Shadowlord spread his wings, Yonah still in his arms. Nier, a heap on the ground, desperately reached out for her.

"Give my sister back . . ." he croaked, his words empty as a tomb.

As the Shadowlord and Grimoire Noir broke through the crumbling ceiling and fled into the sky, another screw fell from above Kainé's shoulder.

Then another.

Then another.

The sky was visible through the ceiling, but the Shadowlord was nowhere to be seen. The color of the clouds, which had hung low and heavy not long ago, seemed thin. Perhaps they had been blown away by a stronger wind far above. It wouldn't be long before sunlight managed to pierce that scant cover.

"The fight's over," said Kainé. "And I think we lost."

There was an awful smell in her nose. She thought she'd gotten used to the putrid scent of blood and mud, but each breath now hit her like a hammer.

"We?" Emil repeated, lifting his gaze from where Nier was cradled in his arms.

"Sorry, guys. I think this is it for me too." There was nothing else for it—the door would be down in moments.

"Kainé, no!" Emil shouted in a voice thick with tears.

"Oh, quit crying."

Get a grip, she told herself. *If anyone sounds like they're gonna start crying, it's me.*

"Look, before I go, we need to take care of this guy."

At least she had a plan. Even if they couldn't kill the creature, they could still lock it away.

"*Whoa, hold on!*" cried Tyrann as he began to piece together what she intended to do. But this was her show now, and she paid him no mind.

"I want you to petrify me."

The corners of Emil's lips went lopsided. Even from a distance, Kainé could tell he was biting the inside of his mouth.

"You can use me to keep this thing locked away down there."

Even if Emil could, simply turning the door to stone would not be enough. This Shade was so powerful, it could live on even as just a head and would likely shatter a stone door with ease. They needed to fight fire with fire to seal it away for good—they needed the power of a Shade.

"Are you freakin' KIDDING me right now, Sunshine? You gone soft in the head or something? Because I am NOT cool with this!"

I didn't ask for your opinion, Tyrann—but feel free to leave my body if you want . . . Oh, that's right! You CAN'T!

Nier languidly lifted his head from Emil's arms. "Kainé . . ." he croaked. "Stop . . ."

"He's right!" Emil chimed in. "It's suicide! You can't do it."

Kainé smiled at him. "Your powers exist to protect others, right?"

I'll use my Shade to protect others too. That's been the plan for a long time now.

"Stop it, Sunshine! I don't want this!"

Tyrann began appearing on her skin but didn't attempt anything further. In truth, he *couldn't* do anything more than that, and though he might have been insane, he at least understood that much.

"Just do it, Emil," said Kainé.

"But—"

The more they argued, the more the door shuddered in its frame. Would it crack first, or would the remaining hinge finally pop free? Either way, no one would survive if things got to that point.

"We don't have a choice!"

After a moment that was both an instant and an eternity, Emil nodded. His slim shoulders and slender hands trembled as he untied his bandage. Large droplets rolled down his cheeks onto the floor below. It was the first time Kainé had ever seen his eyes, and they were *beautiful*.

"No more crying. Okay?"

Suddenly, she felt her limbs grow heavy. She tried to look down to see what was happening and found she couldn't move at all. The petrification had begun.

"Grow strong," she said to Nier. "Never lose hope."

Do it for your sister. Save her from the Shadowlord.

She didn't know if Nier replied—she knew only that he was there.

"*I don't want this!*" cried Tyrann from the depths of her increasingly foggy mind. "*I need more! I wanna kill more! Destroy more! I want to make your body my own and do whatever I want! No! No, no, no, no, noooo!*"

Though he was throwing an increasingly noisy fit, she could no longer feel the writhing left half of her body. As her field of vision began to darken and narrow, something popped up in front of her.

"Weiss . . ." she began.

"Spare me the goodbye, hussy. I imagine it will take more than this to kill you."

"Heh. I doubt it."

Brief as their time together had been, Nier, Weiss, and Emil were the friends whom she fought with—and the first people in her life ever worthy of the name. She would never forget them.

No matter how much time passed—and even from within walls of stone—she would never forget them.

All was quiet. The noise from moments earlier felt like a dream. Tyrann was silent. If this was her reward for turning to stone, then maybe it wasn't so bad after all.

And with that, Kainé's time stopped.

REPORT 08

This is a report on the Jack invasion that occurred five years ago, including what happened in the intervening years and up to the present situation.

As we detailed in the emergency report filed after the incident, the incursion by the creature code-named Jack was orchestrated by the Shadowlord. Its purpose was to use Jack to create a diversion, permitting the Shadowlord to kidnap Yonah.

Casualties were severe. There were a staggering amount of dead and injured, and most of the village was destroyed. The walls and ceiling of the library sustained substantial damage, and we hold little hope of ever repairing them. Additionally, Jack's head remains sealed away in the basement.

Though we had long feared an attack from the Shadowlord, it manifested in the worst possible way. We were lax in our awareness of the situation, and we paid the price.

Nier was despondent over the loss of his sister, and we feared for a time that his mind was permanently broken. He has thankfully calmed a bit after half a decade, and now devotes himself wholly to searching for his sister and slaughtering Shades.

But Nier is not the only unpredictable aspect

in our lives; every villager lives in an increasingly desperate state, and sightings of Shades have become commonplace. To be frank, we never expected things to get this bad.

The Shadowlord has remained completely out of sight since the incident, which means we still have time to get a handle on the situation. We must do all we can to avoid any setbacks on Project Gestalt, which means it is imperative to locate the Shadowlord and stop him by whatever means necessary. End report.

Record written by Popola

The Man 1

1.

THE WORLD WAS white. Nier slowed his steps and tilted his head. Every step created a creak in both sound and sensation. It felt like he was walking through the desert, but the colors were all wrong. Sand wasn't supposed to be white.

But this wasn't sand. It was salt.

He glanced at the narrow sky above and found a series of staggeringly tall buildings clustered together. Looking at them made him dizzy, so he quickly lowered his gaze. As he did, he spotted a red tower among the haphazardly placed structures. It was tall and thin, the tip bent slightly like a sword.

Suddenly, the red tower vanished; a powerful gust of wind had stirred the salt into the air, blocking it from view.

Strange. Had he always known this white powder was salt? He'd never tasted it or smelled it, after all. And while it felt exactly like sand, it looked more like snow. The way it sat in heaps around him reminded him of a picture book he'd read to Yonah as a child—the story of a girl from a cold, snowy land who was searching for a stolen boy.

Searching? Stolen?

Yonah.

I have to find her. The Shadowlord took her, and then . . .

Nier began to run. For some reason, he knew exactly where to go: a squat building located nearby.

I need to get back right now.

But why?

I killed them. I killed them all. I need to tell her it's okay.

Killed? Who? Shades? The Shadowlord?

No. That's not right. I haven't killed the Shadowlord yet.

As he rushed into a dim building, he noticed his feet had begun to make a dry, scraping sound. Looking down, he saw they were clad in a strange pair of shoes.

What are these?

His clothes were also odd, as was the stick in his hand. It was some kind of metal; its compact size belied an impressive weight. When he saw it was sullied with Shade blood, he understood it was a weapon.

How did I get this? And what about my sword? I hope I didn't lose it. That would be bad.

He whirled around, determined to find his trusty blade, when a thin voice stopped him in his tracks.

"You're back?"

It was the voice he'd been so desperate to hear. The one he'd been searching for this whole time.

It was Yonah.

But was it *really*? He was terrified of turning around to see for himself, despite knowing he could never mistake anyone else for her.

Finally, he forced himself to move. It was no mistake. He was not imagining things. She was there.

"Look," she said. "I found this while you were gone."

His sister was cradling a flat canister containing a single cookie. They were Yonah's favorite, and . . .

Hold on. How do I know there are cookies in there? And why is Yonah wearing those weird clothes?

"Here. We can split it."

Still, her clothes didn't matter. *Nothing* mattered so long as he finally got to see her.

"Yonah . . ."

As he leaned in to give her a hug, it dawned on him that she hadn't grown. It had been half a decade since she was stolen away, and yet the little girl before him was nowhere near twelve years of age.

His heart clenched when he thought about the missing time. Five years since the Shadowlord appeared. Five years since his only remaining family was taken—the little sister he loved more than life itself. He'd been through so much for her sake, and then she was just . . . gone. Not a day went by that he didn't think about her. She was a part of him always—even in his dreams.

Dreams.

This is a dream. Of course it is.

He suddenly understood why he wore such strange clothing. Why he wielded a metal pipe instead of a sword. Even the heaps of salt began to make a kind of sense.

This was all a dream.

"You need to eat," said Yonah, as she offered him half of the small cookie. She was smiling, which made him happy. All he wanted was to see her smile, even in dreams.

Forever.

"Yonah!"

As his cry escaped his lips, his vision went black.

"What is it now, lad?"

Another familiar voice—one that was the picture of eloquence, even if it did often overstep the line into general annoyance. A voice belonging to a friend of arcane power and outstanding intelligence.

"Hey, Weiss," murmured Nier. He opened his eyes to find the

tome floating near his head. This was his house, his sword was an arm's length away, and Yonah was nowhere to be found.

"I thought you a bit old for nightmares. What manner of midnight reverie had you crying aloud in your sleep?"

Nier knew he'd been dreaming but couldn't remember it. All he understood was that Yonah was there—the rest had melted into shadow the moment he'd opened his eyes.

"I don't know. But it couldn't have been that bad."

He could even consider it a happy dream because he got to see Yonah. And though he couldn't remember where he'd been, there was a strange sense of familiarity deep in his chest.

"Are you sure you've not contracted some other fell dream from the Forest of Myth?" asked Weiss cautiously. The tome had no desire to relive the Deathdream—an opinion Nier shared wholeheartedly. Thinking of this caused a wry smile to tug at his lips, remembering the troubles they went through five years ago. But this dream had clearly been no Deathdream, because he could remember the details of the Deathdream after waking up.

"I don't think so," he replied to Weiss. "I haven't been to the Forest of Myth in a long time."

"Yes, I suppose we've not heard tell of any Shades showing their faces there."

The lack of Shades didn't mean they couldn't pass through to see the villagers, but Nier simply hadn't made the time. Instead, he'd spent every waking moment of the past five years hunting Shades. He needed to find the Shadowlord and get Yonah back—and since that creature ruled over the Shades, he figured killing them would eventually lead him to his goal. They'd used the same strategy to track down the Sealed Verses, after all, and that had worked well enough.

To that end, he took on any job and ventured into any dark place that gave him the chance for slaughter, yet he came up empty-handed each time. He hadn't done enough searching. He needed to go to more places, *different* places. His destinations became ever more distant, his journeys longer and longer. And now, panic over the fruitlessness of his efforts had begun to manifest as bizarre dreams.

"Are you not returning to sleep, lad?"

Nier had begun readying for the day, prompting the query from Weiss. It was much too early for anyone to be up and about; most of the villagers would still be in bed.

Though, over the course of the past five years, the time of day had come to have less effect on people's activity. Instead, the weather ruled their lives.

In the past, the town and village gates had remained closed only at night. Most settlements, Facade aside, had left them open during the day so as not to interrupt travel, posting a few guards as a precaution against random Shade incursions. But now gates remained shut no matter the time of day. If a traveler wished to pass from one side to the other, the guards were forced to unbolt the barrier from the inside. It was a lot of work, but necessary in order to keep the Shades at bay.

During these five years, Shade attacks had been increasing at an alarming rate. It was now dangerous to venture out even during the day, unless the sun was high in a cloudless sky. Whenever it rained, the people locked themselves away and prayed it would soon be over.

But that was not the only disturbing trend on the rise. Though it was not readily visible, the Black Scrawl was starting to claim more and more victims. People who contracted it long after Yonah had now perished weeks or even days after getting sick. The same affliction that used to do its grim work at a slow, methodical pace now burned through victims like wildfire. And if that was the case, it meant Yonah might be—

Nier shook his head and grabbed his sword. He couldn't afford to let his mind wander to dark places; he needed to think about eradicating Shades.

"You received a letter from Emil, did you not?" asked Grimoire Weiss. The way he was floating suggested he wasn't sure what to do with the time on his hands—not that books have hands. But after five years of traveling together, Nier had come to see his mannerisms in a human fashion.

"Yeah, I'm thinking about visiting him," replied Nier. "He said he wanted to talk about petrification." In much the same way Nier had focused his efforts on eliminating Shades, Emil had been frantically searching for a way to reverse his petrification spell and save Kainé.

"In which case, we should leave with all haste," said Weiss. A smile formed in his voice as he continued, "Since I assume you plan to sweep clean the entire southern plains of Shades as we go."

2.

EVEN THOUGH NIER left the village long before the chicken-keeping couple was up, the sun was brushing the horizon by the time they arrived at Emil's manor. Shade activity had increased greatly in the southern plains, and it now took nearly a full day to clear them out and make the crossing—a chore that he could have finished by noon only a few years before.

Once they opened the rusted gates and stepped into the manor grounds, however, time felt much the same as always. The familiar chill descended around them, making their skin clammy before settling into their bones.

"This wretched place remains a haunted mansion no matter what hour of day we step inside," complained Weiss. His distaste for the manor was another thing that hadn't changed over the last half decade; he still clearly believed the house was cursed.

"Oh! Hey there, guys!"

As the butler brought them into one of the manor's many rooms, a gleeful Emil rushed over, causing Nier to smile in reply. When had they last seen each other? He began counting months in his head and was shocked to realize nearly an entire year had gone by. Yet with so much time between meetings, it struck Nier just how little Emil had changed. Children were supposed to grow a lot in a year; perhaps being cooped up in the manor had stunted his growth somehow.

"You haven't aged a day," Nier commented.

"Oh, uh, yeah. I'm sorta . . . special that way."

Emil's hesitation made Nier regret bringing it up. He had the power to turn things into stone, so it only made sense that he wouldn't age like any other child. The toll such a thing must take on his body was unimaginable.

"Fair enough," said Nier in an awkward attempt to change the topic. "So, uh, sorry it took so long to get here. I know you sent that letter ages ago."

When Nier had finally returned home from his last excursion, he'd found the mailbox crammed full of unopened letters. His absence wasn't the only reason; letter carriers also came less frequently these days, which meant mail came later than usual.

Indeed, with people only able to move about during the sunniest of days, long-distance travel was slowly becoming impractical. Sadly, even the sun wasn't a guarantee of safety anymore, as some Shades had taken to wearing armor to protect themselves from its rays. These creatures had given Nier trouble in the southern plains earlier that very day, and he could only imagine what kind of horrors they might lead to if left unchecked.

Annoyed at his brain's constant stream of terrible thoughts, Nier launched into the reason he'd come: "So, have you found a way to undo the petrification?"

"Not quite," replied Emil. "But I did find this." He groped around the table before handing Nier a piece of paper that had clearly been readied in advance. It was old—very old, in fact—and had both crumbling edges and faded writing.

"Archival . . . storage?" said Nier as he squinted. "Recent incident with Number 6 . . . Planning Room? Damn, this isn't easy to read."

"Pray allow me," said Grimoire Weiss as he peered at the document from above. "Project . . . Snow White. Notice: Archival

Storage. Following the recent incident with Number 6, we have decided to establish a Planning Room."

"Incident? What's it talking about?"

"Silence, lad. Let me continue."

"Right. Sorry."

Grimoire Weiss cleared his throat theatrically before moving on. "This room will hold records on the methods used to control and/or cancel all forms of magic—including petrification and bestial transformation—as well as allow other projects to move forward. Specifically, this should make it easier to complete a long-term storage solution for Number 6, as well as proceed with our work on Number 7."

Nier's gaze snapped toward Grimoire Weiss. He desperately wanted to say something, despite Weiss's clear orders to the contrary, but somehow managed to hold his tongue.

"All employees are required to keep the courtyard entrance to this new room secure. Failure to do so is considered grounds for immediate termination."

The moment Weiss fell silent, an excited Nier leaped in. "You said something about controlling all forms of magic *including* petrification, right?"

"Control *and/or* cancel, yes."

He hadn't heard wrong: there were records about a way to control Emil's powers of petrification and undo the spell on Kainé. Or at least that's what the old document seemed to say.

"The information we seek is presumably contained in this Planning Room."

"And the entrance to that is in the courtyard . . ." observed Nier, trailing off into thought. If they went to this Planning Room, they'd be able to both free Emil from his uncontrollable power as well as bring back Kainé.

"Let's go find it!" he cried.

"I doubt it will be so easily found, lad. Likely it will be well disguised enough to escape notice; the entrance was meant to be secure, after all."

As they followed the same path as they had five years prior—venturing through the far door in the dining room and into the hallway, then into the courtyard from the hallway—they found Grimoire Weiss's prediction to be off. The first thing that they noticed when they entered the courtyard was the central fountain. Even at a glance, it was clear there was some sort of mechanism there.

"Why did they put it in such an obvious place?" asked Nier.

The fountain sat in a spot that would strike anyone as suspicious—it couldn't even be called secure as a form of flattery. The bigger question was why they hadn't noticed it five years ago. True, they'd been struck by the frightening faces of the statues surrounding it, but that was still no excuse not to see it for the obvious mechanism it was.

"Only time could pull off such a trick," Grimoire Weiss remarked. "Look."

"What am I looking at?"

"The stone there is a different color from those around it."

Nier looked to where Grimoire Weiss indicated and saw he was correct. It almost looked like someone was *trying* to highlight the mechanism.

"Perhaps there was once some sort of ornamental element here to better disguise it."

"You mean whatever it was fell off sometime in the last five years?"

"Considering the age of this manor, it's a miracle any of its outdoor handiwork still exists at all."

"I'm sorry," Emil said. "All I did was search the library. If I'd realized sooner, we could have—"

"It's okay," interrupted Nier. "You found the document that led us here. You did exactly the right thing." Not to mention Emil might not have found it if he had searched earlier; the decoration mentioned by Grimoire Weiss had clearly not been missing for long.

"The question is, what are we supposed to *do* with this thing?"

Thinking, Nier casually placed a hand on the exposed spot, which immediately caused a low rumble to begin shaking the entire courtyard.

"What the hell?!" he cried.

"Guys!" yelled Emil as he desperately tried to maintain his balance. "There's a weird sound coming from over there!"

Nier turned and his eyes went wide—the small staircase connecting the manor and the courtyard was *moving*. Apparently the entrance had been under their feet the entire time.

Grimoire Weiss floated over to it and peered down. "A hidden staircase, is it? Delightful!"

"Wait, does that say *warning*?" asked Nier. He was pointing at an old label on the floor alongside a rusted, tattered chain. Likely it once acted as a seal at the top of the stairs.

Nier leaned close to the label and squinted. "Um, yeah. It says, 'Warning, this facility . . .' I can't read the rest. Something about a seal? Help me out here, Weiss."

"I am flattered you think me powerful enough to conjure writing already lost to time," muttered Grimoire Weiss, who clearly appreciated the attention regardless. "Still, if someone bothered to attach a warning to this area, I doubt our venture inside will be an easy one."

That said, the information both Emil and Kainé required was hidden somewhere beyond, which meant the companions had no choice but to brave the dangers and press on.

As Nier glanced behind him, he saw Emil doubled over and clutching his head. "Emil? You okay? What's wrong?"

"It's nothing," said the boy as he stood. Despite his assurance, the pallor of his face told a much different tale.

Grimoire Weiss floated closer to Nier. "Take care not to stray too far from the boy," he instructed.

"Got it."

With that, Nier began venturing down the stairs and into the darkness below, mindful of Emil's every step behind him.

3.

AS THEY DESCENDED into the basement, Nier's first thought was that he was entering the Junk Heap all over again. Though it seemed devoid of people, the spacious facility's equipment was very much alive. It was as bright as noonday, despite the complete lack of sun. And the similarities didn't end there.

"Is that all of them?"

After mowing down Shade after Shade, Nier finally sheathed his sword. Though the Junk Heap had robots instead of Shades, both places still held considerable enemies of considerable strength—and both made it very difficult for outsiders to proceed.

"Why are there Shades here?" he wondered.

"We encountered the creatures within the manor, yes?" Grimoire Weiss pointed out. "It stands to reason they might appear in the basement as well."

His words made sense, but Nier still wondered how Shades managed to pass through such a tightly sealed entrance. While the chain keeping the entrance closed may have been rusted away, the door at the bottom of the stairs had been shut tight—and the lock required a keycard to boot. It was hard to imagine Shades being intelligent enough to use such technology.

"Emil is falling behind," warned Grimoire Weiss suddenly.

Nier whirled around and began retracing his steps. Emil had been right behind him a second ago, but now he was gone. The basement facility was even more of a maze than the Junk Heap, and though the rough sketches of the layout scattered here and there on the floor kept him from getting completely lost, he knew he'd quickly lose his bearings if he let his guard down. If he and Emil got separated by any kind of distance, they might never meet up again.

Luckily, Emil hadn't gone far; Nier found him crouching behind a rough stack of crates and trying to stay out of sight.

"I feel like . . . I know this place," Emil murmured, his face buried in his knees.

"Well, it IS right under your house—you might've come down here once or twice before." Nier realized this was a thoughtless thing to say as soon as it came out; there was no way a child would have made it down here.

"You're probably right. I'm sorry. I'll be fine."

Emil scrambled to his feet, and Nier extended a hand to help him up. The boy's fingers were frighteningly cold, reminding Nier of how Yonah's hands felt before she came down with a fever.

"What is this? National . . . Weapons Research Laboratory?"

Grimoire Weiss's voice extinguished the image of Yonah in Nier's mind. Weiss was peering at a scrap of paper on the floor; as Nier scooped it up, it felt like it was going to crumble apart in his hands. Like everything else in the facility, it was old and significantly degraded.

"It's another document. Something about Project Number . . . 6?"

"A progress report," said Grimoire Weiss as he began narrating aloud. "We have completed the initial research into Number 6, and are ready to initiate the startup experiment in the coming days. As this will likely mark a great leap forward in Gestalt research, the National Weapons Research Laboratory has made the completion of the Number 6 project its top priority. Budgets for all other projects are to be frozen, effective immediately."

"Experiment?" wondered Nier. "Gestalt? I don't understand any of this."

"They were attempting to build weapons, lad. I believe this building was once some manner of magical research facility."

"What kind of weapons?"

Before Weiss could answer, something fell from the piece of paper and onto the ground. When Nier retrieved it, he saw it was a photograph of a girl, the colors long since faded. She looked to be slightly older than Yonah—perhaps around Emil's age—and was staring into the camera with a blank look. When Nier flipped the picture over, he found a single word: *Halua*.

"Halua? I wonder if that's her name."

Emil suddenly groaned; it seemed his insistence all was well had been a front. As he bent over double, Nier placed a gentle hand on his shoulder.

"Why don't we turn back for today? We'll get some rest and come back another—"

"No!" cried the boy. "No. We need to keep going. I'm fine."

Despite the power in his voice, his lips were pale, and faint beads of sweat glistened on his forehead. Suddenly, he stood and began to walk with confident steps, almost as though he knew exactly where he was going.

They proceeded down long corridors, fought off hordes of Shades, then descended more stairs and did it all over again. Rinse and repeat. It went on for long enough that Nier lost all track of how far they'd traveled; if not for the floorplans, he would have been hopelessly lost long ago.

"Basement third floor," mused Nier as they entered yet another new area. "What's this room for?"

"I can scarce imagine," replied Weiss. The rooms they'd

passed through previously had been square and filled with boxes, but this one was octagonal. They'd have to move through it in order to reach their final destination: the Planning Room.

"This is a weird shape for a room," said Nier as he stared at the entrance.

"Indeed," agreed Weiss. "I would not be surprised to encounter something dangerous inside, considering the document we previously found."

Said document had been resting on a stair landing. It began with a bit about "a solution for long-term storage of Number 6," and also mentioned "disguising the laboratory's aboveground facility as a mansion." So far as everyone could figure, Emil's manor was the disguised aboveground portion of the facility, the National Weapons Research Laboratory maintained the overall structure, and the place they were presently walking through was some kind of containment area.

"Let us proceed with caution," continued Weiss.

Nier didn't need to be told twice. One hand gripped his sword while the other slowly pushed the door open. But what greeted them on the other side of the door was not a Shade, nor a robot, but instead what appeared to be a child's playroom.

That said, Nier couldn't imagine having a playroom like this; every child in his village could run around here with room to spare. There were two slides, a massive jungle gym in the center that resembled a birdcage, and enough blocks, balls, and other toys for an army of happy kids.

"Watch your step, Emil," he said. "There are toys all over the place here. Guess no one ever made these kids pick up after themselves."

"Amusements are not the only things on the floor. Look there."

At Grimoire Weiss's command, Nier looked down and saw

another piece of paper. "More documents? I'm starting to get sick of . . . Wait, hang on. This one's different."

This one consisted of several pieces of notepad paper protected by a thick cover with the now-familiar words *Progress Report on Number 6* written on it. Unlike the other documents, however, the cover had kept these pages perfectly legible.

"The donor body Halua has been chosen from among the seven candidate subjects to proceed to the next stage. In the interest of protecting state secrets, all but one of the remaining subjects will be disposed of. The donor body . . ."

Grimoire Weiss suddenly fell silent; something about the text was bothering him. Nier leaned over to see what was the matter, and his heart immediately sank as he read the next line aloud.

"The donor body Emil, however, will be kept in storage as a fail-safe measure."

Was it all a coincidence? Nier flipped the page over and found two photos. One was a shot of the same young girl labeled *Halua* on the back, and the other was a young boy who was clearly related to her. Nier didn't even need to turn it over to know it was Emil.

Nier took a deep breath, trying to calm his nerves, and placed a finger across the boy's eyes just to be certain. He wondered briefly how the researchers had been able to take the photo without turning to stone, and thought perhaps Emil had not yet developed his petrification abilities.

"What the hell was going on down here?" Nier muttered.

The seven candidate subjects mentioned in the report had likely been children, with Halua being the one who moved on to the next stage of the Number 6 Project and Emil serving as the backup. Everyone else had been "disposed of."

Not wanting to think about what that might mean, Nier placed the covered report back on the ground where he found it.

As he did, Emil began to groan, pressing his hands to his head and breathing in short, ragged gasps.

"Another headache?" asked Nier as he hurried over to Emil's side. Though he didn't answer, the way his hands were digging into his temples suggested he was both trying to suppress pain and remember something. He'd claimed to know where they were earlier, so likely something in this room had triggered a memory.

As if proving Nier's suspicion, Emil lowered himself to the floor and began feeling around with his hands.

"What is it?" Nier asked, but Emil didn't answer. Finally, he came upon the object of his search: a strange toy that looked like a combination of a blue cube and black discs. He ran his fingers over the black discs slowly; they rattled dryly as they spun.

"Why . . . ? What was . . . I doing . . . ?"

As the toy clattered to the ground, Nier cupped the boy's clammy hands in his own. "You're gonna be okay," he said.

"Am I? Am I really?"

"Yeah, you are. I promise."

The new document only proved what Nier had been suspecting for a while: Emil was no ordinary child. If the power of petrification hadn't been proof enough, the fact that he hadn't aged over five years cinched it.

"Your past makes no difference," continued Nier. "We'll support you no matter what."

"Indeed," Grimoire Weiss added in a dry tone. "At any rate, you would hardly be the first member of our merry band to have issues."

"Now let's go," Nier said as Emil nodded hesitantly. "The Planning Room is just up ahead."

The party moved through the playroom, down a long corridor, and into the vast, circular area of the Planning Room. The ceiling loomed far above their heads, reminding Nier of the test site in the Junk Heap.

And just as in that place, a monster was waiting for them.

The thing was chained to the wall at the far end of the room. It was massive—nearly the size of the Shade that had attacked the village five years prior. Its limbs were shriveled skin and bone, its globular head was far too large for the rest of its body, and its lower torso was disproportionately puffed out and round.

After a moment, Nier figured out what it reminded him of. The large head and round belly were reminiscent of a baby. That explained why it seemed especially dreadful and eerie.

Stranger still were the countless nails that had been hammered into it, as well as the layers upon layers of thick chains wrapped around its body. While the monstrous creature gave Nier a faint chill, he was more concerned by the way it had been so firmly bound.

"What is this thing?" Nier wondered aloud.

"Number 6," whispered Emil.

The term had come up countless times in the old documents they'd found on their way. Could this really be that creature? Perhaps more important, how did Emil even know it was *there*?

"Can you see it?" asked Nier.

"No. But I know where we are." Though Emil's lips were still pale, his speech had regained a degree of calm. "We used to play in the room back there."

Nier recalled the photo of the girl who looked so similar to Emil. "We? You mean Halua?"

Emil nodded, his voice shaking like a leaf in a storm. "I had forgotten at some point, but . . . I remember now. I remember everything. We used to be humans. Normal humans. Just a bunch of regular kids like you'd see anywhere."

The emphasis on the words *used to* led Nier to think he meant the time when the photographs were originally taken. According to the dates on the back, that was September 12, 2026—hundreds of years ago.

"And then we came here," Emil continued. "They wanted to turn us into weapons, so they used magic to perform terrible experiments on us. Eventually, they succeeded. They managed to create a perfect weapon."

That had been Number 6. Nier was suddenly reminded of the horrible phrase on one of the documents: "all but one of the remaining subjects will be disposed of." Perfectly normal children had been murdered in the interest of keeping state secrets.

Emil lifted his head toward the wall. Though he was blindfolded, Nier knew exactly what he was looking at.

"She's . . . my sister."

As those words left his mouth, Number 6 shuddered. The two dinner plates that were her eyes began flashing red.

"This thing is alive?!" Grimoire Weiss exclaimed.

Oh, it was indeed. The documents had talked about storage for Number 6, not disposal—and on top of that, the seal had been applied hundreds of years prior. It would be no surprise if the petrification effect wore off with time.

"But soon they lost control of Number 6," continued Emil, "and the experiment was deemed a failure. They had to create a weapon that could petrify Number 6 and seal it away. So they created me. I'm Number 7. I'm . . . I'm a weapon."

Nier suddenly understood why Emil's petrification ability was so powerful: It had been created to stop another weapon after it got out of control. So long as the scientists could petrify Number 6, nothing else was required—including the search for a way to control or even undo the power.

Nier remembered the chill he'd felt when he saw the nails

and chains holding Number 6 in place. They spoke of the fear her creators felt for their creation—fear of a magical weapon far beyond the capabilities of any human.

"Weapon or no weapon, you're still Emil to us," Nier reassured him. After a brief silence, Emil smiled and replied.

"Thank you."

Behind him, Number 6 shuddered again and strained against her bonds.

"My sister is the greatest weapon ever made. And with her power, I could eradicate my petrification curse."

Number 6's shriveled arms began to move. Perhaps it was not time that was awakening her from her slumber, but the voice of her brother after so long.

"First you have to promise me something," said Emil.

Chains shattered. Nails popped from the wall and past Emil's head before embedding themselves in the ground, causing Nier to yell out a warning. But Emil seemed not to notice, instead taking a step toward the danger.

"If my sister somehow manages to swallow me up . . . If my original self becomes lost . . . I'm afraid I may try to hurt all of you."

Another nail. Then a rain of them. But Emil kept going. In that moment, Nier finally understood what Emil was trying to do: He was going to obtain his sister's magic.

Emil turned to face his companions, the corners of his mouth lifted in a clear smile.

"And if that happens—then I want you to kill me."

Nier rushed toward his friend, but another nail flew into the ground at his feet and blocked his way.

"No, wait!" he cried. "Come back!"

Now completely unbound, Number 6 reached toward her

brother as he extended a hand to her. There was no doubt he was trying to claim the might of the world's most powerful weapon for his own.

A crack began to spread across Number 6's head—a crack that suddenly revealed itself as a mouth. The giant opening took up half of the creature's entire face.

"Emil!"

Before Nier could act, Number 6 swallowed Emil whole and raised a magical barrier that sent Nier flying. By the time Nier had scrambled to his feet, Emil was gone. Though the boy had been attempting to take his sister's power, she had somehow reversed the plan and consumed *him*.

"You have to get him out of there!" Grimoire Weiss cried.

"I'm on it," Nier called back. "We're not going to lose anyone else."

Yonah had been kidnapped. Kainé turned to stone. And now Number 6—humanity's greatest weapon—was trying to absorb Emil. Nier could not permit such a thing to happen.

"Hurry!" Grimoire Weiss urged. "There's still time to save him!"

"I know!"

He *would* save him—he had no doubt in his mind. But just as the resolve came to him, Number 6 unleashed a fearsome attack. They were magical bullets, the same ones Shades so often used, but there were so many more of them.

"Weiss!"

Nier used the spell he'd learned back at the Junk Heap—the one that allowed him to absorb an enemy's magic and wield it as his own. The more powerful the attack he absorbed was, the more powerfully the counterattack struck the target; such a spell would be incredibly effective against an enemy such as Number 6.

"This thing is way too quick!" Nier griped. Though Number 6

was the size of the Shade that attacked the village five years ago, her movements were far more nimble, and she was an incredibly powerful jumper. She also scuttled up and across walls at an astonishing speed, forcing Nier to unleash magic spears in desperate attempts to slow her down.

When one of his strikes finally hit home, Number 6 fell to the floor and landed on her back. As she struggled to rise, Nier drew his blade—but Grimoire Weiss was quick to stop him.

"Sheathe your weapon! Such attacks will hurt Emil!"

"So how is magic any different?!"

"Because Emil is highly resistant to it!"

"If you say so!"

Unfortunately, this exchange took precious seconds; by the time Nier's magic fist was flying toward the target, Number 6 had already leaped away. She then began stomping her feet like a child throwing a tantrum. Though she looked like a monster on the outside, she was clearly still the young Halua within. And though most of her sense of self had long since been lost, the situation still caused something to tighten in Nier's heart.

Still, there was no choice; if he didn't take her down, Emil would be consumed utterly.

"Hold on, Emil!" Nier called loudly, as much to shake free of his own guilt as anything. "We're coming for you!"

I only want to help my friends.

As Number 6 fled up the walls again, Nier sent more spears flying. Orbs packed with powerful magic rained down around him, almost as if she was letting them fly without understanding why. Nier dodged, firing his own magical bullets at her as he did, then found a safe place from which to launch a spear. A moment later, he began the process all over again.

"Come back to us!" cried Grimoire Weiss as Number 6 fell to the ground.

I'll get her this time, Nier thought as he concentrated on his magic. His spears pierced her swollen stomach, her exposed ribs, her circular head. They pinned her to the wall, causing her to shudder violently enough to shake the entire room. Heavy blasts of air forced Nier to shield his eyes with his hands. Though he was calling for Emil, he couldn't hear himself—but he did feel like he heard someone yelling Halua's name.

The shockwaves and blasts of air came to a sudden halt as silence descended on the room. When Nier opened his eyes, Number 6 was gone. The place where she had been moments earlier was now covered in a black mist, with magical circles surrounding the small space. Despite how quiet it was now compared to moments ago, he could feel powerful magic.

"Emil?" called Nier tentatively as he tried to make out what was happening in the mist. "Are you all right?"

"I'm still alive!" came Emil's excited voice from the tangle of mist and barrier. "I feel my sister's power inside of me! I think I can control my abilities now!"

"Yes, we're all quite pleased," said an anxious Grimoire Weiss, who'd always had something of a soft spot for the boy. "Now get out here already!"

"Just a second. I can't see very well . . ."

As the black mist began to fade and the magic circles vanished, the silhouette of a person was eventually revealed. Suddenly, Emil cried out, his voice at once bewildered and shocked.

"What's wrong?" asked Nier. For a moment, he wondered if his magic had injured his friend; Weiss had never said Emil was *immune* to it, after all—just highly resistant. Panicked, Nier dashed forward, hoping to aid him in whatever way he could.

"Stay back!" yelled Emil suddenly, his voice filled with desperate tears. "Don't look at me!"

Finally, the mist and barriers vanished completely, permitting everyone to see what had become of Emil.

"Good god," whispered Grimoire Weiss.

Skeletal hands clutched at a globular head. Though the size of the body was the same as Emil's original form, he now resembled the horror that was Number 6. He had obtained her power while retaining his sense of self, which meant he had both absorbed and merged with her. But though his thoughts were still his own, he had not been able to retain his appearance.

As Emil sobbed, Nier approached and pulled the boy's bony body into a massive hug.

"Welcome back, Emil. You've been through a lot." He lightly patted his palm against Emil's back, much like he did when he calmed a fussy Yonah.

"But . . . my body . . ."

"Yeah, I know."

"I can't stand to be with you when I look like . . ."

His sobs erased the last of his words. Nier placed a hand on Emil's head and began stroking it. All traces of his once-soft hair were gone, but there was no doubt the shudder he felt on his palm came from Emil.

"What'd I tell you?" Nier said. "We're here for you. No matter what."

It didn't matter who he had been in the past, or what sort of person he might turn out to be in the future. Emil was an irreplaceable person in his life, and that was why he held the boy in his arms as Emil cried.

As his sobs finally abated, Emil looked up at Nier, his eyes a pair of perfectly round, perfectly dark circles.

"Can you see my face?" Nier asked.

Emil nodded, realizing that though he had lost his human

form, he had regained something else. "You look just like I thought you would. You look really cool."

"Heh. Sure."

Emil didn't need his blindfold anymore. He didn't need to stay cooped up in a lonely manor. He could go wherever he wanted and experience the joy of light and freedom, even if it came at the price of no longer looking human.

"I think I'm okay now," he said as he climbed to his feet. "If this is how I look now, then so be it. I was terrified at first, but it's not all bad, you know? I have the magic I wanted, and I can use it to bring Kainé back to us. Still, I sure hope seeing me doesn't petrify her . . . You know? In fear?"

"I see this transformation has not stolen your terrible sense of humor!" snorted Grimoire Weiss.

Nier could feel the corners of his mouth lifting in a smile. *Weiss really is soft on him*, he thought.

4.

"WHENEVER I INTERACTED with Kainé, I was re-minded about something from my past."

Emil spoke softly as the trio stood in front of the petrified Kainé, who continued to guard the basement door in the village library.

"Maybe my mind has been confusing her with my sister this whole time."

As they traveled back from the manor, Emil told Nier and Weiss stories about the time he spent with his twin, Halua. The two had lost their parents in an accident and been taken in by a facility that falsely advertised itself as an orphanage. Once there, they were subjected to countless tests under the guise of health checkups, before being forced to go through body modifications—the same experiments that ultimately turned them into magical weapons.

He had forgotten all of that, but the moment he saw Halua, it was like a knot had suddenly been undone. In a way, it might have been expected that he would forget about something that occurred centuries prior, but the way he suddenly recalled all of it, all at once, was highly unnatural. Perhaps some sort of spell had been controlling his memory.

"I saw my sister," he continued. "When she absorbed me, I passed out, but then I came back thanks to you."

Perhaps he'd even come into contact with what was left of Halua's consciousness when he fused with her.

"She held my hand, just like she did all those years ago. Then she told me to wake up in the exact same way, and said she was always going to watch over me."

Even as she slumbered in a state of petrification, Halua's desire to watch over her brother had surely been as powerful as Nier's protectiveness of his sister. No matter who we are, the love we hold for the precious little ones in our families always brings us to the same path.

Grimoire Weiss's scolding tone pulled Nier back to reality. "Are you done daydreaming? The moment the petrification is undone, that Shade will make its entrance."

"I'm ready."

All that was left of the massive Shade was its head—the one part of the enemy they'd failed to defeat five years ago.

"I'm ready," echoed Emil. Nier nodded. The fight was on.

Emil used his staff to paint a magic circle in midair, then began emitting magic from his hands. The magic grew in strength as it passed through the circle, then poured into Kainé's petrified body.

Suddenly, a bright light exploded, causing Nier to instinctively shut his eyes. When he opened them again, he saw Kainé slowly slipping into Emil's arms. The door to the basement was no longer stone, but wood—just as it had been five years prior.

"The beast approaches," Grimoire Weiss warned.

"Oh, I know," Nier replied, drawing his sword. The door splintered in the next moment as a black mass leaped forth. Countless appendages protruded from the head; the thing was just as unpleasant as it had been half a decade ago.

"What anger this creature must have!" Grimoire Weiss exclaimed. "How did it even survive these past five years?!"

"I'm not going to let this happen again," Nier replied. "It dies today!"

He slammed his blade into the Shade's snaking legs in an attempt to slow it down. He knew the creature could regenerate at an incredible rate, so he intended to cut it to pieces before that could happen.

"My sword feels lighter!" he cried. Five years ago, he'd struggled to pull his weapon out after plunging it into the Shade, and he'd needed to put all of his weight onto the handle in order to cut into the Shade when swinging. Now he could stab, withdraw, and slash with a single hand. Had the Shade become weaker after spending five years locked in the basement?

"It's not the blade, but the skill of the user," Grimoire Weiss said smugly, as though he were speaking of himself. "Strike it down!"

Nier didn't need to be told twice. After weakening the Shade by hacking at its limbs, he smashed it with a magic fist and dragged it into the air. The massive head soon lost its original shape, and a moment later, it collapsed to the floor and melted away into a black mist. It seemed impossible that the thing could ever have caused him so much trouble.

"How's Kainé doing?" asked Nier when he was done. Emil looked up and shook his head; Kainé lay still on the library floor, almost as if she'd not been freed from the petrification at all. Worried, Nier reached out and put his hand against her forehead. She was warm, at least, and such warmth meant life.

"She's been asleep for five years," said Nier. "I think she'll be fine. It's probably going to take some time for her to wake up."

But Emil did not seem content to hold her and wait. Instead, he leaned down to her ear and began calling her name over and over—an action that reminded Nier of his younger self. He'd tried so hard to bring Kainé back after killing the Shade in The

Aerie, fearing she might slip away entirely if he let up for even a moment.

"Grandma . . . ?"

In a strange coincidence, Kainé murmured the same word she'd said when waking on that fateful day. Nier knew what would come next: her lashes would shudder, her lids would twitch, and light would finally return to her eyes.

"Oh, hey . . ." she said weakly. As she moved to sit up, Emil placed a hand on her back to support her. Though his face couldn't change anymore, Nier could tell he was brimming with dazzling joy.

When Kainé turned around to see who was supporting her, Emil flinched and turned away. As Kainé stared at his perfectly round head, the corners of her eyes lifted slightly.

"Emil. You were the one calling me, weren't you?"

"You still . . . recognize me?"

"Of course. I knew you right away."

"Thank you, Kainé."

It was a short conversation, but more than enough. With just a few words, she had dispelled enough of his shame that he no longer felt the need to look away.

"Welcome back, Kainé," said Nier as he extended a hand.

"Wow. You grew up."

She climbed to her feet, wobbling slightly as she did. Standing next to her, Nier realized he was now taller than she was. It wasn't unexpected after so much time, but it still felt strange to look down at her after looking up for so long.

"So . . ." she began slowly. "How long has it been?"

"Five years."

"Shit. That's a long time."

She dropped her gaze for a moment before suddenly speaking

again, as though something had come to her. "Any luck with Yonah?"

The answer was obvious, but Nier didn't want to put it into words. She wasn't back yet. Not yet. Not yet. *Not yet.*

It was Grimoire Weiss who answered in Nier's place. "We are still no closer to finding her. We need a way to locate the Shadowlord."

As Grimoire Weiss and Kainé conversed, Nier reached out to one of the bookshelves and withdrew something he'd placed there before the battle to keep it safe.

"This is for you," he said, holding it out to a wide-eyed Kainé.

"Is that . . . a Lunar Tear?"

Somewhere along the way, a traveling merchant had taught him how to cultivate Lunar Tears. Though it was exceedingly rare for the white blossoms to grow naturally in the wild, they could be crossbred with a little human help. All one needed was time and effort. Nier never thought they'd be ready by the time Kainé and Yonah returned, but it turned out the Lunar Tears had bloomed long before he'd freed either of them.

"It's not as good as your grandmother's, but . . . I tried."

Though it wasn't the perfect decoration it was supposed to be, Kainé still wove it into her hair. As Nier watched, it struck him that they had *finally* reclaimed something they'd lost—and if Kainé could come back, that meant Yonah could too.

The sky hung high above the shattered library ceiling, the same sight Nier had beheld with despair five years prior. But things were different now; he'd struck down a Shade he had once been unable to touch, and they had Kainé at their side once more.

We'll get her back this time, Nier vowed as he gazed at the light above. *I swear it.*

JUN EISHIMA was born in 1964 in Fukuoka Prefecture. Her extensive backlist includes stories set in the *Final Fantasy, NieR,* and *Drakengard* universes. Under the name Emi Nagashima, she has also authored *The Cat Thief Hinako's Case Files,* among other works. In 2016, she received the 69th Mystery Writers of Japan Award (Short Story division), for the title "Old Maid."

YOKO TARO is the game director for the *NieR* and *Drakengard* series.

TOSHIYUKI ITAHANA is an artwork and character designer at Square Enix. Major works include *Final Fantasy IX, Chocobo's Mystery Dungeon,* and *Final Fantasy: Crystal Chronicles.*

Cover Illustration: Kazuma Koda

Frontispiece Illustration: Akihiko Yoshida

Interior Illustrations: Toshiyuki Itahana

Japanese Edition Design: Sachie Ijiri

JASMINE BERNHARDT is a translator of Japanese popular media, including such works as *NieR Re[in]carnation, Spice & Wolf,* and *My Happy Marriage.* She lives in Wales with her husband.

ALAN AVERILL has worked on dozens of video games, including *NieR:Automata* and *Hotel Dusk: Room 215.* He is also the author of *The Beautiful Land,* a novel about love and time machines.

8-4, Ltd.

Translator: Jasmine Bernhardt

Editors: Alan Averill, D. Scott Miller

Coordinator: Tina Carter

Special Thanks: Graeme Howard

English Edition Cover Design: Ti Collier

English Edition Text Design: Jen Valero